THE ANGER BENEATH

PAUL HARLAND

Ordering Information:

Prime Seven Media
518 Landmann St.
Tomah City, WI 54660

Printed in the United States of America

To Denise
with love,
once again

Acknowledgements

I thank my friends and family who have encouraged me with my growing obsession with writing, and especially those who said, and wrote, good things about my first book, *A Windfall of Secrets*.

This time around, I have had very positive feedback (about *The Anger Beneath*) from those who read the opening chapters and now want to know "how it all works out". Well, now they shall find out!

It is incumbent on me to acknowledge the continued inspiration from the many writers who have 'helped' me through the dark hours of indecision. They really are too numerous to mention, but here's my shortlist anyway: P.B. Shelley, Hermann Hesse, Allen Ginsberg, W. Somerset Maugham, Franz Kafka, Albert Camus, J.G. Ballard, James Baldwin, A.E. Housman, Jack Kerouac, George Orwell, Stephen Fry and Walt Whitman.

Special thanks to Joe Harland for the title page design.

The anger of the years gone by,
falling from the sky,
it seems the young have found a way,
of trying not to die.

1971

22ⁿᵈ May 1956. Nottingham.

"Not another bloody bomb!" The sudden anger created its own explosive effect. Ellen Carter, responding to her husband, moved behind his armchair, leaned forward and peered at the newspaper, the dark waves of her hair brushing the side of his face.

He continued his outburst. "It was the Russians a couple of months ago, then it was us, now it's the ruddy Yanks!"

Ellen straightened up, closed her eyes and sighed deeply. "It's awful."

"It's more than that, love," he asserted, folding the paper messily, "it's madness!" Flapping the newspaper angrily onto the footrest by the hearth, he stood up energetically and turned to his wife. His face wrestled itself into something between a grimace and a smile. He was lost for words, so he sighed with a clear thrust of annoyance.

Ellen looked at him sympathetically, and shared, as she always did, his obvious frustration. "We don't ever 'uninvent' weapons, do we?" she said, thoughtfully, almost helplessly.

"Exactly."

"I sometimes wonder where this will all end." With that she moved to the table and started clearing the breakfast things away. She carefully removed the rogue crumbs of toast from the damask covering, depositing them onto a plate, before brushing any remaining particles from the edge of the cloth onto the same plate. "I often wish we could just hide away from it all," she remarked absently, as she stopped to stroke the slight swelling of her abdomen with her free hand. The new addition to the family was still months away, and the joys and responsibilities of anticipated parenthood had been informing their thoughts lately.

"Me too," agreed Ken Carter, "me too." Ellen placed the crockery and the cutlery on the breakfast tray and carried them into the kitchen as Ken stepped slowly towards the window. The bright, late spring sky returned his gaze. This was the same sky which was, more than once, filled with the sound of a hundred German bombers bringing terror to Nottingham, to the teenaged Ken Carter, to his family, to his neighbours during the Blitz. An unforgettable experience, an unforgettable memory, an unforgettable part on his history. The force of the bombing, the power of the explosions could never be worse than he remembered. These horrific images would last forever. But later, at seventeen, on the newsreels, he would witness the new horror, the modern horror, which was Hiroshima and Nagasaki. So things could get worse. He frowned. His fist unclenched.

Hide away from it all, he thought. His eyes burned with a passion. Was that really possible? To escape the insanity around you which you can't control? Turning away from the light outside, his eyes set upon the polished walnut of the mantelpiece clock and the gleaming brass of an old, but well-cherished miner's lamp. He thought about these consuming ideas, over and over, until he realised the clenching of his fists had left his hands feeling weak.

10th December 1989. South London.

With a flourish of the handset, George Ford switched off the television and pondered briefly, before carefully punching in a series of digits on the pale blue telephone which rested on the small table by the side of his sofa. Steel grey eyes wandered thoughtfully across the room and settled on the window and beyond. He sat calmly and waited patiently for someone to answer his call.

"Ah, Derek, it's George here. What we were talking about the other day.... the Cold War thing. It has become quite critical, I think. We need to talk....yes....properly. Can you reach Felicity? And we need a group to meet. Decisions. As soon as possible, there's been quite a bit of dissent so we could do with calming everyone down. Try Lesley and Ken and maybe Alan. Yes. And anyone else you can think of. Probably by the end of the week." He stared at the blank television as he listened to the faraway voice. "Okay, see you soon. And Derek, I think this is rather urgent. Mmm. Goodbye."

Having replaced the receiver, George left the comfort of his sitting room and turned into the hallway and walked towards the back of the house. The hallway led from the vestibule at the front of the house towards the kitchen, a dining room and a spacious conservatory. Halfway down the broad passageway was a door, on the wall by the stairs, which to the unassuming eye would have been the access to a cupboard. The door waited for George's approach. He reached into his trouser pocket, extracted a key and undid the lock and opened the door. This was not an under-stair cupboard containing implements of domestic cleaning activity, but an opening to a flight of narrow stairs leading into the darkness of a basement area. George replaced the darkness with the bright glare of strip lighting with a flick of a switch, just inside the door. As he descended the steps he fumbled with the other keys, choosing a particular one for his use. The air had a staleness about it, as if this room was rarely open to the freshness of the day. Although a long rectangular carpet adorned the floor, it was old and worn and could not hide the fact that underneath lay a cool expanse of concrete. George reached the bottom of the stairs and deliberately looked from side to side. Along the wall to his right stretched a robust, but old cabinet running almost the whole length of the basement room. The second key was used, and a sliding, reinforced door panel was pulled back with a moderate jerk of both his arms.

George stood back and surveyed the sight before him, his steel grey eyes fixed, almost trance-like. Inside the section of cabinet he had just opened was a row of six old handguns, each secured carefully and displayed, almost ceremoniously like exhibits in a museum, as if waiting for something to happen. Placing the key on the bottom shelf of the open cabinet, he reached slowly, almost theatrically, towards one of the weapons. With a tentative reverence he rubbed his finger along the barrel of his chosen gun, withdrew his hand, then reached forward to stroke this sacred implement of conflict. His knowledge of guns was incidental to his current state of mind. George felt his brain in torment and turmoil, his reluctant admiration for these deadly objects taking all attention away from his thought processes. A mixture of the sophisticated and the visceral.

For several minutes, George Ford stared at the passive weapons in front of him. He consciously controlled his breathing. He remembered his first experiences of guns, towards the end of the war, as a young man. Memories which stung him, memories he would prefer to forget, responses he remembered, vividly vied for his attention; an intrusion beyond his control it seemed. He brought all this together, inside his head and continued to stare. A word from his erstwhile telephone call came back. Decisions.

Almost without notice, a tear escaped from his eye. He blinked. He stared, as if blind, trying to focus on images which weren't there. They were in his imagination, but he knew that some of them would be given life and his world, maybe the world at large, might never be the same again. The burden of choice, of making decisions, of taking responsibility was upon him. A point had been reached and he needed to stare into the barrel of consequence. Some things were simply unavoidable.

8th August 1990. Scottish Highlands.

He stood, steadily and breathlessly, by the solid outcrop of grey granite, scanning the distant horizon with a feeling of satisfaction. Above, wheeled a buzzard, hang-gliding on a thermal current of summer air. The clear day had opened up the distance and a crystal sharpness defined the edges of mountains and forests. The view was inspiring. It had been years since he last reached the summit of anything more modest than an English fell. Why had he waited so long to renew that wonderful feeling of satisfaction which accompanied this outdoor sense of achievement? The feeling of fulfilment fuelled by accomplishment. The knowledge that a coveted plan had come to fruition. The excitement of appreciating the sense of occasion of something special, something different.

And, of course, there was always the view. It was truly inspiring.

He sat down against a half-buried boulder, a clump of coarse grass pressed against his backside like a cushion, and waited for his two companions who followed somewhere behind, trudging doggedly towards him, from further back on the well-worn pathway. The slight breeze sang almost silently; an eerie whisper under the Scottish sky.

Two pairs of lightweight boots were making their contributions to the wear and tear of the narrow passage between the jagged teeth of rock, which decorated the way to the top of Ben Ochin. These boots approached, wearily climbing towards the triumphant figure slumped in the granite shadow. The first pair, belonging to a young woman, stopped a few yards short of the outcrop and its satisfied guest. The woman rested her hands on her hips and breathed out a measured sigh.

"Patrick, it's not a race. We lost sight of you!"

The man smiled. "I was carried away. I was enjoying myself. Still am."

The sun blazed down as Patrick leaned forward, arm outstretched, and pulled the woman up the last few steps. She carefully sat down and rubbed the back of her wrist across her forehead. Her breathing subsided to a regular rhythm and she permitted herself a satisfied smile as her eyes closed with an accompanying well-paced indulgent sigh. A second man joined them, blowing out his red cheeks with great effort. He half fell as he melodramatically stumbled to the ground, beside his two companions.

"Sustenance, you old bugger, I need sustenance," he exclaimed, reaching for Patrick's rucksack.

"Sheila, give him the hipflask in the side pocket. He looks as though he needs it. And have one yourself," said Patrick with a flourish of mock generosity.

"I'll make do with my water if it's all the same to you boys." She extracted a small pewter hip flask from the pocket of the rucksack and handed it to the second man, who held it briefly, towards the sky in a theatrical gesture. He brushed aside a flop of fair hair and scanned a section of impressive horizon.

"If I am to die on this wretched mountain, I want the taste of whisky on my lips when it happens," insisted the second man, "and anyway, the deal was Scotch on the Rocks!" Sheila looked at him quizzically.

Patrick now had the flask and slowly drank a brief tot of whisky. "Edward's right. That was the arrangement. Our deal, so to speak! To drink Scotch whisky on top of a Scottish mountain. And here we are! The drink," he brandished the flask, "and the mountain!" He swept his arm in a great arc of confident flamboyance.

Sheila shook her head, amused by the silliness surrounding her. "Men or boys?" she half whispered to herself. And above them the sun continued to blaze undisturbed.

Calm and contented minutes drifted by, with the occasional laugh, from the group of three, cast out into the air above the high fells. Buzzards continued to glide high overhead and the shades of the glens below gave a mystery and a dimension to the vista, which lay beneath a virtually cloudless sky. Before much time had passed, the trio gathered themselves together and headed off towards the steeper of the two approaches, a renewed collective spring in their steps.

As the pathway gave way to a more open space, the three companions increased their pace. Flickers of breeze flirted with their feelings of freedom as they progressed through the welcoming afternoon. The thrilling walk felt like an exploration of new territory. Which way to go? The luxuriant grassy expanse before them stretched and curved downwards towards the edge of a pleasant body of woodland and into a glen. There seemed no discernible single path, rather the odd indication of wear and tear around the sides of the occasional boulder or outcrop of rock, which decorated the otherwise fertile shapes of a glacial past.

Patrick strode to one side, taking the gentler descent and believing he was leading the way back to their departure point. Swooping birds, too quick to identify clearly, distracted Sheila and Edward. They briefly halted and turned towards the steeper slope which dipped in the direction of a gap in the trees which Edward assumed to be a fire- break. Optimistic thoughts of deer-spotting and catching clearer sightings of the swooping birds inspired the careful and quiet climb with which the two were engaged.

Further to their left, oblivious to his separate sojourn, Patrick contentedly ambled around a particularly large lichen-pitted boulder, the size of which was about to obscure his view of his two companions. He glanced back and realised he could not see the others. Had he strode too far ahead of them again? The near side of the boulder offered a rough step for him from which he thought he'd be able to catch sight of Sheila and Edward. Carefully mounting the solid rock outcrop, he surveyed the area immediately below him, on the other side of the rock. He was standing some distance, perhaps twenty feet above a small, natural bowl-shaped scoop in the landscape. From his vantage point on top of this small cliff he stared, mouth slightly open, at the scene below him.

As Sheila swung around in response to the shout, she caught sight of Patrick waving frantically at them.

Edward had now turned too.

"Is he trying to scare everything away?" he commented indignantly.

"Has he seen something, do you think?" suggested Sheila.

From his rocky perch, Patrick was clearly beckoning.

"Let's see what he wants." Sheila moved back up the slope.

Edward joined her and the two walkers trudged across the grassy expanse towards their energetically waving friend.

"Look," Patrick pointed downwards as Sheila and Edward arrived, breathlessly.

"Good God," exclaimed Edward as the pair peered over the rim of the rock. The three of them now stood together. Staring. At the body of a dead man.

9th August 1990. Inverness.

Detective Inspector Colin McNab sat back in his chair and gave an ironic, tight smile to the man sitting at the other side of the desk. McNab, avuncular of manner, sandy hair thinning on top, was an experienced police officer and often felt that the excitement of policing in a more metropolitan area would have brought more intrigue, more variety and more pressure to his life. He had settled for his present lot with ease and the north of Scotland had been more than a compensation for this absence of excitement in his career, and he probably felt less cynicism than he would otherwise have felt in the environs of Glasgow or Edinburgh. Cataloguing his most interesting cases in his mind, he was beginning to suspect that the current incident under investigation may just turn out to be a highlight worthy of his retirement speech, which he had pencilled in for next year.

"So, what have we got, sir?"

McNab tapped on the buff folder lying on his desk, "What we have, Baxter, is a body with no apparent identification, a bullet through his heart and not a lot else."

"No-one reported missing.....er.. locally, I suppose," mused Baxter, "any chance it's a shooting accident, sir?"

"Unlikely. He was shot with a handgun, apparently. However, we have a problem with the actual shot which killed him. The evidence doesn't really match up. Our man had only been dead for a maximum of half-an-hour before he was found by those three walkers. All three of them are certain, absolutely certain, that they heard no shot. Mister Davenport, the first one to spot the body, insisted that the only sounds they heard, for the previous two hours, were natural; birdsong, running water and the like. Sheila Phillips commented that they were specifically listening for sounds; they'd come for the wildlife….bird-spotting in particular. We have no other reports of any body else hearing anything like the discharge of a firearm. Not only that, there were no sightings of anybody else up there. We've had officers out trying to confirm any sightings, you know, strangers and the like, but nothing as yet has materialised. Our killer appears to be invisible, very, very clever or incredibly lucky! And there are some unusual aspects to the body itself. He was wearing work boots rather than walking boots. Rather strange if he was a visitor. And overalls of sorts, as if he was at work or on his way from work. But no identifying marks, logos or whatever on his clothing. No wallet, credit cards, cash or documentation of any sort."

"Hell's bells," exclaimed Baxter, "where do we start?"

"That's what we need to decide…"

Baxter interrupted, "sorry, did you say no cash at all? So he walked there and hadn't the need for bus fare, so he's local?…. Or he drove, so there must be a parked car somewhere. A nearby bed and breakfast?"

"We're working on that now, but no-one, as far as we know, has failed to return to their accommodation; tourist or worker. No missing persons. Nothing."

The two men sat in a brief awkward silence. McNab continued to lean back in his chair, and Baxter shuffled into a more comfortable position in his. In the stuffy atmosphere of the office there was an invisible whirl of thinking as both men searched for something relevant to say, something to ignite their considerations. The harsh, jangling intervention of the telephone broke in. McNab reached for the receiver.

"Yes, McNab here. What is it?" He listened attentively to the new information, a series of facial expressions translating vague impressions to Baxter, who waited for some welcome diversions from his absence of ideas. "I see, that certainly is interesting," he smiled and half-laughed ironically into the phone, "yes, interesting, but not necessarily helpful, eh?"

With measured anticipation, Baxter took out a notebook and pen and prepared to write down the obviously- new information which had come to light. He was expecting to be sent off to carry out some specific investigatory task. That was what he was hoping for. McNab thanked the person on the phone, replaced the receiver and gave a wry smile to Baxter. He indicated Baxter's pen with a nod. "Make a note," he paused, "AD365."

"A...D...3...6...5.." Baxter dictated to himself as he wrote. He looked up, "is that it, sir?"

McNab nodded.

"But what is it? A date? And what has it to do with our dead body?" Baxter mused.

"It's a tattoo," McNab answered, "found on the deceased's left foot!"

"So, unlikely to be a date. AD could be a person's initials," reflected Baxter, "I suppose it will turn out to be a serial number of some type...it just seems very strange that it has been tattooed on a person's body."

"Mmm....exactly. It smacks more of an organisation, a cult of some sort? Forensics seem to think it is, as far as they can tell, a relatively recent tattoo. They estimate the body in his early forties and the tattoo may have been done when he was in his mid to late thirties. Not an obvious age to chose to have a tattoo."

"If he did chose to," suggested Baxter.

"What do you mean?"

"No one asked the inmates of Belsen or Auschwitz if they wanted their tattoos, sir."

"I see what you mean. That could be a tricky complication." McNab's look indicated he probably could have done without this helpful suggestion from his junior. "Ah, there was another piece of curious information I was given by Forensics, which adds more mystery to our man."

"What's that, sir?"

"His boots. Remember they were work boots," McNab emphasised, "the dirt in the tread did not match the soil or the material at the location where he was found. It was more dust-like, ground rock and concrete, only 'superficial local debris' they said."

Baxter was shaking his head slowly, "God, another mystery! Still, it's a while since we had a real challenge to contend with." A note of enthusiasm was evident and the younger officer physically shaped himself for action. McNab observed the growing interest exhibited by his junior partner and raised the level of intrigue.

"One positive thing, mind you. He didn't have multiple broken bones." McNab asserted with a firm nod.

Baxter looked confused, "how does that help?"

"Well, that proves he didn't simply fall out of the sky! That was going to be my first suggestion."

With rotor blades slicing noisily through the highland air, the police helicopter swept purposefully above the hillside, followed by its undulating shadow across the rugged terrain. Inside the aircraft, the officers squinted into each crevice of glen, and each wrinkle of gorge with a buzzard's concentration. Isolated vehicles were inspected, initially through binoculars, licence plates reported and checked over the airwaves. This was an aerial search conducted with an earnestness, quite warranted by the discovery of a dead body, but vainly in the cold light of day. There would be no evidence to find, no further clues to aid the perplexed investigating police officers, nothing to be discovered, no way forward for quite some time. The search would continue for several hours in the brisk summer freshness of the Scottish air.

12th August 1990.
North Somerset Coast.

The two young children skipped ahead of the couple, across a cobbled pathway, next to a row of small stone cottages. Seascape. Thrift Cottage. Blue Yonder. The end dwelling appeared not to have a name. As the sun blazed over the sloping street and their happy offspring headed further off towards the beckoning sea front, Mr and Mrs Anderson gazed with open curiosity at the individual cottages, assessing their suitability for future holidays. These ones were much closer to the sea than the current one they were occupying for their family holiday. They perhaps had a bit more character too, more traditionally built.

Diane Anderson had noticed the end cottage, the one without a name, had a small paved area at the side which would have made a lovely patio with a fine view of the coastline, but the owners had clearly not acknowledged this potential and had just left the space unadorned with garden furniture or any semblance of decoration. Diane felt that was a terrible waste. Her husband had stopped to take a photograph of the quaint thoroughfare they had come down, trying to capture some of the West Country character they obviously admired. She was having all sorts of ideas about what she could do with the end cottage, visualising terracotta plant pots, wall-climbing flowers, patio furniture and a selection of other homely bric-a-brac, when she noticed the front door of the cottage move slightly ajar.

Feeling awkward in herself, as she had stopped walking past the cottage, she began, self-consciously, to pick up her pace while still watching the door as it opened slowly. Very slowly. Before she fully realised what was happening, a figure had emerged from the doorway, staggered for a couple of erratic steps, slumped forward and sprawled on to the paved area by the painted garden gate.

"Colin," she called urgently, as she swung the gate open, and knelt beside the prone figure. Her husband was beside her almost instantly, bending down towards the prostrate man, anxiously trying to assess the situation.

He noticed the blood; there was a wound, probably a bad wound. "Find a phone, love, he needs an ambulance!" Diane retreated, leaving an anxious husband to assist.

A low moaning came from the man as he lay on the ground. He was trying to articulate something, he was trying to speak, he croaked. "Locked in......I've locked him in. Ach!"

"Easy, mate, try to lie still and save your energy," was all Colin Anderson could think of saying. He watched the dark blood spread from the man's torso and knew this injured man had little time left. On the cobbles behind him, Colin was aware of a small crowd gathering, and he could make out snippets of concerned conversations about the scene before him. He knew he could do nothing to help. He was supervising the final minutes of a fellow human being. This was not a part of the holiday he had planned for his family.

14th August 1990. Bristol.

A brisk breeze blew from the open sea across the skeletal jungle of aerials above the headquarters of the Avon and Somerset Constabulary. The benefits of the cooling air were not felt by those working inside the drab building. The blues and whites of the cloud-flecked sky could be seen, but not fully appreciated from the window of Detective Chief Inspector Gates' office.

"A tattoo? Is that it?" snarled Gates, into the telephone receiver. He raised his eyes towards the ceiling in a gesture of annoyance and frustration. Detective Sergeant Frank Harvey watched his superior's face pensively, and with the usual trepidation he required in order to cope with the unpredictable temper of his colleague and mentor. The tone, and content, of the current telephone conversation did not augur well for the anticipated exchange to come. The telephone receiver was replaced firmly. Harvey held his curiosity and waited.

"A Scotsman with a tattoo!" Gates announced dramatically. "And nothing, it seems, in the damned cottage!"

"So, that's all we've got at the moment." Harvey inwardly cringed at what he had just said; stating the obvious in front of Gates was not a particularly effective strategy. "I could take another look at the cottage, sir," he now suggested, to give a more positive element to the exchange.

Gates growled a "hmmmm," and stood up, surprisingly calmly. "That may be a good idea, Harvey. At the moment, it seems there's more chance of us gleaning information from the cottage than there is from the body." He was standing with both hands deep in his trouser pockets, shaping up for one of his perceptive monologues which Harvey, and his other colleagues, had accepted as a sort of 'thinking aloud' approach to summarising where his ideas were coming from. This familiar method was wholly acknowledged by his fellow officers, but never ridiculed; it had been, and still was, an excellent way of focusing on the business in hand, and allowed others to find their own focus on points that may have otherwise slipped by the wayside. "Our main witness, Colin Anderson, was absolutely clear about the deceased's accent. Scottish. Readily distinctive, so we have that. Now, the actual words spoken. Again, Anderson was very clear about that... .'locked him in'.....must be a reference to the cottage....i.e. where he'd just come from. A search of the cottage has revealed very little of help, particularly the absence of anyone being locked anywhere!" Gates paused, while he paced back to his desk. "The local lads, however, have discovered an uncertain history, recent history, concerning that particular cottage. It is considered a bit of a mystery by the neighbours. It appears, on the surface, to be just another holiday let, but the clientele seem unusual. Well, the range of clientele, I should say! It does not appear to be as well-frequented as the other cottages. There's no obvious reason why that should be so. Rarely are there the customary comings and goings one would expect and, although the property has more than one bedroom, no one locally has any recollection of any family staying there." Gates had very much emphasised the word 'family'.

Harvey was intrigued, "so the cottage is worth another visit, eh?" The question hung in the air, unacknowledged it seemed by Gates. As Harvey moved towards the door, half-expecting to be called back, he noted the thoughtful nod of his superior officer; the assent he needed to try for a special step forward with this investigation.

15th August 1990. Inverness. 8 a.m.

Puddles of recent rain peppered the surface of the police station car park, as DS Baxter tightened the laces of his walking boots. He looked skywards to confirm that the weather was clearing and the earlier mist and drizzle were finally disappearing. Turning towards the nearest Landrover, he noticed the earnest approach of DI McNab.

"Ah, Baxter, before you go, I may have some crumbs for you from the Forensics table," announced McNab.

Baxter was perplexed, "crumbs, sir?"

"Information. Such as it is. AD365, more or less, crawled to the spot where he was found. The point we've been bearing in mind is how far could he realistically have travelled? Well, some microscopic remnants of moss….I won't give you the technical name," he smiled ironically, "have been found under his fingernails and on the fabric of his clothing, which suggest he'd been somewhere near running water. The Achna Burn splashes its way near there, down towards the river…. so you may want to focus on that, it's slightly west of the body's location….and before you ask…..no, I'm not quite sure what we're looking for. But there must be something more up there……surely. There has to be. Best of luck, Baxter."

With a determined sense of purpose, Baxter and his team dispersed to their respective vehicles, ready for the gruelling task ahead. In truth, Baxter was looking forward to this. His sense of adventure was being nurtured with every inch of the journey and his enthusiasm for what lay ahead could not be faulted. In a flurry of exhaust fumes, the police entourage turned into the road towards Ben Ochin.

15th August 1990.
North Somerset Coast. 11a.m.

If Frank Harvey had had a lot of hair, he may seriously have considered pulling some of it out. He was exasperated. He felt defeated. His near two hours in the cottage on Lundy Lane had proven pointless. From a police point of view, more specifically, clueless. With the exception of the front door and the back door of the abode, he had found no other places where someone could be 'locked in'. He had begun to assume that the words, which Colin Anderson had thought emanated from the Scotsman, had been misheard. Perhaps it was a particularly thick accent? Harvey found himself wandering through the kitchen of the cottage, then into the bigger of the two bedrooms, mouthing aloud in outrageous versions of Scottish accents, dialects, trying out the words….reaching the point where he was simply being stupid. All in an attempt to make some meaning out a small morsel of information.

One last throw of the die, he thought, as he picked up the bundle of original crime-scene photographs which lay on the lounge coffee table. He stared at one now, unaware of what he was staring at. It was a photograph of the hallway which ran from the front door to the kitchen at the back of the cottage. In the picture he could clearly see the smears of the victim's blood on both sides of the hall. The photo of the kitchen doorway gave the clear indication of where he had been shot. Because there had been no evidence of blood in the kitchen itself it was assumed he had been shot in the kitchen doorway, then staggered to the front door. Despite the absence of any gunshot being heard, the 'kitchen doorway theory' prevailed, although there wasn't a single officer wholly convinced of this 'thin' idea. At least it was regarded as a 'starting point'. DS Harvey, in particular, needed to be convinced this was actually a plausible theory. Harvey lifted up one of the photos and held it at arm's length. He stared intently. Blood on both walls. Harvey walked into the hallway to look for himself.

As the victim staggered down the hallway, it was thought, he would have brushed both walls as he swayed from side to side. A reasonable assumption. Harvey checked. And saw something which didn't ring true. He looked at what wasn't there. Along the final section of hallway, that part which approached the front door, there was no blood on the walls, but enough on the floor and on the door. Harvey turned towards the kitchen and looked again. The photos told the same story. Harvey realised what he was looking at. The kitchen doorway was not where the man had been shot. This was where he had stopped and turned. Some way down the hall was a 'cleaning' cupboard which, presumably, had been checked earlier as part of the crime scene. But perhaps not checked as well as it should have been. Harvey, in his mind's eye, saw the victim coming out of the cupboard, brushing along one side of the hallway's wall, stopping in the kitchen doorway, then turning and brushing the other wall before moving more purposefully towards the outside door.

With a clear and assertive confidence, Harvey opened the cupboard and found himself looking at a blank wall between a fixed shelving unit and an array of various household appliances. The space which was clear was easily the size of another door. A small box just below the low ceiling flashed its red light. A security device? Something to do with an alarm system? There had been no evidence of burglar alarms or other security systems anywhere in the house when the first investigations had been done. The presence of the red flashing light had been taken for granted. DCI Gates would definitely be expressing a view on that aspect of the investigation. Harvey avoided feeling smug, but was genuinely excited by what he had found.

One minute later he was calling Gates on the portable radio. There were much clearer ideas now of 'someone being locked in', further ideas to relieve the bewilderment surrounding this killing. Harvey was presenting his chief with the next step. He was going to be talking about electronic locks and what made this particular holiday cottage different from the others on Lundy Lane.

15th August 1990.
Scottish Highlands. 11 a.m.

Having laboured for some time just to reach the 'crime scene' of the discovered body, Baxter and his team were organising themselves purposefully in the careful preparations for their search for any signs of anything like a clue in this curious investigation. Baxter was excited, but not very optimistic, about the possibility that the team would unearth something of use. Each member of his team was checking the equipment and the territory of their investigations. Local knowledge was at a premium and this had been a major consideration in how Baxter had allocated the personnel. Generally the officers worked in pairs. The challenge before them was not helped by the guiding advice that they were looking for nothing specific. It was unlikely they would find the weapon, for instance, and there were no obvious 'missing' items belonging to the victim. Anything unusual which was found may prove impossible to link to either the killer or the victim. But this operation was critical if progress was to be made in this peculiar case.

As Baxter traced his finger along the route of a blue line on the laminated Ordnance Survey map, for the benefit of Constable Malone, his chosen colleague for that section of the search, the sudden clear blast of a gunshot rang out. The echo cracked the air and the party of searchers stopped in their tracks.

Across the rugged terrain, shouts from various officers called out; warnings, exclamations and other incoherent words. "That way!" "Over there!" "Sir, down there!" The last call was from an officer gesturing wildly and indicating the direction of the source of the gunshot.

Baxter, acting quickly, ordered some of his officers to spread out further up the mountainside. Others were ordered to move further down. His almost-instinctive thoughts had pictured two people, shooter and shot-at, therefore two areas of concern needed to be addressed. Control of this new situation was vital, and Baxter instantly assessed the changing scenario. This was the excitement that Baxter had hoped for. It could turn out more dramatic than he imagined. The ensuing movement of the officers was fluid, well-organised and gave Baxter a strong sense of satisfaction. Any idea of a wasted trip up Ben Ochin had quickly disappeared; something was happening now. In his own mind, Baxter was already convinced that this new incident was linked to the finding of the body a week earlier. This was more significant than a 'found' clue. Things were moving in directions not normally associated with the Northern Constabulary and Baxter felt that he had been thrust into a new and very significant arena.

A shout rang out. "Near the burn! Straight ahead!" There was a brief pause while everyone checked their bearings; locating the place in question. "There's a man!"

Two of Baxter's group changed the direction of their pursuit slightly, one of them waving to Baxter and indicating the new focus of their search. Within seconds Baxter could see the figure of a man, about a hundred yards away, clearly having difficulty as he scrambled, erratically and desperately, in an attempt to follow the water course towards the lower slopes of the mountain. Overwhelmingly, it was clear from the pace and panic exhibited by the man that he was running away from something, someone, escaping, trying to evade something awful. He was clearly injured in some way. At one point he tripped, and tumbled over a tussock of coarse grass and appeared to lie still as if exhausted. Slowly he pushed himself up to continue his escape, but his efforts were suddenly very laboured and he looked, once more, at the point of collapse. The police officers closed in quite rapidly now, the man reduced to a drunken-like stagger. He seemed to reel about blindly, uncertain of where he was. In that moment Baxter confirmed in his own thoughts, that this man was clearly the one who had been shot. Baxter stopped and swung round, peering across the summer landscape, looking at the various rock outcrops, the shadows, the random boulders on the slopes and the narrow ravines which made up the immediate landscape. Where was the gunman? The victim was accounted for; where was the assailant?

From the broad belt of his jacket, Baxter plucked the police radio. He needed medical support and armed support. His team had only been equipped for the expected search duties and were carrying only basic medical provision; nothing to deal with gunshot wounds. The original scenario had changed drastically and now further medical back-up was necessary and a manhunt required. It may already have been too late for their mysterious victim; he seemed to be in a bad way. There had been no sighting of the gunman. Having confirmed that the necessary assistance was on its way, Baxter turned his attentions to determining the position of his men regarding the location of the gunman. The search was to continue; a case of 'locate and monitor', rather than 'approach and apprehend'. None of his men had firearms, someone out there did.

Clambering down towards the shooting victim, Baxter looked across to the other side of the tumbling stream of water as it sparkled its way down towards a distant river and on to the Moray Firth. Two policemen had reached the man and were talking to him as he lay prone among the grey outcrops of rock. As he approached the wounded figure he noticed something familiar about the clothing of the man. He was wearing the same overalls as AD365.

Baxter knew for certain, in that moment, his assertion that the recent gunshots were linked to the previous week's body had been confirmed. He instinctively knew, when he looked at the latest victim, that beneath the man's left sock there would be, no doubt, a tattooed serial number.

15th August 1990.
North Somerset Coast. 2 p.m.

The flurry of police activity at the cottage on Lundy Lane was providing an intriguing diversion for the families of holiday-makers and passers-by. The blue and white striped tape which discouraged the public from trespass fluttered in the light breeze. Officers in uniform had a strong presence and overall-clad forensic personnel and members of the technical team came and went with clear indications of purpose. It was a busy time. It was an exciting time for Frank Harvey. His discovery earlier in the day had transformed the investigation and he felt as if this 'new line of enquiry' would bode well, at some point, for his promotion chances. He had dismissed the suggestion of some of his fellow officers that he had 'been lucky' when uncovering the mysterious door after the first team of officers had missed the evidence. Angry words had been thrown around and gossip about formal warnings had been doing the rounds and some anticipated backlashes had been voiced. Harvey had kept his focus and made no comment on anybody else's possible shortcomings. The talk, back at the station, had amused him, but now he felt he was, justifiably, in the front line of the action, as he watched over proceedings inside the cottage.

"Can't we just break through it, sir?" asked a young police officer, indicating the newly-discovered door inside the narrow cupboard.

"We may need to," returned DCI John Gates, before adding," how are the electronics going? Any joy?" The officer addressed shook his head sheepishly. "This is a murder investigation, I'm not waiting for bloody paperwork, get smashing!" He noted the glee on some of the faces. "But be careful…only the door itself, right?" He and Frank Harvey stood back to let the damage begin.

In a remarkably short period of time, there was a substantial opening where the doorway, previously posing as a wall panel, had been. A cool current of air blew into the hallway from this new portal, but peering into the newly-opened space, the eyes of the police could see nothing but darkness. Rough stone steps sloped away from the hole, but there was no light.

"Torch, please," instructed Gates to no-one in particular. A heavy-duty torch was produced and the revealed passageway was illuminated.

Along one wall, at intervals, were lamp fittings for electric lights, but a careful search around the entrance did not reveal any switches. The passageway was long and, apart from the first few yards, seemed to be naturally formed. The section closest to the entrance seemed to have a concrete floor for several yards before giving way to a solid rock floor and appeared to be a cave. As well as the lamp fittings there were various cables, running along one wall, fixed at intervals onto brackets. The passage widened at the point where the beam of the torchlight ended, so it was impossible to tell what stretched beyond. There was a clear idea of the volume of space which lay ahead as the cold draught emanating from the darkness continued like an indoor autumnal breeze.

Gates inhaled slowly and turned to one side. "Right, lads…..who's going to play hero and go in first?"

15th August. Inverness. 4 p.m.

"Ah'm not sure whether I can take all this excitement, Craig," explained DI McNab to his sergeant, as they sat together in the sparse disorder of the Inspector's office. Baxter raised his head in surprise at the use of his first name. McNab smiled back at him sagely, before continuing in a more serious manner. "We have, at last, made some headway with this mess. At least we have some names to work with, but we now have two dead bodies to deal with."

Baxter seemed uncertain whether his senior officer was choosing to be ironic or simply allowing the newly-ascertained facts to undermine the progress which was being made with this extraordinary and curious matter.

"We do have the bits of information we managed to get from Bernard Todd….it was so useful to have the deceased's name this time …. and this strange business about tunnels," said Baxter, in an attempt to capitalise on this new positive point of progress.

"Yes," mused McNab, "and there's this name, Alfred Craddock, to follow up. Todd was certain, very distressed apparently, about the other victim probably being Craddock. It seems they were friends?…..Clearly mixed up in something that frightened him. Todd was very fearful, you reckoned, at the time of his collapse."

"He was….in a highly-agitated state. He knew that the person who'd shot him was likely to pursue him to make sure he was dead. No name, just 'they'. 'They' were after him and he was sure that Craddock had been a victim too. There was an implicit feeling of 'two sides' of a conflict…..somehow….

like gang warfare, I suppose, it was difficult to be certain." Baxter paused as he remembered the desperate emotional condition of Bernard Todd during his final moments. "The references to a tunnel were difficult to make out. It was clear that was where Todd believed the killer to be. We think that Todd was trying to explain that he himself had come from this tunnel. The inference was he was escaping from something… or someone. That would be an obvious deduction to make. I don't know. It didn't really make sense, sir."

"This 'tunnel' idea is a strange one, but we must treat it seriously," pondered McNab. "The suggestion being made here is that there's a tunnel of some sort halfway up Ben Ochin! A bit far-fetched, if you ask me….but it would explain the sudden appearance of dead bodies and the just-as-sudden disappearance of their assailants!"

"Todd and Craddock's names have been passed on to Scotland Yard, sir. This new computer system, HOLMES it's called. Supposed to be a wizard at finding missing persons…. or at least matching their details anyway," enthused Baxter.

"Well, we're pretty clever at finding dead ones!" blurted McNab.

"At least we don't need to refer to them as AD365 and AA47 anymore, sir! The Yard explained that we would have the information, if there was any, within the hour, but I need to speak to someone else now, about caves and tunnels." Baxter gathered up his notebook and pencil and moved towards the door. He looked towards McNab and noticed the quizzical frown on the older man's face "I need to speak to a chap from the University, sir, and someone from the National Parks…. about this idea of tunnels, caves and other underground business. It's not something we've had any dealings with. My knowledge of geology, and…er…geography.. is a wee bit lacking. This part of the country isn't known for its caves is it?….And constructing tunnels is hardly something you can do in secret! So, I'm after a crash course in tunnel construction and engineering so I can learn about such possibilities from the experts. I'm hoping it will give us some clues to help us locate any likely tunnels or caves that might be out there." He paused, as if for effect, and seemed quite pleased, almost exuding a boyish smugness, with what lay ahead in this investigation. For a moment, within this pause, there seemed to be an utter change of heart, as if he suddenly realised that this particular direction may be futile. "Tunnels, though, sir. We also need to know why? Why would anyone build tunnels here? What's it about? What would be the reason?"

Baxter regained his composure and gave a confident, knowing nod and, armed with his fervour and his great thirst for knowledge, he headed out of McNab's office. The Detective Inspector watched him go. The benign look on his face indicated a silent encouragement for this younger and vibrantly-keen officer and the sincere wish that Baxter would be destined to a long and worthy career ahead of him. This next generation of officers would move in a different world from the one he himself had occupied; even in this relative backwater, in the north of Scotland, policing was changing….had been changing for some time. McNab was also acknowledging that he himself was probably involved in the last major case of his own career; a pretty unusual one by all accounts. Soon, he would be embarking on a long and quiet retirement, comprising fishing in rivers, drinking in lounges and reading about the exploits of other detectives.

16th August 1990. Scotland Yard

Above the radar-mimicking rotations of the gleaming name-sign of Scotland Yard, a sheer wall of offices pushed up towards the summer sun. Occasional glints of sunlight flashed innocently into the eyes of passers-by, giving no clue to what was happening inside the building. This citadel of the British Establishment presented a rather nondescript face to the world, but its famed reputation of mystery, and its ability to find solutions to these mysteries, was embedded in the public psyche; an everyday excitement to be relied on.

And here it stood, in all its steel and glass glory. Inside, there had been a flurry of activity in the offices and operations room of Chief Superintendent Shackleton.

"There is clearly something going on here," asserted the tall, bearded figure of Chief Superintendent Oscar Shackleton, noting the looks on the faces of the group of officers before him. "And, yes, that is an understatement…. but we need to keep a close eye on what we divulge to the public. These individual deaths we're concerned about have already been reported in the press, but nothing that suggests sensation or anything more interesting than local curiosity. No link between the incidents has been presented to the public and, as far as things are concerned at the present time, that is the way it will remain. This could turn out to be very contentious, I know. Any hint that there is control over any information passed to the media….and we're on a hiding to nothing."

The ensuing silence from the other officers meant they were unsure about the Chief Super having finished his diatribe. He scanned his audience with his narrow eyes and continued, "Cummins, remind us of the facts…the facts we are now suggesting *are* linked in some way. We have evidence that *is* the case, but intelligence is rather thin, at the moment, and the nature of the killings is of great concern. No apparent motives and, it would seem, not linked to any other crimes as yet. Cummins?"

"Thank you, sir. The two victims in Scotland have been identified as Alfred Craddock and Bernard Todd, both from the West Country. The body found in Somerset was Ian Buchan who came from Morayshire in Scotland." He paused briefly, as if to allow those details to sink in. There were frowns and quizzical looks exchanged amongst the officers present. "The coincidence of these 'reciprocal corpses' is something we are aware of, but as yet any connections are circumstantial. The information we have, concerning the men in question, is perhaps of greater significance. Todd disappeared eight years ago in curious circumstances…it was thought, initially, that he had run off with someone and left his family; simply a domestic matter. He left his job, as an electrical engineer, without notice. He just failed to turn up one morning and that was it. But quite soon after this, his wife and two kids vanished without trace, again very suddenly. Within weeks, the house was sold and no contact with friends or neighbours was maintained. One big mystery." Once more, Cummins savoured his pause, before continuing. "Our second big mystery is our Scotsman found in Somerset! It's the same story. 1983, that's one year after Todd went AWOL, Buchan, also an electrical engineer, apparently runs out on his family who also vanish within weeks. No notice of leaving his job and a very quick house sale to follow. No contact with any neighbours or friends was ever maintained. We are trying to ascertain whether any of the family can be traced; benefits claims, housing lists, school rolls, the usual. Our third victim, the first one to be killed, was Alfred Craddock, a computer analyst. He was thirty-seven when he and his wife vanished from their rented house. It appeared to be a moonlight flit, although his parents pestered the police for several months about the unexplained disappearance." Cummins breathed heavily, then entered the 'final straight' of his lecture. "So, all these men and their families (Craddock had no children) have vanished from....er ...everything...and the men themselves have now turned up dead. The photographs you have seen indicate the scant information which seems to connect the three men; the serial number tattoos on the left foot and the work overalls they were all wearing at the time of their deaths. Remember, all were shot within a short time of their discovery. As yet there are no obvious explanations how no gunshots were heard. The final words spoken by Buchan and Todd suggest there is a link to tunnels of some sort. The discovery of an underground area at the Somerset property on Lundy Lane is being investigated as we speak, and the possibility of a tunnel of some sort in Scotland has alerted us to the possibility of some sort of organised crime operation or even terrorist activity. As the scale of these events appears to be nationwide there will be a coordinated approach to this case involving a number of agencies. Each member of the team here will be allotted specific tasks, while officers in the field, and other operatives, will continue to follow up a variety of leads. Thank you. Are there any questions?

17th August 1990.
South London. 8 a.m.

"It's too late; questions have been asked and it's only a matter of time before the whole network's rumbled!" George Ford held the phone tightly. He was anxious, angry and unshaven. For several days now, his life had moved to the edge of an abyss. And staring into it had not been part of his plan. "Our man at the Yard was in a briefing yesterday and they are taking this mess seriously.....they've linked the killings, and any other ones.....and there will be other ones....I know....will be on their radar immediately."

The voice at the other end of the phone tried to steady the conversation, but Ford's eyes told a fearful tale. His desperation seemed to visibly grow and there was little improvement to his agitation when he replied. "I am not sure we can handle it. I do not share your optimism.......I know the bastards are in a minority, but they've taken advantage quickly and we aren't in a position to stop it, or keep the lid on things."

Frustration crawled out of every pore of George Ford as the fateful conversation continued with no relief to the pressure he was feeling. His distress was palpable. This was a man fast approaching breaking point.

"After all those years, this is not the nightmare we were always afraid of.....this is something else, but as this is real, it is happening....it's unspeakable! Everything we believed in, isn't just compromised, it's disintegrating....completely. It's Pandora's Box, for Christ's sake! I never ever thought we would go public.....not in this way....not in such appalling circumstances." Ford pulled his hand over his rough, unshaven jaw and carried on with his announcement, "I shall see what happens over the next forty-eight hours and then….well….we must face all this…….. out in the open."

17th August 1990. Inverness

McNab held the phone with a certain amount of confident assurance. He had good news to impart to his Scotland Yard counterpart and felt pleased that he was helping to dispel those stereotypical assertions that 'country coppers' were slow-paced, quaint and slightly out-of-touch. He turned to the bright sky outside his window and wondered if the sky was as blue as this in London.

"D.I. Cummins? Good, it's McNab here. Inverness. Yes. We've found a tunnel which we strongly believe is linked to our two bodies. Quite astonishing to be honest. The entrance to it was quite ingenious, really very clever.....it was concealed in such a way that no-one would ever had known it wasn't an ordinary piece of rock. It had been done like a piece of stone cladding, the sort ye get on town houses, so there was no clear indication that it was there. It was the blood marks and the skid marks of boots which gave it away. We were very lucky. The passageway in is about fifteen yards, a sort of vestibule, I suppose…and that leads to another door with some sort of electronic security system, which we intend to bypass when our specialist lads get there." He paused and sat back while he listened to Cummins' questions.

"It's halfway up a mountain, actually, so getting a team with the necessary equipment up there is not a wee job; it may take some time. I'll get back to you tomorrow, whatever happens. Aye, that'll be fine. Goodbye."

18th August 1990. Scotland Yard

Tie slightly loosened and silently sweating, Samuel Cummins stepped towards the large television set mounted on the bland beige wall of the operations room. He glanced with irritation at the air-conditioning unit and asked himself whether it was actually still working; the heat was gradually becoming quite oppressive and he needed to make sure the team of officers were on task and able to focus on the new revelations he was about to present to them.

"Watson, could you open that window a little more, please, and then close that blind. I want us to be able to see this recording as clearly as possible." Cummins waved a video cassette above his head.

The small group of officers took up positions to view the television. Three sat in available chairs, the others stood or perched on the edge of desks making themselves comfortable. What would they be watching? And how long would it last? With the cassette slipped into the machine, Cummins confirmed he had full attention before embarking on his 'live documentary' with recorded support.

"It seems," he began, "that we have another related killing on our hands. Two days ago, in Cheddar, there was a fatal stabbing in a car park. A number of people, mainly visitors but some local residents, witnessed the attack, so we *have* details about the attacker this time, and a corpse with the serial number tattoo again. It is clear from the witness statements that this attack was clearly meant to result in a death; it was deliberate and frenzied. The killer fled the scene only after he was sure the man was dead. Not a mad moment out of the blue. This killing was wholly intentional and the person we are looking for is right here." He pointed to the screen. "Yes, we have some footage of the killer." His tone was almost triumphant. The other officers stared at him. A self-conscious flush appeared and disappeared, as his hand, hovering over the play button, pointed at the screen. Cummins continued. "The video you are about to see was taken from the newly-installed CCTV system at one of the public caves. It's in two sequences; the first shows a party of tourists being led into the entrance of the cave by the resident guide. The second sequence is the more relevant and interesting one. Please take note of the group which emerges from the cave after the tour." He pressed the button and the recording started. The officers watched the screen, rapt, but uncertain of what they should be looking out for.

At the beginning of the second sequence, Cummins paused the video. "You will all have noticed," he began, trying not to sound patronising in the least, "that the initial party of visitors was, twenty plus the guide." He allowed the information to sink in. "But you will also notice, I'm sure, the difference when the same party comes out of the cave fifty minutes later." The video resumed.

Within half a minute an officer in one of the chairs exclaimed, "there's more of them!"

"Two more, to be precise," enthused Cummins, sounding rather like the slightly smug teacher who clearly knows more than his students, but wishes to reward good work. "After a lot of replays, we were able to visually identify the two newcomers." He rewound the tape a short way and then paused it. Stepping up to the screen, he took a pen from his shirt pocket and stood to one side. "Here is the party emerging, after their tour. All of them, as you can see, are wearing the safety helmets. The ones belonging to the cave company have black numbers on the side towards the back, but these two characters," he indicated the figures with his pen, "were wearing helmets without the black numbers. This was what alerted the Avon and Somerset boys when they were given the video as a result of an appeal for photographs and information from the public, from the time of the killing. A couple of stills...not brilliant definition...have been taken from the video footage of our killer and victim."

Cummins moved over to a side table, where he picked up a set of photographs and began to hand them around each officer. "This is our man. Approaching six foot, thin, dark features, dark hair.... at the time unshaven...he may still be unshaven, as he'll be, as they say, 'on the run' and is unlikely to have a refuge of any sorts. We don't know that, of course, but given the circumstances, that *is* the more likely scenario. Predictably, he was wearing exactly the same clothing, these unmarked overalls, as worn by the victim and the other three bodies we have already identified." He paused for breath and then added, "from the CCTV footage and the witness statements we have built up a 'story' of the final minutes of our new victim. Having discarded the helmets.....they were found amongst the tourist ones later.....the victim, ie. the target of the attack, tried to mingle briefly with the crowds.... the assailant followed him closely until the target made a run for it...there was a certain amount of barging into people, which helps to account for the number of witnesses. A full-blown chase ensued...down from the caves, passed shops and restaurants, over the road bridge, passed a public house and into the main car park. The attack was vicious, face slashed first...this disabled him...then more blows to the body, straight thrusts aimed at the heart...more stabs and slashes to the head. As I said before, a number of the witnesses were convinced that the attack continued until the attacker knew the target was dead. And that was the case; the paramedics declared him dead at the scene.

Eyes scanned photographs, earnest looks were exchanged and a light buzz of comments drifted through the room.

This whole mystery deepened, and this team from Scotland Yard had been charged with drawing the different incidents together and trying to fathom it. Intriguing, fascinating, horrifying but at the moment quite exasperating. D. I. Samuel Cummins waited for a resumption of the rapt attention he had had earlier.

"Now to the crux of the matter. If we simply look at this incident as a car park stabbing, we have a man-hunt on our hands. A dangerous man, clearly. That is bad enough. But. The big concern is the business of these two men emerging from the cave. It is this issue, specifically, which indicates the grave nature of this whole business. We've spoken to the people who run the cave as an attraction, checked the safety regulations, all their security practices, everything…. the conclusion is, that these two interlopers entered the public cave from *inside* the underground system itself. This appears to match the idea, the ludicrous idea we had at first, that there is a tunnel/cave network or networks we know nothing about, but some very dangerous killers clearly do know a lot about."

The observant officer from earlier spoke up, "so, are we looking for a terrorist group sir?"

Cummins gave a timely grimace, "we don't know….as yet. The possibility is undeniable. Whoever they are, they seem to be well resourced, well organised and very determined in their aims. In the absence, at the moment, of any communication from the Intelligence community we are treating this as a purely criminal matter. The suggestion it could be some sort of gang warfare is another possibility, judging from the details and nature of the Cheddar attack. Witnesses compared the assault to something out of a gangster action movie….the sort of violence you don't associate with ordinary crime…if there is such a thing!"

An hour later the team of investigators were about their various businesses. The fact that it was a Saturday and the sun was shining was now lost to any of the doubters. Their professionalism had come to the fore, and thoughts of possibly more bodies was enough motivation to keep them focused on this awful new phenomenon facing them.

19th August 1990. Central London.

The air was warm with the pink glow of the approach of sunset. The sky was like a painting, worthy of admiration, and a source of inspiration to those melancholy poetic types who gaze upwards when wishing to feel suitably abstracted by beauty. Even the subtlety of a wistful breeze provided an element of sweet distraction as this part of the metropolis lazed beneath an invisible canopy of evening delight. Indulgence and fun were the reasons why the locals, and the passing visitors, drifted between the bars and restaurants of this pleasing neighbourhood in a dreamy state, soaking up the remnants of this glorious summer Sunday. Along the streets the people were relaxed as they walked back and forth. Instinctively, one would feel this was the classic idyllic London evening when the capital was at its best.

Bursting out from the shadow of a side street, from a fashionable row of mews cottages and apartments, sprinted a young man in a wild panic. Swerving violently to avoid colliding with a taxi, just pulling away from the kerb, he half-tripped but regained his balance erratically and sped across the road and straight into another side street. His ungainly arm movements suggested he wasn't a regular or practised runner and was running more out of a need to survive, rather than a need to keep fit. His frantic efforts, narrowly missing lamp standards, parked cars and concrete bollards, soon brought him to the end of the short street, where a narrow alleyway took him to yet another street and another line of obstacles to hinder his escape. For the first time he looked behind with fear-filled eyes and a look of exhausted terror on his face. His thick blond hair stuck to the sweat on his forehead and neck and his breathing was alarmingly out of control. A series of agonising gasps brought him concerned attention from an older man who had been standing in a shop doorway admiring the contents of the window display.

"You alright mate?" the man enquired.

The runner made a motion with his head which could have been a shake or a nod. He attempted to wave his arm as if to indicate he couldn't answer, then gave up and rested his hands on his knees as he bent forward as if ready to drop. As he stumbled towards the refuge of the doorway there was a squeal of car tyres from further along the road. Passers-by slowed and turned their heads towards the ominous sound of the squealing car, which was quickly gathering speed as it moved swiftly and shark-like, the only vehicle in the middle of the road. The young runner, now a contortion of emotion, gave another desperate gasp, high-pitched this time, as if recognising a threat from this long black marauder, and staggered from side to side in an obvious panic, his lightweight jerkin flapping madly.

Silently, the nearside back window of the approaching car slid down and the tip of a crossbow bolt protruded into the summer Sunday air. The car slowed, briefly, and within a couple of seconds the deadly bolt was on its way towards the target of the gasping young man, as he reeled about hysterically.

The smash of the shop window, exploding into the evening air, brought screams and instant confusion to the street and the realisation that two figures lay on the ground in a mess of glass fragments added to the shock of the bystanders. The black car was off and away, screeching tyres and fumes in its wake. Shouts from stunned people seemed futile and helpless in the aftermath of this appalling incident; they had seen something, something shocking, a flash of violence, an attack on others in the street, their evening shattered by something dreadful.

On the pavement lay two men. Very still at first, but gradually the window- shopper pushed himself up with blood-flecked hands where he had been cut by the exploding glass. "Bleedin' Hell, mate, what was that?"

A low groaning beneath him told him the runner was still with him, still alive. He was not dead, as the purpose of the attack was meant to achieve, for the bolt from the crossbow had ripped through the young man's loose jerkin and grazed the inside of his arm, before continuing its deadly path through one of the panes of glass in the shop doorway, and embedding itself in the abdomen of a manikin wearing a striped summer shirt. The relieved young man lay for a while, still panting heavily, still trying to catch his breath. Exhaustion kept him on the ground as people gathered around to help the two men. Within minutes, the sound of approaching sirens brought a tired smile to the lips of the erstwhile runner. The closeness of the pavement soothed him and he could sense the warmth and the light of the sky above him. Moments before, he had earnestly expected to die. He believed that there was no escape. He had battled the demons inside, and outside, his head. He was about to be saved. He was about to survive.

20th August 1990. Scotland Yard

From his office window, Oscar Shackleton looked out across the dull London landscape towards the Southern edges of the city. So much was hidden. So much could not be seen. Although Shackleton believed that the majority of any population were honest and law-abiding, he knew there was always that certain proportion of people prone to bending the rules, breaking the rules and even showing a complete disregard for all rules and all morality. In a vast city like London, this 'proportion' translated into a large, potentially large, *raw number* of undesirable persons. Perhaps this was part of the challenge which had led the young Oscar Shackleton to join the police force all those years before. The apprehension of criminals, the protection of the public, the upholding of justice and the correct concern for good order; these were important to him, and he hoped they were important to others. This latest challenge seemed to set a new level of mystery, a new slant on those rare occasions when violent killings were apparently random and without motive; the greatest horror for all detectives. He was about to share this experience with his colleagues.

The information he had just received, Scotland Yard had just received, gave a whole new meaning and significance to what he understood by 'hidden'. It might even bring a whole new meaning to what he discerned as 'criminal activity'. The sheets of paper lying on his desk gave a chilling testimony of a situation confronting the police which tested the powers of his imagination. The scale of the problem, Shackleton knew, threatened to become an issue with the other security and intelligence agencies. He could see the clear possibility of an internal power struggle ahead, and this aggravated him intensely. The previous evening's attempted killing on the streets of London had outraged him and the good fortune of new intelligence, new information, coming from the would-be victim had proved both helpful and alarming. His imminent briefing of his team of officers would need to be firm and uncompromising. The local difficulties of some of the provincial forces would be urgently tackled as there was now a 'national' dimension to this 'case'.

Shackleton picked up the papers, adjusted his tie in the mirror by the door, then swept out of his office and down the corridor to the briefing room where his team grimly waited. His confident entrance brought a sudden focus and the meeting began.

"Gentlemen," he began, "and er ladies," as he noticed two pairs of stockinged legs on the front row, "we have a grave situation confronting us. Something very new it seems. Even our more experienced officers will find themselves facing a unique scenario which we are learning more and more about by the hour." He halted briefly to ascertain that the correct note of gravity had been utilised. The facial expressions in front of him confirmed this to be the case. "To be specific, we now have information.....and are gleaning more as we speak.....from a young man.....he's nineteen years of age..... who was the target of an assassination bid yesterday evening in the Bayswater area. I use the term 'assassination' because, in the circumstances, it seems more appropriate. He has told us...*is* telling us....of a network of...er....well....tunnels, caves, underground areas, which have been developed over a period of thirty years by an organisation founded during the Cold War years of the Fifties by peace groups, anti-nuclear groups and such like, for the purpose of protecting a future Britain in the event of a nuclear war. Now, however far-fetched this may seem, Pickering.....the young man is called

Andrew Pickering…has spent his entire life living the double life of a member of this organisation. Details he has given us, about personnel and locations, are being investigated, but the problem outlined by Pickering….and he is a *very* frightened man…..revolves around a 'falling out' between factions of this organisation during the past year which, this month, reached critical point and there is now a….. what Pickering calls it…..a civil war….largely underground….but as we now know, from the experiences of the past ten days or so, has now spilt over into the 'outside world'."

Shackleton paused to check something on one of his sheets of paper. His inclination was to turn this 'information briefing' into some sort of address, a rallying cry, something more appropriate to the beginnings of a dire conflict, but he resisted the temptation, but he continued with a stern voice. "The ferocity of the violence we have encountered so far leads us to believe that we are dealing with the stop-at-nothing types we dread to face, but must face, must confront, for the sake of the public at large. Pickering is being protected in a secure location. He has no major medical needs, but it is clear he is distressed about still being a target for assassination. It has been agreed that protecting him has the utmost priority; he has more to tell us, most of it historical, but some information about locations, underground locations, will prove highly important as this investigation develops."

Shackleton paused. Not for effect, but to compose himself before the next injection of explanation and information. The next section of his oration required him to refer to his papers. He held one up, as if about to announce the winner of a literary prize, then stared at his audience, moving his head in a slow horizontal arc. Then he continued.

"Andrew Pickering's father, Alan, was a mining engineer who vanished from his home and job in 1968. The circumstances were akin to those of Craddock, Todd and Buchan. This is a very common pattern with the members of this organisation. They generally refer to themselves as 'the Network', but this is a loose label and does not appear in any documentation or insignia of any kind. I will remind you, at this point, about the uniform overalls worn by the early casualties in this case; these, along with the foot tattoos, remain the only identification evidence we have. Back to Alan Pickering. As a mining engineer, he had obvious skills and knowledge which would prove invaluable to the organisation. Experience with excavating and explosives was paramount to his usefulness and, perhaps just as important, he was an active member in the peace movement, being a member of CND and a participant in Vietnam War protests. It was by mixing in these circles that he became a target for recruitment into this highly- politicised secret underground….and this can be taken literally….movement. I believe it is vitally important to stress here, that in the early stages of this phenomenon, there would be very little likelihood of criminal activity. The *raison d'etre* of these people is essentially benign, at least that would be true of the original founder members and those who later joined for the same 'honourable' reasons. If Andrew Pickering's information is to be accepted at face value, then it would seem only *recently* has there been evidence of dubious or criminal activity." The faces in front of Oscar Shackleton were staring back at him, serious and concerned. This was new territory for them. So, were they dealing with a group of peaceful lefties who were compromised by an influx of violent killers? More attention to detail should answer the question.

The bearded figure of Oscar Shackleton proceeded with his monologue. "Over thirty years; Andrew Pickering believes it may be thirty-two or thirty-three, the 'Network' has built up a series of underground areas….bases, if you like…across the country. Many, apparently, are linked to tunnels and cave networks stretching for miles underground. The entrances are protected with intense security and secrecy. Some have 'doorways' from extant public tunnels. Pickering knows, because he has been to these places, of extensive networks accessed from a whole range of locations; Nottingham, Newcastle, Manchester, obviously London, and more rural areas....Scotland and the West Country we already know about. There are, however, examples of *inner* doorways where what is, or has been, discovered is *not* the whole thing. For instance, our investigations into the property at Lundy Lane, where the body of Ian Buchan was found, have reached an impasse...a physical impasse....the cave under 'exploration' contains nothing of significance; it appears to be an empty space! Buchan's 'locked in' reference strongly suggested his killer made his escape through this 'empty space' into another, deeper underground area.....but at the moment we are confronted by another mystery. It is very likely that there will be more of the same in the coming days....and weeks, no doubt."

Once more, Shackleton's hand reached up to stroke his beard, pulling the fingers together until they perched at the point of his chin; a picture of profundity. "So, we have a number of unfortunate aspects to deal with in the days that lie ahead. It may take weeks to achieve a breakthrough. We will need a level of vigilance, perhaps, that few of us have experienced before, and it is crucial that the public remain unaware of all this for as long as possible."

He stopped deliberately and slowly perused the group of people in front of him. The differing views about public knowledge of ongoing enquiries was always a sensitive issue; Shackleton's sweep of the gathered faces tried to discern the general reaction. The earnestness was palpable, but he felt he needed to reinforce his own thinking on the matter. He straightened his back and proceeded.

"Vigilante groups would make a meal of this. Professing to be assisting the police in areas where they perceived us as being under-resourced. Taking opportunities for identifying scapegoats of all types. Instigating their own man-hunts for ill-defined reasons and pursuing a whole range of other potentially- undesirable activities. And all of this should remind us that membership,…if that's the right word … of this organisation, is not a criminal activity. Clearly, we are dealing with deadly killers, but as Pickering has told us, most of these….er….underground people….are innocent. These have been the only victims so far."

As Shackleton came to the end of his deliberations, there were brief murmurings and side glances as the officers assimilated the weight of the information confronting them. An assertive hand stood out. Shackleton gave a flicker of a frown then encouraged the response, "Watson?"

D.S. Maurice Watson spoke, articulating the question that was probably forming in the minds of quite a number of the officers present. "What will the strategy be with regards to firearms, sir? There seems a strong likelihood of 'confrontations', sir?"

The repetition of 'sir' slightly irritated Shackleton; he almost felt it may have been intended as a calculated slip into sarcasm. He dismissed the idea. "Good question. The issuing of firearms *is* being addressed, as I'm sure you would expect. There will be some intense activity on the training front and other operational aspects will be communicated to those concerned as soon as is necessary."

20th August 1990.
Scottish Highlands.

The team had worked hard, battling at times through a range of varying weather conditions. The early mist had cleared eventually to give way to a steady bout of rain, which swept in with a chill wind from the Moray Firth. Considerable effort had been harnessed to effect progress inside the mountain. The highly unusual task of locating and exploring beyond the 'vestibule', as McNab had called it, to reveal the secrets of the mystery tunnel had been the talk of the local community for several days. Everyone had voiced a theory or a speculation. Some of these airings had kept the officers both entertained and focused in their endeavours to find the answers. Specialist equipment had been carried over the difficult terrain, painfully and laboriously, before a request for aerial support, and a change in the weather, had brought a certain amount of relief in the shape of a heavy-duty helicopter. Ultimately, the operation in practice had turned out to be more professional than first assumed. McNab had been pleased to take advantage of the 'Scotland Yard connection' to add weight to his request, realising some time later that the 'request' had become a 'demand'. He had pointed out that his men were trained officers, not labourers.

Given the gravity of the operation, McNab had chosen to oversee the operation at first hand. It was important, he conceded, that his men should have his physical presence to give authority to what was a unique piece of policing and also to give visual support and guidance during the hours of their toil. He now stood, overlooking the taped-off area below an outcrop of solid rock, wondering what was in store for his officers when they entered this strange and unlikely tunnel. Oxyacetylene burners had been used to cut through the inner door after several attempts to deal with the electronic security system had resulted in repeated failure. The 'old school' McNab had had mixed feelings about the technical team's impotency when their 'technological solutions' had failed to solve the problem. The utilisation of the gas burners convinced him that this more 'direct' way, a sort of 'break-the-door-down' sort of way, was the way forward. He wasn't a real Luddite, or even a technophobe, he just had a healthy suspicion of new things which seemed too clever, or too flash, being used to achieve something relatively simple and straightforward. How straightforward this tunnel business would be, remained to be seen.

Within half an hour, the interior entrance of the tunnel had been breached. The scorching of the metal on the surface of the door presented a strange and dramatic witness to recent police activity. A number of officers were checking equipment; caving helmets, torches, police radios and firearms, before their assault on the inner sanctum. For a moment, the gaping hole in the doorway was ignored. McNab spoke.

"Well, gentlemen, the first unit inside will ascertain the 'lie of the land', for want of a better expression! We simply don't know what is inside…or who. We have no idea how far this tunnel goes. There may be other adjoining tunnels or other entrances. Exits! What we do know is that at some point recently there was, most likely, a killer in there. They may still be in there. That may sound unlikely, but we will take no chances. D.S. Baxter will lead. Irwin and Malone will make a full visual check on what's in there, every nook, every cranny. Alright there lads?" The two constables gravely nodded assent. "Murray and Forster will give firearm support if necessary. We are hoping this will not be needed. Talk to each other.

Each of you should know what the others are doing. Is that clear?" A gruff chorus of 'yes' was heard. "Best of luck."

The inner vault Baxter was now standing in was almost pitch black. The air was cool, several degrees lower than the sun –heated air of the outside. He was aware of, and surprised by, the feeling that this was a significant space. There seemed nothing cramped about his new surroundings. He peered, then squinted, at the second surprise. There was a distant, vague smudge of pale light which seemed to indicate an opening about twenty yards from the entrance the police officers had just climbed through.

"Malone check left, Irwin right. Are the walls clear?" Beams of bright torchlight waved across the stone walls, revealing a number of tubular shelving units, one with a clothes rail behind a heavy plastic transparent screen like those found in a clothing factory or warehouse. There were four sets of the ubiquitous overalls, identical to those worn by the two shooting victims, hanging on a length of the rail. "Clothing, sir," informed Malone, "and footwear too," as he spotted several pairs of work-boots beneath the overalls. Other containers, worthy of exploration, could be seen.

"More doors, sir," announced Irwin as he swept his beam of light in a tight line along another stretch of wall where three doorways were situated next to more shelving units, some holding several large, heavy-looking boxes. As Baxter turned towards the doorways, there was a soft scraping sound ahead of them.

"Hello. Police," shouted Baxter. There was a silent pause after the brief reverberations of his voice.

"Sir, the light's gone," whispered Malone, "look!"

The vague smudge of light ahead had disappeared. Baxter immediately assumed an opening had closed. Someone had closed it. "Switch off all lights on the count of two, for two seconds," ordered Baxter. "One, two." Click. Total darkness. There was no other light source. "Okay." The torches came back on. "This way," led the detective sergeant, as he moved cautiously towards the spot where the original faint light had been.

In a sudden crash, which the people present would talk about for years, all hell seemed to break loose. The deafening report and resonance of a gun shot filled the space around them and seemed to ring in everyone's ears for minutes, but it would have been only seconds. Shouts of "Police" echoed against the walls and low ceiling, and then another shot rang out and a shattered torch was dead. The confusion instantly generated meant Baxter had no idea who had fired the second shot. Or in fact from whereabouts it had come, in this dungeon of a space. He had no idea what was going on, other than it wasn't part of their plan Another loud crash followed by another gunshot brought complete turmoil to their operation. Someone was yelling, then moaning. Was it the same person? Baxter was aware of a sudden movement and someone was running away from the immediate space. Towards the spot where the light had been earlier. Someone else was giving chase. In the remaining torchlight, Baxter saw two figures, pursued and pursuer. The chase happened so quickly and finished so abruptly, that Baxter always remembered it like the flickering of an old silent movie.

As the figures were about to become one, the front one turned and seemed to kick out. Then a sudden glow of light appeared. Malone's voice gasped and exclaimed, "You?" before another almighty crash of the final gunshot. The glow of light vanished and the chaos caused by the interloper remained, waiting to be cleared up. Cordite hung in the air like a disease and the muffling and panting of bodies added to the utter catastrophe of this dark and darkened incident.

"Torch, someone, over here!" shouted Baxter. One beam of light obeyed. "Hell! Malone's been hit. He's in a bad way. We need help. Get the paramedic!"

"Will do, sarge," came Irwin's voice, "the others'll need one too, the bastard pushed the shelving on top of them!"

Lying prone on the ground Jamie Malone was trying to say something to Baxter. "No, Jamie, no, don't you talk, just rest. You keep your breathing steady. We'll take care of you in a wee while."

And in the near darkness, with the groans of two of his officers somewhere behind him, and shouting from the outside world, D.S. Craig Baxter watched over his youngest officer for a few poignant moments before help arrived, and shed the tears that no-one else would ever see.

21st August 1990. Bristol.

John Gates' team of officers, the cream of the Avon and Somerset Constabulary, sat earnestly and expectantly, around the briefing room waiting to be told, in greater detail, of the morning's success and its consequences for them. The early apprehending of a vicious killer was always going to be good news inside any police station, so the atmosphere in the room was bordering on buoyant. In the presence of Detective Chief Inspector John Gates, the level of buoyancy was measured, rather than lively.

"As you have already been informed, no doubt, we have apprehended the suspect for the Cheddar murder, committed five days ago. He was found asleep in a barn just off the B3151 after a tip-off from a local farmer, whose brother-in-law happens to be one of our fellow officers. A stroke of luck there perhaps…. but we're not complaining. The suspect made a determined attempt to resist arrest, but was unsuccessful in his efforts. He sustained minor injuries in the process and has been examined by the police surgeon, who has confirmed there is no need for hospitalisation and he can be held in custody right here! We have him downstairs at the moment and, in keeping with others involved in this current business, he has no identification, and is resolutely refusing to cooperate with us over the matter. The fact that he had not travelled far from the scene of the crime is interesting. He has clearly been sleeping rough, but seemed to chose to stay relatively close to Cheddar. Remember, he came from the cave in Cheddar Gorge!" Gates realised in an instant what that sounded like; a tabloid headline or a title from a B. movie. One or two officers 'heard' it too. A few wry smiles appeared in the assembled group. Gates continued after a slightly embarrassed shrug.

"Scotland Yard is coordinating this business, but they are not 'moving in and taking over'. We are at the sharp end, like our Scottish colleagues, and our local knowledge and intelligence may prove to be invaluable in taking these major investigations forward. I don't need to remind you of the shocking nature of the Cheddar killing, but I do need to add something very pertinent about the people we may be dealing with. I was informed earlier today that a young police officer near Inverness, in Scotland, was shot in an incident underground, while taking part in an operation to investigate a suspicious tunnel and apprehend an assailant, who also injured two other armed officers, before making his escape." The emphasis Gates placed on *'incident underground'* and *'armed'* was deliberate. A number of shocked faces stared back at him. In their own minds they had emphasised *'shot'* and *'young officer'*.

Any doubts that the officers may have had about the nature of this present 'case' were dramatically removed from their thoughts and speculations. The shooting of a police officer on the British mainland was still something rare and shocking. The exchanged looks and hardened faces told their own story.

"The national dimension to this business is becoming more apparent and in some sense may seem a complication, but *our* focus, 'on the ground' so to speak, is the search for the suspect in the Lundy Lane murder and the interrogation of the Cheddar assailant, who remains the only person, anywhere in the country in custody over this matter." There was a guarded smugness almost in the way Gates expressed this last fact, as if it was something his force could be proud of, albeit as a result of a stroke of luck. He reminded himself of a similar lucky break which had lead to the capture of the Yorkshire Ripper in the 70's.

"An officer from Scotland Yard," Gates continued, "will be here later today to coordinate any relevant information and consult on operational matters. We will give him full assistance, obviously, but we may also be able to glean further information from him to help our own efforts here. D.S. Watson will also be taking a look at the Lundy Lane property with our own D.S. Harvey. There are some issues here which may need to be reassessed in light of the Scottish incident. Okay."

As his officers quietly and purposefully dispersed, Gates was all too aware that he had not planned to finish on such a sombre note and now the moment was lost.

21ˢᵗ August 1990. Central London.

The anticipated caffeine rush was savoured by George Ford as he held his hot cup of coffee in both hands. Mystery seemed to surround the physics of the absurdly-shaped object with a single, overly-small handle, and an equally absurd-sized cup attached to it. Ford's abstracted state allowed him to ponder, meaninglessly, on the whole business of weight distribution as it affected the cup of coffee in front of him. Such distractions helped Ford to avoid focusing on the matter in hand. Any flight of fancy would have been welcomed as long as it occupied Ford's thoughts and feelings on subjects of no consequence. Perhaps the caffeine had been an ill-judged idea; he did not really want to be so over-stimulated. He continued to use both hands and took another careful sip of the hot liquid. Then he placed it back onto its saucer. The physics of a coffee cup. There was the irony. He caught a glimpse of himself in the mirrored wall adjacent to the table he occupied. This was a man who had planned, and helped execute, one of the greatest physical projects of human endeavour. An unbelievable and largely unknown masterpiece of engineering had been constructed beneath Britain, completely unacknowledged by the wider society above ground, but appreciated by a few thousand committed people who had joined his adventure, joined his dream. But now the legacy of recent dissent and division threatened to turn this unlikely dream into a breathtaking nightmare. That which had been his benign empire was now the great burden of his life. He simply did not expect the near future to bring anything but chaos and heartache. By some means or another, it had all changed. The Vision had gone; tarnished compromised, embattled, destroyed. He couldn't bury his head in the sand; he knew what was buried there.

Meeting 'in secret' had become something new to George Ford. For almost half his life he had led a secret life; perhaps half a secret life anyway, but not in the sense that he needed to actively evade people. Now was different. Now, there was another 'side', an 'opposition', an enemy. So much had been re-defined. Now there were people he must avoid. And some of them, probably most of them had, at one time or another, been his friends. Now it wasn't just different, it was also difficult.

There was a brief flurry of activity at the door of the coffee shop, with a lively group of students leaving noisily. The straggler of the group redeemed himself by hanging back to hold the door open for an older couple and a single sun-glassed man. A short cheer went up from the other students already on the pavement as their 'hero' emerged through the cafe door, wrapped in coy embarrassment.

The couple sat at a window table while the 'bespectacled' man gave a slightly self-conscious scan of the tables, before removing the sunglasses and discreetly acknowledging Ford. He stepped uncertainly towards the counter and ordered his coffee and fumbled for a five-pound note. His long coat contradicted the weather outside.

Two minutes later, George Ford and Ken Carter were locked in a stern and tense conversation which fizzed with tension. It almost glowed with raw, restrained and restricted emotions which did even less for the health of their digestive systems than the strong coffee they were consuming.

Ford was articulating his view in measured, but earnest tones, "I did as you suggested, Ken. I held back on the idea of going public. You were right about that. I realised that the media was not the way to do it anyway. But we do need to make some decisions now. We can't delay when people are being killed!"

Ken Carter nodded assent, "I know, I know. I had hoped for something to change, something to prevent things from escalating, but....I do think now that any chance that would happen has gone. It's out of control. Certainly ours!"

"And it *is* Derek and Henry who are leading them?" inquired Ford.

"Well, yes I suppose so. They were clearly the primary instigators, but to say that the pair of them are 'leading' anyone or even 'in control' may be an exaggeration. It's more like anarchy from the reports I've been getting. I think the brutality has been frightening. Frankly, it's a nightmare!"

"What about us....is Ellen okay? The Pickerings? I've lost all contact with them since they were due to be top-side, not even a phone call. That's bloody worrying. And Felicity? Although, she may be out of the country this time of year."

"Ellen is back in Nottingham, looking after her mother who is getting worse. Ellen will be fine, she'll be able to keep away from anything nasty. David knows what's going on and is concerned about some of the others. I worry he might try to do something rash, you know how committed he's always been. He won't be able to let go. Alan Pickering was due to come back to London a couple of days ago. I've heard nothing further." Carter seemed to run out of heart as his update came to an end.

"The other people who we've lost contact with.....do we know any more? I know some will be in hiding, but, to be blunt, there could be a lot of dead bodies around. It could be a bloodbath, for God's sake! Bodies out of sight that no- one will ever know about." Ford stopped suddenly, as if he had listened to his words for the first time, and they had registered the real magnitude of their meaning. He stared directly into the eyes of his old friend Ken Carter. "It worked for so long, Ken; our dream. A generation of good intentions gone, virtually overnight. We can only hope to salvage something from it all if we come clean with the authorities somehow. We've never been here before. No-one's ever been here before. There are no precedents, no rules, no right way to do it. I just don't know."

The dregs of the coffee were cold now as they languished in the absurd cup. The two men were hunched over the table looking like a pair of losers recently turned out of the bookmakers for one last time. Two men drained of life, drained of confidence. Two men who needed a final chance, perhaps, to limit the appalling damage of a broken dream and all its dreadful repercussions.

Ford spoke. "Let's get off now and make the video. I think we both know what needs to be said. The camera is set up. It won't take long. I can put some arrangements in place quickly. The police will have it by the end of the day and we shall see very soon what they make of it all. At least we can give them more pieces to the jigsaw. And give them an idea of how big the picture is."

21st August 1990. Inverness.

A chilling mist rolled in from the Moray Firth, obscuring the distant view of the Black Isle and the mountains beyond. Craig Baxter pulled up the collar of his jacket to guard against the dampness in the air, locked his car and strode purposefully towards the main entrance of Raigmore Hospital. With a troubled mind he set off grimly to the room in the Intensive Care Unit which was solemnly playing host to Constable Jamie Malone. The perilous state of Malone's injuries was the prime concern of Baxter's troubled thoughts, but there was something else which niggled him about his memory of the awful moments before Malone sustained the gunshot wound.

By the time he reached the room, he had decided not to press Malone about his worries until the young man was further on the road to recovery. The constable's parents, Davy and Mags, sat grim-faced by the bedside holding hands on top of Davy's right knee. Baxter smiled awkwardly at the pair and stood, at the bottom of the bed, looking at the young constable's sleeping face and the paraphernalia around him silently assisting his recovery.

"You've a grand lad there, Mrs Malone, Mr Malone," started Baxter, "and he should be fine, sooner than you think."

"Aye, but it was touch and go at first, ye know," commented Davy Malone.

"Yes, it did not look good. I shall never forget that moment, Mr Malone, for as long as I live. Maybe we had some good fortune in that cave," said Baxter looking upwards sagely. Mags Malone crossed herself and nodded. Baxter continued, "there was a great team though; the paramedics and the helicopter boys did us proud and, as usual, the medical people here were brilliant." He stopped himself from going into lecture mode, realising that the Malones knew all this, and also remembering that Jamie Malone's fiancée, Dora Doig, worked as a nurse at this very hospital.

"What was our Jamie doing when he was shot, Mr Baxter?" asked Mags, trying to understand the circumstances where someone would want to take her son away from her. The look on Baxter's face hardened, briefly, then just as quickly softened as he looked at the faces of this bewildered mother and this confused father.

"Well, this is not straightforward," he announced. "The person who shot Jamie may have killed two other men over the last fortnight. He's a very dangerous man. However, the circumstances of this particular investigation are far-reaching and somewhat er, confidential, I suppose." He noted the expression on the Malones' faces. "I know this is not sounding very satisfactory as an explanation, but believe me," and he turned towards the bed-ridden young officer," that lad is a good copper, he's a brave young man and when this whole story comes out a lot more people will realise that."

"Thanks for that, Mr Baxter, we know what you're saying. And we're already proud of him. He'll be back working with you pretty soon, I'm sure," said Davy Malone.

"I shall see you tomorrow hopefully, when I pop in to see him; he still hasn't given me his report about yesterday!" he exclaimed with mock seriousness. He smiled and left the room, leaving the Malones to continue their vigil and returning to his own niggling thoughts, and the question he was rehearsing to ask Jamie Malone when he had regained consciousness.

22nd August 1990. Bristol. 8 a.m.

Maurice Watson felt like a spy. Effectively, he was a spy, when he considered the current circumstances of his life.

His reason for being in Bristol was the fact that he was a Detective Sergeant from Scotland Yard assisting in the investigations of two murders, linked to another two murders in Scotland, with a couple of attempted murders thrown in for good measure. All of these crimes were clearly perpetrated by members of a clandestine organisation; an organisation of which *he* was a member. How he felt about this was not easy to grasp. He was utterly aware of a great sense of guilt, but also understood that he had no reason to feel any guilt whatsoever. Confessing to his own membership of this network would not have helped matters as far as the current series of incidents was concerned; his revelation would only have created a needless distraction. *He* would have become part of the story, and he seriously doubted whether he could then make any worthwhile contribution to the investigation. By remaining incognito, so to speak, he might be able to help things along, without the necessity of revealing himself. So that would be his plan. For years he had kept the secret; throughout his training at Hendon. On more than one occasion he had disguised his potentially-incriminating tattoo with some additional artwork with a black pen, cleverly masking the X147 on his left foot and passing the design off as a result of a romantic interlude from his teenage years.

He thought now of those early days when he became involved with the network. The tattoos had been a device to identify people within the organisation and had been instigated from the very beginning. The specific purposes for the numbers had been lost over time, but the practice was strictly carried out. It was something he had rarely thought about until the advent of this recent crisis. The original founders of the organisation, from 1956, had taken the first numbers and had become known as the A Group, and every subsequent year the membership moved one letter at a time through the alphabet until 1982 when they started again with an A prefix and the alphabet sequence following as before. The number was simply the chronological number of each new member for that year. Watson had obviously felt bad about the victims when their deaths were discovered, and he had realised that the numbers, AD365, AA47 and AB124, those of the first three bodies, indicated that they were relatively new recruits, joining some years after his own introduction. He had mentally wrestled with the idea that this may be of some significance to the case itself, but found no real reason for thinking it so. The previous evening, shortly after his arrival in Bristol, he had briefly seen the Cheddar suspect and had toyed with the idea of asking to see the man's serial number. He had decided not to do so. Whether he would do so later, and make the daring suggestion to his superiors that the tattooed numbers may have a meaning, was an idea which had floated around his mind but had not considered whether it should land yet. He needed to be convinced that this information would be of any help to the overall investigation.

Sitting by himself at a breakfast table by the window, Watson cut his last piece of bacon with his final mushroom and brought his full English breakfast to a satisfying end. Across the sunlit restaurant guests were at various stages of their own hotel breakfast rituals, some in subdued chatter with colleagues or friends, others reading propped up newspapers or taking in their pleasant surroundings. Glancing at his watch told him that D.S. Frank Harvey would be meeting him outside reception in about five minutes. A quick top up of coffee from the stainless steel pot would help send him into today's business of mystery and enquiry with a sharpened mind.

Minutes later, Watson strode through the open foyer doors of the hotel as a dark blue saloon car pulled up at the kerb by the main entrance, and D.S. Harvey gave a brief wave towards the passenger door which quietly slipped open. This mutual punctuality augured well for the day ahead.

"Good morning, how was breakfast?" asked Frank Harvey, from the driver's seat.

"Breakfast was fine, thank you," replied Watson, "I hope you're taking me somewhere nice. When I'm in this part of the country I always think I'm on holiday!"

"Well, I am taking you to the seaside!" laughed Harvey, "but don't expect a lot of fun. The exploration of Lundy Lane has reached an impasse, meaning we have not located any new entrances or exits from this inner chamber we found. So that's the physical side of things; that's frustrating enough, but there are other points of concern about the property, namely its ownership. The paper trail has led us abroad. We are still working on that, but something that may be more pertinent is its cover as a holiday let." He checked his mirror with a glance, slid into top gear, left the roundabout behind and accelerated up the slip-road and on to the M5, heading swiftly to the Somerset coast.

Watson tried to visualise the inner chamber Harvey had described previously; it may be something similar to one of those he had experienced himself. He had to concede that the engineering skills used to disguise the entrances to the tunnel system was second to none. Although he had no expertise in the field of engineering, he was proud to be associated with such excellence. Some of the members he had befriended over the years had been responsible for this superb security. Now of course he could not be sure who could be trusted in this elusive mayhem taking place across the whole country. He speculated whether there would be anything familiar about the chamber he was about to visit. Would he 'find the door' if he realised where it was? How could he make that look like a lucky guess? He stared at the cloud-flecked sky, thinking before speaking.

"A holiday let, you say?" queried Watson, "a cover?"

"Well, that's it. A meticulous search has failed to reveal how it was ever booked! No advertising for the property has been unearthed! We were informed by local intelligence; interviewing residents and even making contact with visitors who had stayed at the other cottages on Lundy Lane, and came up with a very clear picture of the clientele. Never any families, with children I mean, usually couples, but sometimes single persons. Apart from the odd 'hullo', 'good morning' or 'good evening' there have been no verbal exchanges mentioned by anyone. And no-one has any recollection of anything being delivered there." Harvey absently shook his head as if he had finished all the known details of this conundrum. He glanced at Watson, half-looking for a reaction. There appeared to be none. Harvey was about to resume his update when Watson spoke.

"So, given the circumstances and meagre information we now have, and putting this knowledge into some kind of context, we are presumably looking at a property which belongs to this network 'thing'….. is part of it, in fact?"

"I suppose so, even though that doesn't make us feel as if we've made any tangible progress. It's all new territory really, isn't it?"

"Yes, and this Scottish incident turns it all into something very nasty. The 'civil war' scenario we've been discussing at the Yard makes a solution, or even an approach, very difficult. It shows us the potential scale of the task, and that's pretty intimidating, if you ask me. We could be dealing with a lot of people who are wholly innocent, it would appear, while some of the others are behaving like psychopaths!" Watson grimaced with annoyance and scanned the widening blue stretches of sky, even though his struggling thoughts were definitely underground. A pensive and mutual silence filled the car as they sped on towards Lundy Lane.

22ⁿᵈ August 1990.
Central London. 8 a.m.

It had been three long days since Andrew Pickering had been truly out in the open air. The light freshness of the late summer breeze helped to lift his spirits and gave him a surprising boost in confidence after his recent trauma and troubles. Being 'held' in a police 'safe' house had been a curious experience for him, his only concern being an inability to find out about his parents' whereabouts. Detailing as much as he knew about the underground network to the police had been an important part of his ongoing recovery from the ordeal he had been through. The secrecy of many years had been challenged and he felt a curious mixture of feelings. In the confusion of his raw emotions were relief, shock, anger, a feeling that he had betrayed others, perhaps even his parents, a sense of associated guilt, a level of vulnerability he was not accustomed to, and a strong awareness of responsibility as he perceived the true importance of the new information he was conveying to the authorities. One thing which was very clear to him was the fact that his recent experience, coupled with the revelations he had now presented to the 'outside world', meant his life would never be the same again. His 'detention' had been a strange, but welcome, relief to his sensibilities and his sense of security. He was ready to face the next phase of this new reality.

Accompanied closely by a plain-clothes police officer, he hastened towards a parked car with a waiting door open to receive him. His emotional recovery from the attempt on his life was not complete by any means, but his determination to move on was evident in the lack of hesitation he demonstrated when the police suggested his participation in a clandestine tour of properties where he knew of 'network' activity, particularly the location of entrances to the mysterious 'underworld' he had been a part of for so long. During his conversations with the police, he had been made aware of other related incidents of great concern to them which gave a context to his own trouble. He was in no doubt of his importance to the whole investigation. And here he was, sitting in a police car, helping them with their enquiries and being escorted towards the scene of a crime.

Slowly, the car moved up the street to the junction of a main road and stopped, waiting for a suitable break in the traffic. Next to Andrew Pickering in the back of the car was D.I. Samuel Cummins.

"We're really grateful for your help with this, Andrew. I realise how difficult it may be, going back to Windsor Mews."

"No, I don't mind. It's important I help you, do the right thing. Something awful has happened with the organisation. And my parents, and some others I know, are missing. I suppose…." young Pickering seemed to run out of steam. He turned to look, nervously, out of the window as tears began to fill his eyes. He brushed them away carelessly with the back of his hand. "I don't fully understand what went wrong; some sort of argument, a division of opinion, pretty strong opinion, I suppose….and it's got out of hand, out of control. I would never have dreamt it could get so violent."

Andrew Pickering paused and looked out at the streets and buildings of London as the police car moved with the morning traffic towards the scene of his recent crisis. He tried to recognise the area of the city they were travelling through, and remembered something he needed to reinforce with D. I. Cummins.

"You do remember that I don't really know this house we're going to, don't you?" he asserted, with a slight edge of guilt. "I mean I'm not familiar with the property. It was a lucky exit, I suppose, that's all." A thought struck him. "Although, I guess it saved my life. Helped to, anyway."

"We appreciate that, Andrew. We just need to find this exit of yours… or entrance, I suppose, if you look at it that way. There are other aspects of the address, the property, we need to ascertain. This will be of great assistance in our investigations. Really." D. I. Cummins gave a nodding smile in Andrew's direction.

The details of the witnessed violence he had given to the police during the extensive interviews over the previous three days in the 'safe' house came back to him. The questioning had never felt like an interrogation; he simply felt relieved to expose his experiences to the forces of law and order. He had been desperate to describe the frightening incidents which told him, very clearly, that things below ground had gone seriously wrong. His own individual experience had shown him that the trouble had not stayed underground. When he was informed that the Cheddar attack he read about in the newspaper was another related incident he was mortified. For all of his life he had been a part of this strange network; he had grown up under its wing. It was a benign presence in his life, but he was also very aware of the importance of its secrecy. Within a brief period of time, his whole life had been turned upside down. Although he was quite a boyish nineteen year old, he was rapidly taking on the mantle of manhood.

Cummins stared sympathetically at the young man and gently touched him on the shoulder. "There's a lot you'll need to get used to, but we will look after you however long it takes." He paused and considered his next few words. "At the moment, you are the only person we know of who can help us with these incidents. Your information could save lives. But I'm sure you realise that."

"Yeah, I know," Andrew nodded, "I just hope there's a chance that Mum and Dad are safe." Cummins could offer no solace on that point and simply nodded his head in tacit agreement.

Some minutes later, the unmarked police car containing Cummins and Andrew Pickering pulled into the short cul-de-sac which was Windsor Mews. The police driver stopped the car just inside the opening of the wide avenue of luxury apartments and cottages. A modern development with the car in mind, Windsor Mews had width enough to allow plenty of room for parking on both sides with adequate space for turning circles, although there appeared to be no garages to accommodate residents' vehicles. As a short stretch of road, with such a wide space for parking, the mews took on the aspect of a courtyard.

Inside the car, D.I. Cummins explained the plan again to Andrew Pickering to reassure him, primarily of his own safety, and the reasoning behind the procedure. "The keys that you grabbed on your dramatic exit from number 8 have been given to the officers who will make the first approach. We are hoping one of the keys fits the front door; we'll know that in about two minutes time. If that is not the case, the second unit of men will batter the door down!" He smiled directly at Pickering, whose eyes seemed to widen in a mixture of alarm and delight. "When the whole house has been checked and deemed safe, you and I will be invited in."

Andrew looked at the front of 8 Windsor Mews and remembered his last, brief experience there; the terrified flight from the building, clearly running for his life, and felt a certain amount of 'unreality' about it. The time he had spent in the house was minimal. He had, in effect, passed through it hurriedly from the tunnel where he had encountered his pursuers and would-be assassins. Any fear of viewing the building again was lost in the ensuing memories of his imagination, rather than in anything tangible like any idea of detail in the passing landscape.

The rasping noise of the police radio broke the general quiet of the parked car. Cummins took the hand-piece. "D.I. Cummins here." He listened intently to the disembodied voice.

"The address you are about to enter, 8 Windsor Mews, has been identified from a series of CCTV tape recordings, as a suspect house. The surveillance cameras we checked, as part of the investigation into the attack on Andrew Pickering, have come up with footage of the identified car going into the mews, but not coming back out. There are no exits or garages indicated on the plans for Windsor Mews."

When the message came to an end, Cummins replaced the radio receiver and turned his attention to looking out of the car's back window. Andrew Pickering followed his gaze. "Ah yes! There it is. See that camera, up on the wall. It's covering the length of the street. Security company operate it as part of the residents' lease agreements. New- fangled idea. We'll be surrounded by them in a few years time, I bet!"

"So that car just vanished....somewhere in this street!" exclaimed Pickering.

"Cars don't vanish. But they can be hidden. I'm interested in those wrought iron gates at 8A." Cummins was looking forward to his invitation to number 8, but had already decided he'd be popping next door to meet the neighbours.

The anticipation in the car was almost palpable, when Cummins and Pickering caught sight of two tall men in dark suits, carrying leather attaché cases, striding towards the top end of the mews. They looked like Jehovah's Witnesses or Mormons.

"That's us!" said Cummins smiling at Pickering and nodding his head towards the two men. "Sometimes they're delivery men, electricity board workers.....all the world's a stage for them," he joked.

As the occupants of the car watched, one of the men took out of his pocket the small bunch of keys which three days ago had fallen into Andrew Pickering's fateful possession. Their value was about to be determined. With the second key, the front door was opened. The two policemen entered the house and lights were switched on inside before an internal check of the building took place. Ten minutes elapsed before the rasping of the radio was heard again. "All clear, sir. It's safe for inspection."

Making the entry to the house look as innocent as possible was part of the plan to avoid causing interest or curiosity amongst the neighbours, but, as yet, there was no obvious evidence that there was anybody around. No movement of curtains, no-one opening front doors. One would have expected some signs of life given the time of day. Nothing stirred. Cummins pensively stroked the side of his face, slowly moving his hand to his chin. Something worried him. It was the street itself. Here he was, on the verge of entering a house, seemingly a normal house…on the face of it…. maybe that was the point. They already knew that No. 8 was *not* a normal house, so what about the others. Surely, all the houses in the mews looked, more or less, the same. Andrew Pickering, having keyed himself up for another visit to No. 8, turned sideways and frowned slightly at Cummins' apparent hesitation.

"Are we going in?" queried Pickering, almost with a sense of eagerness. "Is there something wrong?"

"I don't know." Cummins' reply was slow and deliberately thoughtful, as his eyes quickly scanned the houses on both sides.

As if suddenly spurred into action after a prolonged delay, Cummins grabbed the door handle. "Stay here for the moment. I want to check something before we go in." His tone was authoritative and reassuring and Pickering sat back in his seat and nodded. The detective inspector climbed out of the car and walked steadily towards the open end of the mews, away from No 8. As he reached the corner he signalled to one of the support vehicles which had followed his own car and was now parked out of sight from Pickering's position in the back of the police car.

After several minutes, Cummins emerged purposefully, striding to the first door of the left-side row of houses. He rang the bell and waited. One minute later he was still waiting. With the second ring of the door-bell he stepped to one side and peered unashamedly into a downstairs window. He then tapped, quite robustly, on the glass pane of the window. At the same moment he stepped back to look upwards to the upper floor of the property, another plain clothes officer appeared at the corner and acknowledged Cummins. After a few brief words, the other officer began the same process as Cummins, on the right side of the street. Within minutes of the two officers continuing this strange ritual of ringing bells and knocking on doors, a marked police car slid to a halt and blocked the road entrance to Windsor Mews. Uniformed officers climbed out and, within a minute, had stretched out the blue and white tickertape of a police crime scene, indicating to anyone approaching that they would not be allowed to enter Windsor Mews.

While all of this activity took place around him, Andrew Pickering, watched in rapt excitement and something akin to the beginnings of alarm, as all of the doors remained unanswered. Whatever had irked Detective Inspector Samuel Cummins about this short London street, it had brought him to the discovery of something very unusual.

Half an hour later, Windsor Mews was a hive of police activity. More officers, uniformed and plain-clothes, had arrived, all with clear tasks. Some had been sent to trawl the local businesses for any information about the residents of Windsor Mews. Car radios were utilised for information requests concerning the individual properties. As No 8 had been the initial target of the morning's business, it was here that D.I. Cummins focused. The rest of his men had plenty to occupy them.

By lunch-time, a great deal had been discovered about Windsor Mews. There were no records of individual residents, although property rates had been paid in full since the place was built. The origin of the payments was now subject to an investigation in other quarters. Cummins was perfectly happy for the finance people to chase that; he was chasing dangerous villains and he was surrounded by supporting evidence that Windsor Mews just might be a 'hub' of such activity. The exit used by young Pickering had been found, and a team of officers were working on trying to overcome the electronic security system. Getting out, as Pickering had told them, was always easier than getting in. This was clearly proving to be the case.

But Cummins was particularly pleased with what he considered the major find of the operation so far, the one which linked all this activity to a real crime, was the revelation that 8A was not a real house but a fabricated and false front, rather like a film studio set. And when this 'front' was opened, by a clever electronic sliding-door system, there was the big black car used in the pursuit of Andrew Pickering. The vehicle used in an assassination attempt. Cummins had almost purred with satisfaction when the crucial discovery was made. As Cummins walked back to the police car with Andrew Pickering, he knew that the morning's work had brought a significant breakthrough in this strange case. He was convinced the forensic teams would unearth more gems. The black car would be identified; its ownership, its history, any evidence that was left inside which could lead them to the next stage of the enquiry.

"Thanks, Andrew. This morning has been good. We could not have learnt all this without your lead." Cummins grinned. Noticing Pickering's face, he changed his grin to a more sympathetic smile. "Right, I expect you'll fancy some lunch! And I want you to talk to me about your mum and dad."

22nd August 1990. Inverness. 10.a.m.

Craig Baxter was walking thoughtfully along the hospital corridor, almost lost to speculation and imagination, when he became aware of a figure ahead of him, stopped and blocking his way.

"Dora, isn't it?" He tried to discern the look on her face. "How is Jamie?"

"He regained consciousness a wee while ago, but he still needs rest, Mr Baxter."

"That's great news," enthused Baxter as he made to continue his way to Jamie's room. Dora Doig seemed to stand her ground and gave more than a hint of a frown to the detective sergeant. Baxter held his hands up in mock surrender and gave a twisted smile.

"I promise I won't tire him out. I actually have only one question to ask him," he began to explain, "that's one police-type question, I mean!"

Dora seemed to relent. She took Baxter by the sleeve of his jacket and shepherded him on his way, escorting him along the corridors to the room playing host to her fiancé. As the two of them arrived at the door, Jamie's parents were preparing to leave.

"Ah, Dora and Mr Baxter, we'll just pop home for a time. He's fine and wants a few wee things brought from home. We didna want to leave him alone," explained Davy Malone, turning to his wife to show he was talking for her too.

"We were waiting for a nurse." Mags Malone smiled at Dora. "Ye can have some time alone with him now, hen!"

Suddenly realising she had forgotten Baxter's presence, she finished with an, "oh!"

"I shall be ten minutes, I expect, at the most. I won't be allowed to overstay my welcome. This young lady will see to that!" he indicated Dora.

The Malones left and Dora and Craig Baxter sat at opposite sides of the bed, as the young constable tried a grin on for size and nodded to his protecting fiancée. He then turned to face Craig Baxter.

"It's great to see you, Jamie, awake and looking pretty shipshape. You had us worried for a while," Baxter's eyes took in Dora Doig as he spoke the words. "I'm sure you'll want some time with Dora, rather than me, but I'm temporarily pulling rank; no more than ten minutes." Baxter paused and noted the silent agreement of all parties. "Okay, Jamie, can you remember much about what happened before you were shot?" Baxter inwardly grimaced as he heard the bluntness and insensitivity of his question.

Malone was not fazed by Baxter's approach and seemed surprisingly alert to the business in hand. "It all seemed to happen very quickly, but because it was dark I think I can remember the scenes when there was some light. It's like a series of images, I suppose." This was encouraging for Baxter.

"You appeared to say something to the man with the gun, just before he shot you? Can you recall what it was?"

"Oh yes, I wouldn't forget that," answered Malone, as if there was no doubt in his mind about some crucial detail he was about to reveal. "You see, I recognised him."

Both Baxter and Cora were stunned. They stared at Malone, then looked at each other in disbelief, desperate to understand and gauge the other's reaction.

"You recognised him!" repeated Baxter with a sense of alarm. "You know who he is?" Baxter's eyes opened wide. Dora's hand reached up to her mouth in sudden shock.

"Oh, I don't know his name though. That's the problem. I can't remember it."

Baxter blurted, "but you recognise him? His face? If you saw him again!"

Jamie Malone was certain. "Oh yes. I recognised him from the telly!"

23rd August 1990.
Scotland Yard. 9.30.a.m.

With a grave demeanour, Oscar Shackleton faced the team of officers scattered around the Operations Room. The level of anticipation was high. Each person in the room was expecting more revelations concerning the operation they were embroiled in. Snippets of information, slices of rumour and bits of gossip had inevitably combined to create various versions of what the latest news would be. The nature of this new and unusual challenge was something which occupied their imaginations and fed their sense of intrigue. The apparent scale of the investigation, not just geographically, but administratively, was unprecedented. Whatever was about to be announced would be nothing minor, nothing incidental; that was for certain. Shackleton scanned the crowd attentively and began his latest address, like a general in the field giving a progress report on the state of battle. For a few moments, that was how it felt to him.

"Good morning, ladies and gentlemen. Before I talk to you today about recent Developments here in London, I would like to give you the good news, the very good news, that our Scottish colleague, Police Constable Jamie Malone, has regained consciousness and is on the path to recovery." A buoyant murmur of comments, coupled with smiles and nods, pervaded the room. "We understand that P.C. Malone has information which may help us with our investigations, but this is in the early stages of scrutiny and I shall keep you up to date with any relevant developments."

Like a class of school students, intent on the latest rumour, the officers exchanged looks and whispers. Shackleton nodded patiently and proceeded. "Yesterday, D.I. Cummins and his team; a somewhat bigger team than we originally planned for, made a critical discovery which opens up a whole new avenue of enquiry." His brief pause allowed those people present, who were suitably informed, enough time to spot his word play and smile knowingly. Others sat unaware and waited for the pertinent detail. "In a nutshell, we have discovered a…." he searched for the word,"…er.. bogus street, Windsor Mews in the Bayswater area, which appears to be a front for this network we are investigating. Although there has been domestic activity of sorts in the street itself, in most of the houses in fact, which suggests that people have been living there for some time, there seems to be no real permanent residents and there are some properties which have revealed connecting tunnels in basements, an underground space for several vehicles and all manner of other curiosities which are being dealt with as we speak. As far as this operation is concerned, we regard Windsor Mews as a single 'entity', meaning, in practical terms, it is *one* building. What looks like an ordinary street of mews houses isn't! We now have, for the first time under the streets of London, identified clear evidence of this clandestine system of underground networks. As with the Scottish and the Somerset examples however, we have reached a physical impasse in our attempts to gain further….deeper…access to the system. I have no doubt that other tunnels, and other underground spaces, will come to light as our investigations continue."

Around the room, faces seemed to harden as the realisation presented itself to them that this operation was developing into the proverbial 'long haul', something which would occupy them for much of the foreseeable future. Was this 'big picture' about to become a millstone around their necks perhaps? Or was it destined to become multi- agency?

Would the intelligence services and the military elbow their way into this mysterious business? For the time being, each one of them was determined to follow this beast wherever it went.

Shackleton resumed his performance. "The car used in the attempted killing of Andrew Pickering has been recovered from one of the premises and is the focus of intense forensic examination. Despite the ongoing mystery of this 'case'," he emphasised the word, "we are gaining more and more information every day which provides us with an idea of the bigger picture." Another pause came, while he seemed to be considering something awkward enough to produce a self-conscious and slightly ironic grimace.

"I need to point out here, that apart from the discovery of the suspect car, there is nothing, legally speaking, criminal regarding the unusual nature of Windsor Mews. I am confident, however, that this will be a temporary situation. It would be naive in the extreme to think that this 'construction' has been created for wholly innocent purposes. Some of you present are already involved in the various paper chases incumbent of us in these circumstances."

He moved to a desk behind him and picked up the remote control hand-piece of a television and brandished it, almost jokingly above his head, before returning to his prime position in front of the team of officers.

"The video recording you are about to watch arrived by courier yesterday evening. We believe it is authentic and are treating it seriously. There is enough factual information contained in it to suggest that the person in the recording is well-versed with the substance and the detail of our investigations. While you watch this you may have ideas or information or comments about it. No matter how trivial you think they might be, I urge you to share them. You may wish to make notes, consider questions, anything you feel might be relevant. Listen carefully to what is said; there is very little to look at so don't feel distracted by the man's appearance."

A burst of white noise briefly filled the room as the television came to life with the flick of Shackleton's thumb. The customary distortion of lines flickered on the screen, settled into a discernible shape of a figure sitting behind a plain office table and cleared satisfactorily to reveal a man wearing a ski-mask and a pair of dark-tinted glasses. The effect was, at once, both sinister and even vaguely amusing. The image was redolent of traditional paramilitaries of either side in the Northern Ireland troubles preparing some public proclamation that was unlikely to be offered up as good news. Although it was only a few seconds before the figure spoke, it seemed like an age to many of the officers present, allowing them time enough to put grim interpretations on the nature of the person about to address them. The disguised face looked straight into the camera. The man wore a dark suit jacket with a black scarf covering his neck. His tone was steady and measured, and he appeared earnest at times as the pace of his voice increased when a level of urgency spread into his narrative.

"Please listen to what I have to say. I wish to help you in your investigations. Firstly, I must apologise for the rather theatrical guise I have adopted for this recording. Despite the impression of this unfortunate garb, I am not a criminal. To reveal my identity at this point would be counter-productive for us all; it would merely be a distraction and no doubt hinder the progress of your operation. The resolution to this current problem may be as important to me as it is to the authorities.

I am a founder member of an organisation which came about, for the best of intentions, in the mid-fifties. We do not have a name. Essentially, we embarked on a programme of establishing secret shelters in various parts of the United Kingdom, in response to the threat of nuclear war. Regardless of your opinion, or the opinion of the wider public, we were not cranks or traitors to our country, we were not criminals. For myself and my friends that is still the case.

Our organisation developed. It flourished. We have utilised a considerable level of expertise over the years and created something which is beyond anything you can imagine. The engineering projects, the harnessing of scientific skills and knowledge is immensely impressive. Below the surface of much of Britain is a separate physical world. You must believe what I say, even though your instincts may be to dismiss such mighty claims as nonsense. Already you will have learnt that our underground areas are far more difficult to get into than they are to get out. This is intentional and there are practical reasons why this has been done. This also provides evidence of our advanced technology. The current physical state of our underground network is magnificent; it is a venture we are proud of. The network is probably one of the greatest achievements of the twentieth century, but because of its clandestine nature remains unappreciated. But, this is not as impressive as our other great achievement. The greatest thing we have achieved is the secret itself. More unbelievable than the technology, the living areas, the medical facilities, the research units, all of that….our greatest achievement was keeping it all a secret.

Until now.

Our fears of war and devastation have fluctuated over the passing years, there have been highs and lows. With recent events causing a growing division of opinion about the continued secrecy of our organisation there was a feeling of dissent about how to proceed. This brought about some exchanges of opinion and the airing of a range of attitudes which we believed we could deal with. We now know, from our experience of recent weeks, that for some time, for some considerable time, our organisation, our benign organisation has harboured a Trojan Horse.

Our faith in secrecy has backfired. The Trojan Horse I speak of is a criminal cancer operating inside our beloved network. The incidents which you are currently investigating are the result of *this revelation emerging within our people. At the risk of sounding overly dramatic, I can only describe the situation as akin to a civil war, a very imbalanced war where one side has considerably better access to weaponry than the other side. The ugliness of the last three weeks has shocked me and it has become difficult to see who is controlling what. The spill-over incidents you are aware of will only be the tip of the iceberg. And, like an iceberg, most of it is below the surface. We believe that the other side; I shall refer to them as the enemy, appear to have more access to the key areas of our systems because of their use of coercion. It is now probable that there are areas underground, in different regions of the country, that we don't know about, which are under the control of our enemy. We now know that the enemy have successfully established a 'parallel' network below ground, for the express purpose of aiding criminal activity.*

I wish to remind you that as your operation extends underground you may encounter people who are innocent of anything criminal; they are becoming the unwitting victims of an appalling treachery which is not their fault. The reports I am receiving from my people are very troubling. We are investigating too. We are trying to identify the perpetrators of these atrocities and we shall help you to bring them to justice. Please believe me when I say that my friends and I are not responsible for the acts of violence carried out underground. Your police constable, I believe, is the sole surface casualty. I am pleased to hear that he is recovering well.

You will find it difficult to enter much of the network, even our own part of the network. You will need to guard against the dangers you will no doubt encounter in the enemy's network. I fear they will be less benign than we are. I shall endeavour to inform you of further information which will help your operation.

The image faded and Shackleton nipped the ensuing white noise in the bud and turned to face his team. "Any questions? Any comments?"

23rd August 1990. Inverness. 1.p.m.

D.I. McNab examined the thin sandwich he held in his hand. This 'working lunch' idea was not the best way to gain his nourishment in the middle of the working day. He sat resignedly at his desk and pondered on his forthcoming evening meal, as yet, hours away. The office door opened slowly and Craig Baxter backed in carefully, but brightly, carrying two mugs of hot tea. Placing them both on McNab's desk, he started speaking as if the conversation was resuming after a short pause for breath, although he'd been out of the room for nearly ten minutes.

"Malone's watching the video tapes round about now, sir. I just checked with Irwin. A video player and television have been set up and the bed is screened of. We've had cooperation from the hospital, a little reluctantly at first, but it's fine now," Baxter enthused," and the BBC were superb, sir. They sorted out the tapes for the last eight months or so and sent them up to us overnight. We're hopeful that Malone will spot his man." He took an excited sip of his tea before peeling the cellophane from his lunch-time sandwich, lightly licking his lips in anticipation.

"This idea of Malone's is a little…er…. unlikely… surely?" The doubt in McNab's tone was obvious. "He really believes his man is someone famous?" His direct look at Baxter seemed to hold a slight challenge, as if Baxter himself had called his own credibility into question by going along with Malone's dramatic observation. McNab saw no doubt in the face of his sergeant. In that moment he felt a strange gratification that this officer should have such faith in one of his constables. He hoped this indication of trust, belief and team morale would reap benefits and not end up with everyone with egg on their faces. "Question Time, eh?"

"That's right, sir. He's positive, he has no doubts, that the man who fired the gun had been on Question Time some time earlier in the year. Recognised the face, but can't remember the name."

"So, he could be a politician," McNab concluded in a more worried tone, "that will take some handling if it turns out to be the case!" He tapped the edge of his desk nervously, as if rehearsing the drumbeats and rhythms of a speech. "Perhaps I should be grateful that it won't be me who would need to confront our political friend, once he's been revealed." He finished with an awkward smile.

The two men attacked their respective sandwiches, one with the purposeful enthusiasm of someone about to head off into the fray of an enigmatic and exciting investigation, and the other in a more tentative way, redolent of someone facing the possibility of having to report an awkward piece of information to a superior.

Half an hour later, Baxter had arrived at Raigmore Hospital and felt supremely confident that he was on his way to an encounter with a dramatic event. He was certain that Jamie Malone was on the track of his assailant, however awkward, however embarrassing, however stunning the outcome might be. Baxter felt instinctively that when he next walked along this corridor, he would have a name and the investigation would really take off. Experience told him that having a named individual as a starting point, even a target, was the springboard required for a real investigation. It was the point when the trawling was over and you could look carefully at what was in the net. However, he did not need reminding that this was a national enquiry.

Light laughter came from behind the screened-off bed. Baxter hoped Malone and Irwin weren't sidetracked by the discussions they were watching with so many editions of Question Time to occupy them. He pulled the curtain back carefully, as if not wishing to disturb the two men's deliberations, and gave a friendly nod.

They greeted their sergeant politely but slightly abstractedly, as they momentarily flicked their eyes from the television screen, both officers earnestly involved in an important investigation. The sergeant was pleased by the attitude shown by his men.

"How's it going, lads?" asked Baxter, not really expecting them to reply with a man's name, but trying to ascertain the mood of Malone who was having to dutifully watch all of these recordings when he would probably prefer to be focusing more on his own physical recovery. Baxter immediately felt a twinge of guilt as he acknowledged that his own enthusiasm for the task may have out-prioritised Malone's wish to rest. He needn't have worried. It was soon clear that both men were fully concentrated on engaging with the task in hand, and keen to get a result.

"We're only looking at the openings, sir, when the panellists are introduced to the audience. We've probably looked at about a dozen so far, but I haven't seen him yet." Malone indicated a loose pile of video cassette boxes on the floor by the window.

"You do feel up to this, don't you Jamie?" mused Baxter.

"Oh yes, Irwin's doing all the leg work! With the machine and the tapes anyway."

"This is May now," explained Irwin as he checked the date on the next tape. "We worked backwards from the middle of August to check them all. Just to be on the safe side. Jamie was fairly certain the man in question hadn't been on the show that recently."

The tape was set up and Irwin pressed the play button. For three minutes, the three men were rapt, staring at the screen. Baxter had a sudden feeling of absurdity as he voraciously peered at the screen hoping to see something important. What was *he* expecting to see? Although he had been present when the shooting occurred, he saw nothing but a shadowy figure. It was all down to Jamie, thought Baxter. And it was.

"No," said Malone emphatically. Irwin stopped the machine and ejected the tape, re-boxed it and chose the next recording. After checking the dates written in felt-tip pen on the white labels of the cassettes, Irwin selected the next tape in the sequence. He fed the letter-box opening of the machine and their television investigations resumed.

As the opening titles of the programme slipped over the opening long shot of the panel, sitting at their positions on the broad curve of the long table in front of the waiting audience, Jamie Malone sat up and leaned slightly forward. In anticipation. His eyes seemed to move closer to the television as the camera now focused on David Dimbleby smiling, as he introduced this week's guests. The politicians returned a range of gratuitous smiles towards the studio audience and the viewers at home, and the Chairman introduced the fourth guest.

"That's him! That's the man! That's the bastard who…. er, sorry, sir!" Malone had burst into the joyful rapture of a goal-scorer winning the cup. "We've got him!"

Baxter and Irwin stared at the screen. Irwin's jaw sagged slightly, but Baxter spoke. "Good God! Are you sure, Jamie?" Malone nodded, grinning, as if his assailant had actually been apprehended in the room itself. "It's Henry Hughes. Hell's Bells!"

Irwin turned to the shell-shocked Baxter, "so who is he? What is he?"

"A very rich businessman; industrialist, entrepreneur. He's involved in all sorts of big business ventures, here and abroad. It always seems as if he's into everything."

Irwin had freeze-framed the tape and the man was now in full view, like a portrait on a gallery wall, as the three of them stared, seemingly waiting for something else to happen. Malone perused the man closely as if looking at him in the dock of a courtroom. "So he's called Henry Hughes," Malone said in measured tones, as if disapproving of the name as well as the man, "Henry Hughes."

"Yes, Jamie, that's his name," replied Baxter, "but not quite."

Malone and Irwin looked askance at Baxter, suddenly not understanding what he meant.

"He's actually called *Sir* Henry Hughes!"

24th August 1990. Scotland Yard.

"Sir Henry Bloody Hughes!" exclaimed Shackleton, "Upstairs will just love this!"

Seated around a central table in a rather cramped office, his audience of three stared sympathetically, but nervously, at Chief Superintendent Oscar Shackleton. This was a meeting called in haste, with a certain amount of alarm, and accounted for the unscheduled use of the small office they were currently occupying. Detective Inspector Roger Melville ventured a question, fully aware it may ignite more of Shackleton's blue touch-paper. "Just how certain is this P.C. Malone that Hughes is the assailant, sir?"

"Absolutely and utterly, apparently."

"Oh!"

"Exactly. It goes without saying.......damn, I'll say it anyway....we need to tread carefully on this one. Sir Henry Hughes is not only incredibly rich, he is both powerful and influential. He's a favourite in government circles, has a very visible profile and is generally seen as a popular ambassador for big business. Any investigations about him must be discreet and sensitive. His business interests are universal. I have already put a couple of officers on gathering intelligence about Hughes' recent movements, ostensibly to establish alibis for the pertinent times, so we may come up with information that means we are able to back off before anybody notices!"

Samuel Cummins gave a perplexed frown, "Are we expecting to eliminate Hughes from our enquiries, if at all possible, sir?"

Shackleton stood up with clear impatience. "No. Not necessarily. We pursue our suspects. Whoever they are," he continued firmly, "we just have to proceed cautiously with this type of person. The press and the public would have a field day if there was the slightest inkling of any sort of scandal. The waters would be muddied completely. Any questions about perceived fairness in our investigations would be compromised every step of the way. It would be Hell! Someone upstairs would expect us to treat him with kid gloves and the operation would have to proceed with….. er… shall we call them clear restrictions?"

"So, if possible, eliminate him….." started Cummins, before being interrupted.

"Maybe. Maybe." Shackleton's beard came in for some frustrated brushing, his hand gripping his chin, as if about to pull it off. A distinct display of agitation was more apparent as he seemed to wrestle with thoughts, that may not have been exactly contradictory, but were certainly pulling in different directions. This dilemma was not something he was coping with as calmly as he would like. The other men held back any further comments while a more sedate equilibrium was restored, eventually signalled by Shackleton's pacing coming to an end and him retaking his seat. "Think about this. This situation. Think about what we've been told…by our man on the video. Think about the scale of what's down there. For all that to come about, the technology, the feats of engineering, the communication and transport systems……… there must be some big money behind it. That means someone with power, someone who can call the shots, so to speak. Objectively, we would come to the conclusion that someone like a Henry Hughes could be behind it all… yes, maybe Hughes himself. We can not dismiss him yet. We have an i.d. from a reliable witness. We *do* have a starting point. One of our officers has given us a break. No matter how unlikely that lead might be, we owe it to him to at least follow it up!" He paused, deliberately for effect, "but carefully."

Three heads nodded, almost in unison, an assent which underlined the positive spirit and camaraderie of copper-dom, demonstrated by these seasoned professionals. One head nodded with more conviction than the others. It belonged to Detective Sergeant Maurice Watson, recently back from a fairly fruitless trip to Bristol and the West Country. The Cheddar suspect had continued with his refusal to cooperate, still giving no name or detail about himself. He would remain in custody, with enough evidence to convict him of the heinous car-park murder, so the frustration felt by the police continued, to a degree, but he *was* safely behind bars. Watson's disappointment at drawing a blank regarding the suspect was now countered by the dramatic news he was hearing.

The revelation of Sir Henry Hughes as a possible suspect had had a unique effect on Watson; not an effect shared by the others in the room. Hughes' involvement in the network was something Watson had been aware of, but the idea that Hughes was now emerging as being on the 'wrong' side perhaps, came as a bit of a shock. The frustration of not being able to contribute his extra-curricular knowledge to the discussions in hand was not visible to Watson's colleagues. He knew, at the current time, that declaring his true identity would be an unhelpful distraction. He was playing the party line, the same line as George Ford had followed in his video recording. He speculated how long it would be before some of the key figures in the network, would feel the need to reveal themselves, and exactly how they would, subsequently, be able to directly help the police with their operations. Watson's police mentality, coupled with his police training, combined to remind him that 'active' help from members of the public was rarely encouraged, particularly where there was likely to be a clear danger and specifically, where there was the use of firearms.

Watson would remain circumspect. He knew, once he was exposed, his active participation in the investigation would come to an end. With more and more clarity he could see that he needed, somehow, to affect an opportunity to explore some of the underground areas he, himself, was familiar with. Explore as a policeman, of course. Could he possibly, accidently, 'discover' one of these entrances and subsequently carry out a legitimate investigation? Or could he do something, alone, in his own spare time? The one thing which was not an option was to do nothing.

25th August 1990.
Heathrow Airport. 12.30 p.m.

The growling of the motor, which powered the luggage carousel, had just sprung to life. The vague swishing of rubberised flaps about to convey fully-laden cases and strangely-shaped packages on their respective ways to their respective owners could now be heard. A sense of urgency arose in some disembarked passengers who thought that if their bags were not claimed on the first rotating circuit, their property would doubtless be lost forever in the dark invisible belly of the airport.

Felicity Hood, academic and seasoned traveller, took up her customary position on the first curve of the carousel, peering at the first array of baggage as it moved helplessly forward. Recognising her own piece of distinct luggage as it slipped into view, she felt buoyed up by her luck at being reunited with her case so early in the process. This had never happened to her before. Her time spent negotiating her way out of the airport would be shorter than normal. A good end to a good trip.

Returning from a month's vacation in France and Italy, Felicity Hood was looking forward to the new university term and catching up with her social circle. She had allowed herself a couple of days at home, hoping to sort out her domestic business and prepare for the preparations of the new term. On the third day, she would pick up the phone and re-engage with her London life again. That was her plan.

A figure in a dark coat, who had been standing by the wall of glass doors, cautiously approached her, as if about to cut across the line of her walk. "Ms Hood, Ms Hood," the figure uttered in semi-muffled tones. There was a brief shuffle of the opening of the coat and a small sheet of paper with 'Hood' written in bold ink was thrust towards her. She had not ordered a taxi and was momentarily perplexed by the incursion to her progress. She stopped deliberately and stared at the face beneath the dark flat cap. The man stopped and almost theatrically held the paper beneath his chin, prompting her to look straight at his face. She did so and lifted up her chained spectacles, more confused than irritated and pondered on her unlikely conclusion.

"Ken?" in a moment of possible recognition, "what's this?"

"Please, Felicity, follow me to the car park. Make to wave me away, but follow me at a distance to B level in the car park. It's not a joke. It's urgent. I shall explain later. Please do as I say!" The man's tone was pleading, and the words were whispered harshly; there was no ambiguity about his emotional state. He walked off holding the sheet of paper quite conspicuously. Felicity accepted the curious circumstances and played her role plausibly and cooperatively. To any one observing this episode the conclusion would be that the man had accosted the wrong person.

True to his instructions, she had waved him away, apparently indignantly, but kept an eye on where he was headed. Following at a safe distance, Felicity was slightly intrigued by the 'cloak and dagger' approach of Ken Carter, but had an earnest sense of something which required disciplined adherence to a plan. It appeared to Felicity that Ken knew exactly what he was doing and she respected the methodology of his plan. Her own plans, for the next two days, she felt instinctively, had just been abandoned.

Fuel smells hung on the air like evidence of a poisoning, as she crossed between two lines of parked cars. A few erstwhile travellers were opening car boots, car doors, lifting luggage into small cars, large cars; there seemed to be a natural lull in the busy business of preparing for onward trips. The crowds from minutes before had dissolved into the bright lunch-time air outside. Fewer people were evident now in the auditorium of the car park. Individual sounds could now be distinguished from their echoes. The figure of Ken Carter stood by the driver's door of a silver saloon car, his flat cap making identification easy inside the concrete cave of Level B. He reached down by the door and, within a second or two, the boot swung upwards, indicating the next step of the plan to a rapidly-learning Felicity.

With her luggage out of sight in the boot of the car, Felicity trusted herself to Ken's direction and, moments later, he was driving her away from Heathrow towards South London.

"I am so sorry about this, Felicity. There's no other way, believe me. There is an awful lot of explaining to do, and it's not pleasant. Something dreadful has happened and we only know bits of it. The network has been exposed." This last piece of information brought a look of horror to Felicity Hood's sharp features. She clutched her many beaded necklaces as if anticipating an attempt by somebody to snatch them. Her mind buzzed with questions and comments but felt frozen in the execution of speech. Carter continued. "It's worse than that, Felicity. There's been a Trojan Horse inside the organisation for years." Although certainly not meant in jest, or in any way light-heartedly, the reference to Troy was apt and, with Felicity Hood's great interest in ancient history and knowledge of literature, the dire consequences of the Trojan Horse story, with its everyday interpretations, would clearly not be lost on her.

For one so normally eloquent, the "Oh, my God," was a real surprise to her when she heard herself utter it. In the few seconds when Carter did not speak, she played out countless ugly scenarios suggested by this horrendously bad news, as if the moment lasted a life-time. She felt empty inside when Carter picked up his narrative and described the end of the dream. The dream that had worked for so long, had now been snatched away from them forever.

Overcast skies gathered above London as the silver saloon car continued on its fateful journey. A safe haven was needed for any discussions, any arguments, any speculations that might take place. Felicity Hood had been away for a month and had no knowledge of the traumas faced by her compatriots. She and Ken Carter and George Ford would need to talk like they had never talked before. And everything they would say might not make the slightest difference to the world they knew.

25th August. Bakerloo Line. 2.30.p.m.

Teresa Gomez liked London. The wonderful buildings, the shops, the green spaces; all the things she had read about this city and had now experienced for herself were precious to her. The move she had made to this remarkable city was something she had never regretted. The days when she felt like a tourist had vanished some time before, and now she regarded herself as a local; if that was truly possible in the metropolis.

Her feelings for the London Underground however, were mixed. Of course she realised it was a very convenient and efficient way to move around this capital city, but at times she felt a little intimidated by the hectic nature of the travelling crowds. On occasions it seemed to bring out the worst in people.

On this particular day, she found the carriage she was in, as it rattled north on the Bakerloo line, stuffy and oppressively hot. Her supposed familiarity with particular sections of line was recently compromised when a work colleague pointed out the existence of other stations on the Tube system she did not know about; namely the abandoned stations. The minor revelation that there were such places below ground had surprised her. One of them, Trafalgar Square, was about to be approached by her current train. She wondered if she would be able to catch a glimpse of it.

Almost on cue, the train slowed slightly and she was aware of a change in the light from outside the carriage. With few people standing next to her, she was able to turn and look purposefully out of the window. In a sudden flurry of movement out of nowhere, she saw, quite clearly, two figures fighting in the half-shadowed recessed area where the railway tracks split into two. Both figures appeared to be using objects as weapons, to strike each other, in an energetic and desperate struggle for supremacy. Teresa's very audible gasp at seeing this dramatic sight, was heard by a nearby couple, who followed Teresa's gaze and added their names to the list of witnesses to this awful sight. Other passengers craned their necks for a better view; some spoke, "look at that", "bloody hell" and vainly shouted at the battling pair and hopelessly tapped on the window for their attention. The slowing of the train allowed more people to watch the battle and as this clutch of travellers slipped out of sight, one of the figures was struck a deadly blow, hit the ground and lay motionless. The other man held aloft, in an apparent gesture of triumph, something long and metallic, as if waiting to see if the prone figure would move again. The scene, now having been witnessed by passengers from another carriage, caused consternation and distress, prompting urgent and alarmed chatter to fill both carriages.

Some time later, in response to a series of civilian reports about a violent attack in the Underground system, a pair of transport police officers were sent to follow up the reports and, initially on finding no body, were about to report it as a non-event, when the more observant of the two officers noticed the blood. With further scrutiny, extensive evidence of blood was discovered alongside a section of railway track splattered on the dirt-pitted gravel, on the ancient brick walls and on a discarded long metal lever lying in the grime of the tunnel. In the aftermath of visits from Scene of Crime officers and a forensics team, an urgent report on the incident found its way to the operations rooms of Chief Superintendent Oscar Shackleton at Scotland Yard. Tommy Henderson, one of the young Transport Police officers who made the first reconnaissance of the tunnel, found it all rather curious that such an incident had led to the report moving so immediately, and so far, up the Metropolitan Police food chain.

25th August 1990.
South London. 5p.m.

The glass of red wine in Felicity's hand wavered slightly as her hand shook nervously. This nervousness was exacerbated by the restrained presence of anger. For the previous hour she had had to endure a commentary from two of her greatest friends; a blow by blow account of events which meant her world would be changing irrevocably. It was a torture for all three of them, something devastating beyond their control. It was a result of being complacent and satisfied that everything in the garden was rosy, and then being told of the forest fire. Each of them, in his or her own mind, tried to question the events of their shared past and apply the benefit of hindsight to the situation. In their frustration, they could find no evidence of any naivety, no evidence of misreading clues, no evidence of lax responsibility. Instinctively, there was an uncomfortable indignation that they were blameless of any wrong-doing. To acknowledge their respective roles in creating something which had resulted in such a terrible chaos of suffering and death, was a psychological burden destined for further analysis and deliberation. The nature of this revelation was hideous and had been a bolt from the blue. What they thought was an internal difference of opinion, had turned out to be something catastrophically worse. In Felicity's case, the shock had burst into her feelings of home-bound joy like a bombshell.

A period of silence blanketed the conservatory and the sun shone relentlessly across the rattan furniture and restrained elegance of George Ford's substantial detached house. Outside the double-glazed panes of glass, the greenery of the surrounding trees and bushes colluded in the welcome privacy of the conversations. Many times the three of them, George, Ken and Felicity, had sat in this room, often with others, and relaxed or celebrated their way through a comfortable and contented evening. It seemed to them now that all of that joy had been confined to history, merely a series of pleasant memories of now-unattainable circumstances, never to be repeated.

Felicity uncharacteristically slugged back the last mouthful of wine, and firmly set the empty glass on the long occasional table which was positioned directly in front of a three-seated sofa. "Utterly dreadful. It beggars belief," she declared forcefully. She slumped back and, with a mock smile, continued, "I wish I hadn't bothered coming back!" She realised it was a pathetic thing to say, but she was exasperated beyond reason. Was there actually anything to say in response to the afternoon's revelations? This raw thought lasted for a few moments, then she took a deep breath and asserted an answer to her own unspoken question. "It's planning time, then. I have listened. I have clearly understood." Ken Carter and George Ford raised their eyebrows slightly. "Well, I've understood what you've told me, but I don't understand some of the motivations....from the other side! You're saying that we have unwittingly harboured, for years, a criminal organisation?"

"Well, yes! What's clear, it would seem," offered Ford, "is that Derek and Henry have built up, over a very long time, and evil empire. Yes, I know that does sound rather melodramatic, but I happen to believe it fits the bill. Their criminal activities have obviously been on a grand scale. The exact nature of these crimes is a matter for the police, clearly, but I think we need to accept that our knowledge and experience of the ringleaders may be helpful to the authorities. How we convey that information is just one of the issues we are faced with. Which is why I've asked Maurice Watson here. He should be coming soon." Ford checked his watch.

"Maurice Watson?" queried Felicity.

"Yes, he is our Scotland Yard contact.....er... mole, I suppose. Goodness, that sounds very cloak-and-dagger, very subversive stuff. It is not as conspiratorial as it appears." George Ford added almost apologetically.

Felicity and Carter waited for further explanation, but not absolutely certain that any would be forthcoming.

"Maurice is one of us, and he's a fine policeman, a detective sergeant. He has kept me informed, when he's been able to, about developments concerning a variety of incidents which are linked to our network. It is important to point out that Maurice is not a plant in the police force. He has chosen that career independently and done well for himself. There have been other members of the organisation that have joined the police force. Any convenient coincidence of circumstances is just that. His passing of information about recent events has also been just that. Recent events. Although it is quite fortunate, if I can use that word in these current circumstances, that he has been party to some of the investigations into these incidents which concern the network. Only over the last two weeks has he compromised his role as a police officer, but he has done that for the best of reasons and with honourable intentions. If he was exposed, the help he is giving to the police and ourselves would end. At least the police realise, largely due to the attempt on Andrew Pickering's life, that there is a benign side and an evil side to the underground network. Now, of course, we know that some of the network 'parts' may not be ours. The Scottish one, the one near Inverness, I believe is not one of our making. It is also the one which has unearthed Henry Hughes as a possible killer." Ford reached for the bottle of wine and indicated the empty glasses with an offering gesture. His two guests nodded assent. "Neither of you have met Maurice, I know, but he can be trusted. Our recent experience could easily taint our view of human nature, indeed, but…….." he left the words trailing, and poured the wine.

As the evening descended slowly, the three friends shared their personal and specific worries about mutual friends. Ken Carter reiterated the concern he and his wife had about their son's whereabouts. It seemed that no news was bad news in this scenario. Similarly, Andrew Pickering's parents were overdue from a short break. The stories in the public domain i.e. those known to the police, seemed to demonstrate a hunting down of innocent members of their network by the members of the criminal element in the organisation. The general despondency and bitterness of the talk galvanised itself into an exchange of memories about their varying experiences of Derek Martin and Sir Henry Hughes, culminating in a stark diatribes about the nature of betrayal.

Shortly after six o'clock, the doorbell rang. Ford excused himself and left the conservatory. He returned with a slightly jaded-looking Maurice Watson. Ford placed one hand on Watson's shoulder and looked at his other guests, "Maurice, this is Felicity Hood, and this is Ken Carter." With an almost paternal smile, added, "Detective Sergeant Maurice Watson."

Watson smiled warmly at Felicity and took her offered hand, "it's good to meet you. I just wish the circumstances were different." He took in the light eccentricity of Felicity Hood's appearance, seeing the visual evidence of a stereotypical near-Bohemian, peace activist from the 1960s. His smile broadened. He had known what to expect, because he knew about her from George Ford and was genuinely pleased to meet her. Turning to Ken Carter, he tried a new smile and took the second offered hand of the evening. Compared to Felicity, Ken looked like a more ordinary specimen, but there was something about the nose and the eyes which seemed to jar in the back of his mind. He thought it might have been a recognition at some subconscious level. He wasn't sure. The hand-shake came to an end with a short nod of the head.

The evening's discussions stretched towards midnight and the many frustrations caused by the limited amount of hard knowledge available produced a number of half- plans, qualified strategies and countless suggestions about how to proceed. The first certain point of agreement was that Maurice Watson's membership of the organisation, as far as the police was concerned, must remain secret. He was the best conduit of information, in both directions. Finding more information about Henry Hughes' network was vital. Were there innocent people in the organisation who knew the whereabouts of the alternative 'cells'? The killings had suggested that was the case. Some aspects of the business alarmed them greatly. The existence of Windsor Mews had been a shock to them all. The audacious nature and the scale of this project was a major worry. Such an incredible development, in the middle of London, and not one of them had ever heard a breath of a whisper. Nothing. Were there more such places in London outside their knowledge? Despite the shared animosity they held for Henry Hughes, there was a scepticism that he would ever have put himself in the position where he needed to personally shoot a police officer. Surely that was unthinkable? Surely that was inconceivable? The other incidents had caused much more grief because the expectation, even the likelihood, was that more bodies would be out there somewhere, but probably out of sight, underground. The afternoon's report from the Bakerloo Line highlighted another probable problem, a problem perhaps with dire repercussions for their damaged organisation.

The Underground network of London had many forgotten tunnels and underground spaces. Drainage systems had extensive labyrinths of tunnels and other tunnel systems from London's clandestine history were still in existence. Some of these had been some of the earliest ones commandeered by

George Ford's and Ken Carter's organisation. Although there was limited official use for a number of these underground workings, Ford and Carter's workers had added to, and adapted, the geography of this hidden world. For many of their members, these places were their introduction to the reality of the underground life they were helping to build. With their troubled thoughts of responsibility and a certain sense of proprietary regarding these particular tunnels a stark realisation struck them. The disappearance of the body seemed to indicate that one of *their* tunnels had been used in this terrible crime.

26th August 1990. Inverness.

Glimpsing a rainbow across the distant hillsides, Willie Bolton, the Inverness Courier's top reporter (that's what he liked to believe,) contemplated just how wet he was likely to be, by the time he returned to his car. Broken clouds, jigsaw pieces of blue sky and shafts of sunlight fought an aerial battle with the stubborn showers which crisscrossed the Inverness district. But the rainbow, Willie decided, would be a bit of an omen. By nature he erred on the side of optimism. In his job it would be daft not to! The matter which embroiled his senses today was trying to come to terms with an elusive mystery surrounding the recent incident of the shot policeman. His fascination for the story was the main reason why he was using his Sunday off to further his attempted investigations. He was genuinely keen to succeed in his chosen, and very competitive, profession, and 'policemen with bullets in them' was sensational enough to suggest that an opportunity had presented itself, and was waiting here for him to take advantage and shine. From the beginning, the news released by the police was unnecessarily vague. There was no argument that a young police constable had been badly injured in a shooting incident, but there was not the customary appeal to the public at large for possible witnesses. This was very unusual. In fact, Bolton himself had never heard of such a thing. He had conferred with others, far and wide, and no-one else had experienced such an omission in police proceedings. The information regarding the location of the shooting had also been particularly vague; up on the fells. Why no appeal to walkers, farm workers, campers, bird-watchers, conservationists and the like, anyone out on the mountainsides? There had been some talk of a tunnel, in the mountains, being investigated, but much of this local 'information' Willie Bolton found rather implausible. Trying to find out updates on the condition of the victim had been met with a lack of cooperation and Willie was beginning to suspect signs of a cover-up. An amazing speculation no doubt, but more and more like a real possibility. Why a cover-up? What was really going on? Willie had been keen to discuss his thoughts and theories with an ex-colleague from his training days, so he called him on the telephone the previous evening His friend, based in London, had been hearing of other 'mysteries' on the grapevine. After comparing stories, they had agreed that there appeared to be several poorly-informed news items which newspaper reporters had been hoping would develop into 'the big story' and maybe a couple of these were just over the horizon for both of them!

Dodging the latest downpour, Bolton ran from the car park towards the entrance of Raigmore Hospital. His general plan was to, unashamedly snoop around and tease out more information, if possible, about Jamie Malone's recovery, the circumstances of his injury and anything else worthy of printing for public consumption.

Choosing not to remove his waterproof hat immediately, he scanned the reception area for an unobtrusive place to sit and found one which gave a wide view of the foyer area. With a wry, almost conspiratorial, smile he observed the figure of Dora Doig emerging from an office at the opening of a corridor leading from reception. He could hardly believe his luck. Had that rainbow actually been a good omen after all? He had recognised her from a previous visit and knew that she was the police officer's fiancée. This prompted him to keep the waterproof hat on; the nearest thing he had to a disguise! Daring himself to follow Dora Doig, he was rewarded by the arrival of another nurse who took care of Dora's attention and allowed him to draw closer to the pair. As the nurses approached the small waiting area near one of the out-patient clinics, it was clear to Willie Bolton that the pair were looking for an opportunity to chat. The other nurse took up a position behind a counter by a telephone and Dora, clutching some sheets of paper and a clipboard, leaned against the other side.

Within moments, the pair were engaged in a flurry of chat and gossip, and Bolton had placed himself close by on a chair, cleverly eavesdropping, pretending to be waiting for an appointment. As far as Dora Doig and her colleague were concerned he was invisible.

"Oh, he *is* getting better. Definitely. I don't think he'll be in here for much longer. He'll need to have a lot of rest at home. He doesn't know how long he'll be away from work, though," informed Dora.

"Well, that sounds good. As long as he's on the mend. You must be pleased he'll be able to rest at home?" said the other nurse.

"Yes, I am. They had him working here on Thursday, mind you. It was weird. He had to watch all these tapes…. videos….of that programme Question Time. Loads of them! But he only watched the openings of the show. Then, shortly after Sergeant Baxter arrived they just stopped and they were all very excited about something. It's all a bit of a mystery. He says he can't talk about it yet. But I know he will. Well, when he's out of here!"

"Well, it does sound rather strange, this video business! That programme's all about people talking. So, do you think Jamie was looking for someone, trying to identify someone?" enthused Dora's friend.

"I suppose that's what it looks like….but, it doesn't make a lot of sense, does it?" Dora glanced at the clock on the wall behind her friend. "I'll have to be off. Catch you at the lunch break. Bye."

Inside his anonymity, Willie Bolton agreed that Jamie Malone's video watching didn't make sense. Of course, he also knew that most things *did* make sense. It was a case of thinking carefully, asking further questions, speculating on ideas, sometimes on half-ideas. Something would eventually lead you to a conclusion of some kind, a result. Fully appreciating his astonishing piece of luck regarding his erstwhile eavesdropping, Willie Bolton felt it would be unlikely that he'd glean any more information on this visit, so he decided to decamp, brave the rain, and do some focused thinking, and make another call to his London colleague.

26th August 1990.
Central London. 9.30.a.m.

A background cacophony of traffic noises met the ears of D.I. Cummins and D.S. Watson as they strode purposefully towards the entrance of Piccadilly Circus tube station. The second phase of the morning rush-hour was clearly evident in the earnest dash of people, hurrying, striding, dawdling, shuffling their various ways around the busy streets of the metropolis. Cummins and Watson were on the verge of swapping all that for the dubious and relative quiet of the world underground.

Arrangements had been made for the security and maintenance people, aided by the Transport Police, to provide the high-visibility clothing and necessary assistance to allow the two detectives to check out the underground crime scene. The unusual walk to Trafalgar Square, the abandoned station close to the alleged incident, had vague familiarities for Maurice Watson. A number of years ago he had worked with a team of 'networkers' in clearing the tunnel system as part of a refurbishment operation, so the pattern of tunnels and their 'doorways' was known to him. The thinking behind such access to the underground areas was hardly new; it had been borrowed from the activities of the Second World War, when there was extensive use made of the various tunnels systems below ground in the capital and beyond. One of Watson's recollections which reinforced his knowledge of the place was the fact that he helped to install the signpost system inside the labyrinth of tunnels to aid people's progress and prevent them getting lost. This was always a problem because the cues and clues we take advantage of on the surface are absent when we're below ground.

At a particular point in the exploration, Cummins indicated that was required to confirm the safety arrangements regarding train movement and the situation related to the presence of high-voltage apparatus. The brief delay over, Cummins asserted the area was safe and turned to Watson. "Ah, Watson, I'll catch you up, I'll be one minute. I need a quick word with these chaps." He nodded towards the others who presumed there would be further instructions from the detective inspector.

Keen to push on, Watson crossed the railway track and turned left to pick his way over the gravel bedding towards two separate sections of recessed walls. Stepping with care towards the stretch of wall at the further point, he knelt down to examine the smears and other visible marks of blood which showed the exact location of the observed attack.

Within a minute, Cummins was standing by him, "so you found it, then?"

Watson looked up to meet Cummins' smiling face. Could he discern a slight irony in the smile? Something had just happened which Watson wasn't aware of. Desperately trying to mask his uncertainty, he stood up, brushed his hands and peered around as if looking for a way out. It seemed as if Cummins was waiting for something. Watson did not know what it was. Should he know? In his sudden confusion he seemed to mime a slightly comic, and wholly unconvincing, performance of someone pondering a mystery and searching for the answer. His physical awkwardness was quite apparent and that made him feel at a psychological disadvantage, without knowing how or why. This odd feeling seemed to stretch interminably, and gave him an unpleasant awareness of something not quite right. His unconvincing smile at Cummins was acknowledged by his senior officer.

"So, Watson, where do *you* think the escape route is? Which way did the assailant go? Where did the body disappear to?"

In an earth-shattering instant, Watson realised that he had been discovered. The curious mixture of naivety and enthusiasm for the job had turned explosive and blown up in his face! A torrent of thoughts swept through his mind. He had to make some critical decisions, probably in the next few seconds. He was a police officer. He was a member of the network. Did this have to be a real dilemma? His instincts for both roles *were* compatible. Whatever he did, he needed to utterly establish and reinforce the idea with Cummins, that he was not the enemy. This was imperative and he had to do it now. There was no real choice. Showing Cummins the entrance to the secret tunnels was the only thing he could do now to confirm his true intentions.

Watson took a deep breath and seemed to hold it in, very consciously for a few seconds, then exhaled slowly, gave a rather sheepish grin to Cummins and beckoned him to the edge of a dirt-ingrained wall which appeared flat and featureless. With a few deft movements of his hand along a single line of bricks, Watson caused a brief grating sound to emerge from the wall. Almost imperceptibly, there was a minute shift in the contours of a section of the wall. Cummins peered intently at a raised edge of brick indicated by Watson, who, when he was certain that Cummins knew what he was looking at, reached upwards and tugged at a point on the right-hand edge. A little effort saw a doorway of brick swing open, to reveal a pitch darkness beyond the limited light coming in from the main railway tunnel.

Almost at once, a noxious odour hit the nostrils of both men. Watson grimaced and stepped into the new opening and reached into the dreadful darkness. One press of a hidden switch and light blazed instantly; a surprisingly bright light. Clearly anticipating a grim outcome from this action, the two men braced themselves, knowing what to expect when they ventured further in. Together, they stared at the hunched body of a dead man as it lay, where it had been dragged, against a wall of the tunnel.

"So, it was merely pulled into here to keep it out of sight. There's been no attempt to dispose of it," remarked Cummins as he held a handkerchief to his nose while bending towards the corpse. He turned slightly to peer along the illuminated corridor of tunnel.

"There's no short distance through here to the surface. Moving a deadweight, a dead body, would be very difficult, especially for one person," explained Watson, suddenly forgetting the need to be cagey about what he knew about the background to this unpleasant business. The doubtful situation he had been in previously was now not really in doubt any more.

Cummins stood up and looked straight at his fellow officer, "I think we need forensics here as soon as possible." He glanced at his watch then looked back at Watson. "And we need to talk."

27th August 1990.
Central London. 11.30.a.m.

Felicity Hood had lived in her Bloomsbury apartment for several years. She had turned it into an extension of her personality, oozing eclectic and exotic charm with an ambience of cultured eccentricity. Books, artefacts, paintings, framed photographs, table enhancing sculptures, neat piles of sumptuous magazines and more books decorated every room. This interior landscape was her pride and joy. So many of the objects had stories attached to them, some with tales of foreign adventures, some mere conversation pieces. All of them embedded in her vibrant and varied life. She was her very own Bloomsbury Group, she used to joke when reaching her fourth glass of wine.

The previous forty-eight hours had taken a considerable shine off this treasured archive of joyous living. A distinct hollowness had filled her thoughts and the rich collection of physical memories which surrounded her, now exuded an emptiness, a shallowness of their former beauty and a feeling that the acquisitive drive one may indulge in, innocently and enthusiastically, can crash, unceremoniously, into a meaningless void.

Her telephone rang. "Yes?"

A frantic female voice blurted out, "Felicity, is that you?"

"It is. Who is it?" She was already demonstrating the sort of caution that had been recommended by Ford and Carter.

"Thank goodness, you're all right. It's Lesley Pickering. Something awful has happened, can we come round.

Alan's with me, but we can't reach Andrew," her anxious breathlessness causing gasps between her words, "we've not heard from him since we returned from Vienna. It doesn't look as if he's been to our house for days."

"Lesley, Lesley…..he's fine. Please calm down, dear. He is being protected by the police. I shall explain when you get here."

"Ten minutes, oh Felicity. Thank you!"

Felicity replaced the receiver and pinched the top of her nose and blinked her eyes. Her overwhelmingly full lifestyle had not included motherhood. It was not something she overtly regretted, but from time to time she found herself aware that certain aspects of everyday life may have been missing from her retinue. She could do sharing, she could do caring. And she felt Lesley's distress about her son. Even though he was now a young man, a mother's concern was a lifelong concern. Felicity could appreciate that. Her own emotions had other outlets, but they were nonetheless real as were her sympathies. Taking a handkerchief from the pocket of her braided cardigan, she blew her nose before slipping into her kitchen to put the kettle on.

Having expected the 'something awful has happened' to be an alarming reference to Andrew's apparent disappearance, Felicity was horrified to be told the appalling experiences of the Pickerings over recent days. Some of the grave concerns highlighted by Ford and Carter had already materialised. Lesley and Alan Pickering had discovered three bodies below ground, in an area they were familiar with and frequently visited. A routine refreshing of medical supplies, one of Lesley Pickering's responsibilities, was due on her return from their brief holiday, and on their arrival below ground, at one of the medical centres they maintained, the shocked pair had discovered three dead members of the usual engineering team, all of them with gunshot wounds. The idea of going to the police had been a great source of anxiety. The consequences of their actions had caused huge dilemmas for them. The implications of directing the police into the network were far-reaching, and filled them with absolute panic, as they simply did not know where to turn in these unique and dire circumstances. Would any revelation to the police put Andrew's life in danger? Not knowing the overall state of this underground conflict made them feel paralysed as far as making decisions was concerned. Given an update about Andrew's situation had relieved them greatly, but did make them consider that the attempt on his life may actually have been linked to the dead bodies they themselves had found, and make them question how close to danger they had been, at the time they had discovered the three bodies.

Now that their respective stories had been shared and a level of relative calm had descended on the Bloomsbury apartment, it was time to make some decisions. A clear agreement was reached about ruling out physical engagement with the conflict. The police now knew of the situation and the whole network was compromised. For the time being the 'enemy' had the upper hand. Accepting, reluctantly, that what they had helped to build, was now controlled by criminals was painful and difficult, but had to be done. It was a defeat they had never anticipated, in a battle they had never anticipated. There had been no preparation for such events. The duty they owed to the innocents in their revered organisation was to give the police full cooperation and let the Law deal with the whole ugly matter. All they themselves could do, was then stand back and come to terms with any guilt or recriminations they might feel.

"I shall phone George and explain your position. He is helping the police already. He has a contact in Scotland Yard and has recorded a video which they have seen. The primary problem is to focus on the people who are responsible for the crimes, not the ones responsible for the network. We must make that clear to the police."

27th August 1990.
Central London. 12.15.p.m.

The dark wood panelling of the corner recess gave a sombre feel to the lunchtime glasses of beer brought from the bar by Samuel Cummins. He placed them on the square table which seemed to hem Maurice Watson in, making a quick escape very tricky. D.I. Cummins sat down in his wooden carver chair and took a couple of swallows of beer, then took on the air of a benign interrogator.

"So, what shall we do?" he opened the conversation.

Maurice Watson avoided squirming in his corner seat, and thought the best policy was to be honest, clear and straightforward, because he believed himself to be an honest, clear and straightforward person. "I'm not the enemy, sir," he asserted.

"I'm pleased to hear that."

Watson smiled at the apparent lightness of Cummins' tone. "Yes, I have felt compromised by my involvement with this network and in my role as a policeman. From where you're sitting, that might not look too clever. The organisation as it was originally, and as it was when I joined, is harmless, it is definitely not criminal. To be honest it's not really that political, although outsiders may not see it that way. But, from a personal point of view, the truth is, I have not done anything wrong."

"Relaying police information to civilians?" Cummins' frown and tone were both clearly ironic and seemed almost mocking in a light-hearted way. Was he actually relishing Watson's discomfort?

"But, I didn't. I can't remember……"

"Constable Malone," smiled Cummins. Watson looked confused. "There were five people, as far as I was aware, knew of Malone's recovery when the call came through from Scotland; he regained consciousness on the Wednesday. That was before that video was recorded. Our man in the video knew Malone had woken up the day *before* we told the rest of the team. Someone from the original five must have told him."

Watson looked transfixed at his own naivety, "Oh!"

"My check of the outgoing telephone calls threw up a clue. It was easier than I thought to pinpoint what seemed to be going on. I just needed to be certain."

"So you took me to Trafalgar Square!"

"Yes. That was interesting. Bearing in mind that we've been led to believe this underground network is a considerable size, I wondered whether there was a chance you'd be familiar with that particular part of the system. I suppose it was a bit of a long shot. Your personnel records indicated you haven't spent much time in your life away from London. It naturally followed that any involvement you had with this network would most likely be here in London."

Maurice Watson looked at him with astonishment. "You set me up?" he said with incredulity. "You knew?"

"Not one hundred percent," returned Cummins, "I made a fortuitous guess that your desire to help with the investigation would outweigh your deviousness. I was right."

"And by identifying the correct place in the Underground, I inadvertently gave the game away."

"From the information we had, the description from the initial report, there were four possible places which fitted the description. You saw that report as well. There was a one in four chance you, or anyone else, would guess correctly. When you made a fairly confident beeline for one particular place, I realised I was getting warm. You went for the one you knew was nearest that secret tunnel. It was all rather tenuous really, but my luck was in!" He stared straight into Watson's eyes, "it has to be said, you make a far better detective than you do a criminal!"

Watson stared at the man who had found him out, "so what now?"

"I have the distinct feeling that you will have a lot of information beneficial to our investigations. I know you are a good copper. I also know if you weren't an active part of the team, we would miss out on your input. I also happen to think there may be things you know now, which we do not know are useful…. yet."

Watson pondered on Cummins' deliberations and was gratified by his superior's positive and wise response. "There is a very pertinent piece of information I need to tell you right now. I feel guilty about not passing it on to you, to the team earlier." He held firm eye contact with Cummins' quizzical expression before proceeding. "But you must understand how I couldn't…you would have asked me how I knew."

"Yes, I am inquisitive, like that," Cummins replied with mock modesty, "and?"

"Henry Hughes."

Cummins instantly lost his buoyant humour, "what about him?"

"I know nothing about the Malone shooting, but I can verify that Hughes has been a member of the organisation for a long time and it has now become obvious that he has been leading a……criminal wing…..previously undiscovered by the others. The idea that he, himself, pulled the trigger seemed unlikely at first…largely because of his public profile, we now need to judge him differently. At the very least it is clear that he condones this violence against the innocent members underground, especially if any of them happen to be down there and attempt to escape. If I can use villains' parlance sir, there will be a lot of people who can grass Hughes up! And we know what villains often do in those circumstances. Beating people up as a warning to others may not work as well when it's all out of sight. It becomes more convenient just to kill them; no messy problems running the risk when disposing of the bodies.

Cummins sat, with a profound look on his face, clearly thinking deeply. Both men reached for their drinks and quenched their mouths. There was an unspoken excitement in the air. It was as if Cummins had just come to a monumental decision. "Right you are, young Maurice, this is what will happen. Like yourself, it would be difficult for me to raise Hughes' involvement, without justifying its authenticity. You will continue as before, and if you compromise us I'll have your guts for garters!" The humour was back. "Have you any hunches how we could make inroads to the Hughes part of the investigation?"

"Actually, I have a particular hunch about another aspect of this whole sorry business. I can only reveal this if I can complete a specific piece of investigation while in both my roles simultaneously."

"Are you being deliberately enigmatic, Watson?" said Cummins with a genuine laugh, "that's sounding like a riddle."

"You can call it that if you wish," reasoned a more confident Watson, "but it does allow us a strong chance to make progress and perhaps unearth another inside source."

Cummins nodded thoughtfully, "and you believe this hunch is that important eh?"

"Yes, sir…..for both of us….and both of me!"

28th August 1990.
Scottish Highlands. 9.a.m.

Early mist was steadily clearing from the mountainsides as Tommy McPhail and Alex McDougall sat in the front of the Land Rover and edged their way up a long incline overlooking a breathtaking landscape. Nessy, the sheepdog, perched in the open back of the vehicle, watched the fields rattle by, her tongue lolling about making her look less intelligent than she actually was. Approaching a modest summit in the road, the engine laboured as Tommy dropped down a gear. Sunlight hit the widescreen head-on, out from a gloriously blue sky, and across the whole wide valley there was a clean and fresh sense that this would be a beautiful morning. The summit surmounted, the Land Rover picked up speed as the road bent downwards and to the right, towards the neat stone arch of a bridge which crossed over a rippling, pebble-strewn, shallow stream, glinting like silver in moonlight.

Without warning, from behind the end of a stone wall, a dark figure stumbled into a ditch on the left-hand side of the road. It was a man in overalls having serious problems standing up. From his semi-prone position he waved an arm frantically and was clearly in distress. As the vehicle moved forward, he twisted further in its direction and beckoned wildly to the passengers in the truck. Tommy McPhail duly slowed down and brought the Land Rover to a halt, slightly ahead of the man. The two men climbed down from the cab of the 4X4, while the dog sat and watched from its strategic position in the back. Tommy approached the man first, "you okay there?" he said, knowing that the man probably wasn't okay at all.

Alex invited with, "can we help you?"

Through gritted teeth, the man responded carefully, as if talking was a painful activity for him, "please, I've fallen badly…and I've got to get to the police, and I need my leg seeing to."

"Here, we'll get you into the truck. We'll take you to the hospital, in Inverness." said Tommy McPhail, to reassure the man that things were now under control. "You can call the police from there if you like," he continued.

During the next half hour, the two farm workers used a section of broken gate as a makeshift stretcher to ease the injured man into the back of the truck. Supervised by Nessy, who watched every move the men made, the operation was a surprising success, given that any movement was clearly distressingly painful for the patient. At times, the man threatened to lose consciousness because of the pain and the idea of taking him straight to the hospital was clearly the best course of action. Once the man was safe and secure in the back of the vehicle, Tommy turned it around carefully, very aware how the motion of the 4X4 would affect the man's level of discomfort, and headed for Inverness.

Alex and Tommy, satisfied that they had done the right thing by the injured man, were both of the opinion that he was, however, a bit delirious. When they'd asked about his fall, he'd said he had done so *inside* the mountain and although the fall had been an accident, he insisted that he needed to report a crime to the police. They reasoned that taking the poor soul to the hospital was clearly the best idea.

28th August 1990.
Scotland Yard. 10.a.m.

Detective Roger Melville stood six feet in front of a large whiteboard which was covered in stuck-on scraps of paper, photographs, brief paragraphs written in marker pen, labelled captions, random lines of writing, and dramatic heavy arrow shapes, all presented in a range of bright colours to indicate the state-of-play scenario involving Sir Henry Hughes' alleged part in a deadly nationwide conspiracy. Melville was filled with the feeling that what he was staring at was some form of frustrating jigsaw, which a rather mischievous prankster had left solely for him to solve, while also suggesting that there might be a vital piece missing.

One of the words which often irritated and frustrated police officers, to the borders of demoralisation, is 'circumstantial'. A lot of the information amassed about Sir Henry Hughes seemed to fit into that most annoying of categories. Items which could be regarded as coincidences, or of a tenuous nature, were everywhere. Possible links had been identified, but probably, in the probing atmosphere of a courtroom, they would become loose connections which dissolved in front of the rapt eyes of a jury. The frieze which filled Melville's vision was like an artwork; entitled 'Circumstantial Evidence'. He knew, as all the officers working on this investigation knew, if their prime suspect had been a teenage reprobate or a middle-aged recidivist, he would be warming one of the plastic chairs in an interview room somewhere. Sir Henry Hughes did not fall into that category. Indeed, he was 'protected' by an unspoken taboo regarding the potential scale of universal public embarrassment in the case of false arrest and media misrepresentation.

As Melville studied the jungle of links that had been discovered, and gave his consideration to a series of bright blue arrows pointing to the words 'Windsor Mews', he mentally constructed a set of questions he would like to put to Sir Henry Hughes about his business interests. He interrupted himself by second guessing the matching interruptions, he reluctantly imagined would come from the mouth of a solicitor, representing Sir Henry Hughes. This was a damnable game he was playing and his anger and frustration grew.

The door opened and his colleague D.I. Cummins entered, along with D.S. Maurice Watson. The pair seemed to be rather upbeat, which caused Melville a moment of annoyance as he assumed they were clearly not focusing on the matter in hand, and were probably responding to some light-hearted banter in the corridor. This perception was quickly dispelled when Cummins spoke. "I think we're closing in on Hughes, Roger. We've received information which places Hughes in Scotland round about the time of the Malone shooting."

Melville listened intently to this and excitedly reached for a red board-marker as he anticipated the addition of dramatic new data for his troubled jigsaw. "Just how definite is this? What about timings for instance?" he queried, toying with the red marker.

"On Saturday 18th August, that's two days before the shooting, we know Hughes flew into Dyce airport…that's Aberdeen. There are witnesses that remember it quite clearly. His flight landed quite late, near ten o' clock, and there was a bit of a fuss because of his second flight…" narrated Cummins, until Melville intervened.

"Second flight?"

"Yes. Apparently Hughes was in a bit of a rush, and a bit of a temper as well it seems, as he was due to fly straight out by helicopter for some sort of important business rendezvous. But, the airport has a noise restriction between ten thirty at night and six o' clock in the morning; no take-offs, no landings. Getting the chopper ready to go before the ten thirty curfew was a close run thing. A number of people there commented on his disgruntlement. Not his usual suave and calm self, it would appear."

Melville turned to the table behind him, picked up an atlas already opened at a map of North Scotland. "Aberdeen, eh, on the Saturday. So do we know where he went from there?"

"Not yet. The helicopter was a private one, not one of the usual ones used for the oil workers. That's another reason why people remembered the incident. Although we are trying to find the flight plans for this private helicopter, it could, of course, land virtually anywhere." Cummins stopped for dramatic effect and then smiled at Melville. "But one thing is pretty clear. The chopper set off away from the familiar routes; it travelled west." Melville's finger travelled west, over his atlas. "Towards Inverness!"

Watson, who had observed the growing excitement of D.I. Melville as this crucial information was added to his whiteboard of evidence, felt the strange presence of power born of his own prior knowledge of Hughes' position in the underground network. This power was really a confidence, he supposed, as it was becoming clear that, although the task of bringing this powerful man to justice may be a long drawn-out process, the pieces of this vast investigation were beginning to take shape, and once there were names, real people, to work on, to check up on, then he knew things were moving steadily in the right direction.

"So, this Scottish connection seems a lot stronger than the Windsor Mews links, don't you think?" pondered Melville. "Having established he has a business association with the development company responsible for the property, we need something slightly harder, something more substantial in the form of evidence, before we can move towards the point when we can bring him in for an interview."

Cummins nodded and indicated Watson, as if he believed Melville hadn't noticed the sergeant's presence. On cue, Watson explained, "earlier this morning, sir, I took the liberty of posing as a reporter for a business journal…on the phone, sir….to request an appointment to interview Sir Henry for an article about high-flying entrepreneurs. I was told that he is out of the country at present and not expected back until Friday at the very earliest."

"Well, we might have enough to hang him by then," grinned Melville, clearly buoyed up by this new injection of information. There was a polite diplomatic cough from Watson.

"Ah," said Cummins, in a moment of realisation, looking at his watch, "we two chaps are off to Bristol. We think there may be a lead from the murder suspect being held there."

"I thought he wasn't talking. Best of luck with that then!" he turned back to face his whiteboard, more content now that a slow meaningfulness was growing in front of his previously despondent eyes. As if suddenly remembering another reason for his lifted spirits, he added, "the Pickerings are being interviewed tomorrow. We are reuniting them with Andrew, the son, at the safe house. We're expecting quite a lot from them, although we have been told some of it is going to be unpleasant."

28th August 1990. Bristol. 4.p.m.

"Don't worry, Frank," reassured D.C.I. John Gates, "We are not taking this case away from you. No one is going to do that"

Frank Harvey gave a quick look in the direction of Maurice Watson. Had he misjudged the fellow officer? They seemed to gel quite well on Watson's trip to see the Cheddar suspect, and view Lundy Lane just over a week ago. Was this Scotland Yard interloper trying to play a sleight-of-hand trick and make the West Country man look wet?

Gates continued, "this may seem a little unusual, a little unorthodox, but I have been told, quite clearly by the Yard, that these officers have been given another bite of the cherry to get this man to talk. I have been assured that the highly confidential nature of the new information Inspector Cummins and Sergeant Watson have received has a very good chance of achieving a result regarding the identity of our suspect. When this happens, the ensuing questioning will be carried out as normal." It seemed to Gates that Harvey was some way off from being convinced. "You're a football man, aren't you, Frank?" Harvey frowned and wondered where this was going. "It's all about teamwork," added Gates, firmly, "we're just letting Watson here, take a penalty!"

Watson caught Cummins' eye. The senior officer nodded, then inclined his head towards Frank Harvey. Watson spoke. "I think I know how you feel. We're not standing on your toes. This is a one-off. Ten minutes from now, there's a chance you could have a hell of a laugh at my..our...expense and we could be more embarrassed than you could ever imagine." Watson paused and took in Frank Harvey's quizzical expression. "But," he went on, "I'm confident that will not happen."

The interview room at Bridewell Police Station was as anonymous as one would expect. No distractions, nothing of significance to look at. A room to stare into someone's face or a room to stare into nowhere. The suspect, looking weary and gaunt, did not have the often-hard arrogance of the experienced criminal. There was nothing in his demeanour to suggest he was used to the tussle of a police interrogation There was no tautness of attitude waiting to be exhibited in a series of aggressive posturing, or the casual mock confidence of the 'I've-got-nothing-to-say-to-you' types who find themselves in police custody on a regular basis. This was a man out of his depth. This was a man who looked lost. In his early thirties, but with the vulnerability of someone much younger, this man was a fading human being with the face of a victim.

On entering the room, Watson stepped almost warily towards the prisoner and took up the interrogator's position at the single table. Cummins, although the senior officer present, appeared to take a lesser role, sitting on a chair to the side of the table. However, it was Cummins who, with an almost imperceptible flick of the head, signalled to the police constable, standing on guard behind the prisoner, that it was time for him to leave the interview room.

With his arms folded very loosely, the prisoner looked increasingly uncomfortable as Watson continued to stare at him. Cummins sat back and seemed to be looking at both men, alternately, as if watching some kind of invisible psychological tennis match. The suspect tried to avoid the now piercing gaze of the man on the other side of the table. He unfolded his arms, almost trance-like, and put both hands limply on the edge of the table, nervously moving his fingers as if the dust was annoying his fingertips. The minute that this intense staring occupied, was about to come to an end. Watson's stare, which now seemed to subside into a benign expression of satisfaction heralded the opening gambit of the conversation. It was not the question the prisoner was expecting.

"So, David…" Watson turned the stare back on. The man jolted, his eyes suddenly wide with a mixture of horror and confusion. He swallowed the dryness in his mouth and looked at both men in the shocked realisation that something had just happened which he hadn't been expecting It seemed, for a moment, he might speak. "It is David isn't it? David Carter."

The man's sigh broke, almost into a sob, as he clutched his head and slumped forward. It was as if his body had just been emptied of all its energy. The man inside had gone, and only a shell of fraught emotions was left. The other shocked face in the room was Cummins. He had not known exactly what Watson was going to do or say, and the revelation was stunning. A smile, which did no justice to what he was feeling inside, appeared. A huge relief swept through him, but also the warmness of the rewarded trust he had invested in his junior officer. His risk with Watson's idea had paid off.

David Carter was now sobbing, racked with anxiety, "yes, I'm David Carter." His head came up and the tears were, of relief, of pain and perhaps of guilt. "But how did you find out? No one knows I'm here. Who told you?"

"Your father," replied Maurice Watson.

More shock came from David Carter, "How? Where is he?"

"He's safe, David. But he doesn't know you're here. He doesn't know you're facing a murder charge."

"So how did he tell you I was here?"

"Do you remember me being here last week?" asked Watson, looking more sympathetically at the prisoner.

"I think so, I vaguely remember you," said Carter slightly abstractedly.

"Well, luckily I remembered *you*. So when I met your father, I thought the likeness was too strong to be a coincidence."

"When did you see my Dad? He is okay, isn't he?"

"Yes, as far as I know he is. We can talk about that later. I'm sorry, but I need to remind you of the charges being brought against you, and that the officers here need your full cooperation." Watson sounded more like a policeman again. "We," he looked at, and included Cummins in his explanation, "will do everything we can to help you with your case, because I have great doubts that the situation which occurred in Cheddar is not as it appears at the present moment. We do not think we're looking at a crazed killer."

Carter's ironic smile brought a welling of more tears, "perhaps I was crazed. The man I killed had just murdered my girlfriend and four other innocent unarmed people. I couldn't believe it. He executed them. He shot them in cold blood, but he missed me. When I realised his gun was empty I chased him through the cave. I kept after him. I didn't know he was heading to topside….above ground. I kept after him through the crowd in the cavern. I knew I would catch him. That's all I was thinking about…and Jenny and the others… and when I caught him….yes…maybe I was crazed, but he won't be killing anyone else, will he?" He slumped forward again and rubbed his eyes, and shook his head slowly and resignedly.

Cummins stood up and spoke sympathetically to this broken man. "It's important that you help us, David. There have been more atrocities, like the one you witnessed. When you've made your statement about the Cheddar incident, we'll want to talk to you again about this underground network."

"You know about that too?" Carter replied, as surprised as before.

Maurice Watson stepped towards the chair which had, moments before, been occupied by Samuel Cummins. "Oh, we know quite a bit about the network. But not enough. We need to know more."He placed his left foot on the seat of the chair and pulled back his sock.

David Carter stared at the telltale tattoo just above Watson's ankle, "oh, I see."

29th August 1990.
Central London. 10.a.m.

Teenage sons often present a muted show of affection towards their parents, especially if other people are in attendance. A mixture of embarrassment and coy coolness will invariably win out, and the son will demonstrate a certain reluctance to show filial closeness. None of this applied to Andrew Pickering. When he was reunited with his parents, inside the safe house he had occupied for the last ten days, he released a well of emotion. The collective tears of this family told a simple but powerful story. The circumstances of their separation had been unplanned. Andrew had been working on some safety equipment underground when the catastrophe broke and he could not contact either of his parents who were holidaying abroad. For many days he worried about what might happen to them when they returned to a dangerous situation; he knew they were due to do some ancillary work underground on their return from holiday, but had no way of knowing where they would be. The idea that some homes may be under observation was a real concern. Now that he knew his parents were safe, he hugged them as if he had believed they had fallen victim to the invisible atrocities and had returned from the dead. This poignant display of love and affection brought home to D.I. Roger Melville the fact that he was dealing with a curious type of person who, regardless of the opinions of others, had espoused a grand notion and carried it out. And at its core was the idea of family survival. It troubled him greatly that these benign people were clearly targets of a determined group of criminals, who had already demonstrated a disregard for any human life that they decided was obstructing their illegal activities.

The time taken up by the Pickering's emotional reunion was soon over, and the pressing business of police investigations now took precedence. An account of Alan and Lesley Pickering's discovery of the three bodies was taken down in great detail. The crime scene would be investigated as soon as arrangements could be made for Alan and Lesley Pickering to accompany a team of police officers underground. Melville was very aware of the Pickering's importance to the investigation now. Soon they would lead the police to three murder victims. Soon they would show the police a way into the physical network below ground. Soon they would reveal the everyday dealings which kept this organisation going, and learn how to combat the Trojan Horse enemy. And, he pondered, there may come to light more references to Sir Henry Hughes' involvement in this sordid business.

Before embarking on the underground operation, planned for the following day, there was a need to gather more information about the practicalities of such a venture. Alan Pickering had no hesitation in agreeing to recount his earliest experiences of the network and something of the life below ground.

"I was introduced to a contact in the organisation by a mutual friend whom I had met at a series of CND meetings. I genuinely have no recollection of his name. This was in 1968. It turned out that the network had been in existence for over ten years at that point. I knew that the guy in charge was ex-military; to be honest, that surprised me at first, but as I found out more about how it operated, it seemed eminently sensible to have such experience on our side. There was a huge excitement about the cloak-and-dagger business on the actual day I was interviewed and I felt as if I was doing something terribly subversive, but of course I wasn't. The entrance to the underground area I was taken to…well…to this day….I could not tell you where it was. Somewhere within London."

Alan Pickering stopped briefly to take a few sips of water from the glass on the table he sat at, and took a glance at the tape-machine which recorded every word he spoke. It was as if he was reliving that same excitement from all those years before. An almost wistful smile appeared on his face and he continued with his recollection.

"You must realise that at this time, the late sixties, there was a lot of concern about world events. The Vietnam War. Revolution and rebellion in Africa and South America. The Cold War seemed a daily issue. The Middle East was a tinder box. Protests were everywhere. Student revolts across Europe. Even in the States. And all that nuclear posturing. Well, it didn't look particularly promising did it? Those of us who talked about peace and harmony were derided as subversives, communists, anarchists or any other negative label which came to hand. So the appeal of the underground network was almost overwhelming. The philosophy of the head man; I was told his name was George Ford, but I was also told later that was not his real name, was a philosophy I could relate to and that was it….I wanted to be in." Alan Pickering paused and closed his eyes. "He wasn't really the leader, as such. He was, and still is, a figurehead. Any big decisions are made by committee; that hasn't changed. But I can remember the little speech he gave about what to expect. It was very like an interview, all the same."

16th *November 1968. London.*

"It's a particularly special life, you understand," said George Ford, emphasising the word 'special'. "You need to accept you are living an absurdity. That's what it is ….a measured absurdity. It will become natural of course, over a period of time, but it will always be a secret. That is unequivocal. It always needs to be a

secret. That is crucial. That is an absolute. There is no room for a single doubt." Ford smiled, humourlessly, allowing time for his words to sink in. "You would be joining an underground organisation. Literally." His new smile was more hardened than the first.

Alan Pickering pursed his lips and made thoughtful nods as he absorbed the information, its implications and his own feelings. He was convinced by George Ford's philosophy. It was his own philosophy. The importance of secrecy was paramount. It was essential. It was obvious.

Ford, benign in his observations of Pickering's response, held his hand up, palm forward, as if he was a police officer halting traffic. "Wait. You need to wait. Give yourself time to decide. We will not rush you. There is no coercion, no brainwashing. There is no propaganda to endure. If you are with us, we will welcome you. If not," he paused, "then this conversation never took place."

Pickering's memory of that day was strong. That was to be expected. The breaking of the secret was shattering for him. Life had moved somewhere else.

29th August 1990. Inverness. 10.a.m.

Clutching his battered clipboard, Willie Bolton was back in hospital. His previous visit had been moderately successful and he and his London colleague, were diligently putting together the bones of a story which had all the makings of 'the big one'. What was beginning to convince Willie of his anticipated success was the level of good luck he seemed to be operating on at the present time. His fortunate eavesdropping on the two unassuming nurses had set up an interesting line of enquiry on the Sunday and the previous evening had brought him to some curious pub gossip about two farm workers finding an injured man, who rambled on about all sorts of strange things going on inside a mountain. Other people, including the two farm workers themselves, would doubtless dismiss these ideas as the results of delirium, but there was a familiar aspect to the story as far as Willie was concerned. He had noted who the two men were and had an idea of following up with them later if that course of action looked promising. Finding another opportunity for more information in the mean time meant he was embarking on another adventure of disguise.

Approaching a porter who was crossing the reception foyer, he beckoned him for assistance. "Ah, can you help me? I'm from the Hospital Radio Inverness" he asked, lightly brandishing his clipboard, "I'm new…I need to find some new patients to collect requests from…casualty, and such like."

The porter nodded and pointed down a corridor and began to lead the way, "It's this way to the casualty ward.

There's a policeman with the chap who came in yesterday. He's awake now. You could try him."

Willie's mind was abuzz. On one hand, he appeared to have located the injured man in question with the minimum of effort, but on the other hand there was a police presence. He needed to play this cleverly. As he reached the door of the small casualty ward, he caught sight of a young police constable making notes by someone's bedside. The young officer seemed to stop rather suddenly and indicated to the person in the bed to halt his verbal account and stop talking. He gestured apologetically towards the patient and started moving to the open doorway. P.C. Ronnie Irwin grabbed his police radio, again apologised to the man in the bed, and stepped into the corridor. In a deft and swift response, in a quick moment of slyness, Willie slid into one of the two seats by the ward doorway and took out a pen, flicked over the top sheet of paper and began writing on the pad of paper on his clipboard.

"Yes sir, it's Irwin here. Mister Quinn knows something about some similar incidents to the other ones we're looking into." The policeman walked further away from the door and hadn't noticed the presence of the man in the seat by the door. The reply from the radio was not heard by Willie Bolton. It was Irwin's turn to talk. "Glen Druicht, it's on the other side of Ben Ochin." Willie was now making careful notes as opposed to pretending to make notes A junction in the short corridor allowed Irwin to briefly disappear round a corner while the radio conversation continued. Willie Bolton stood up, in an attempt to listen further, but before he could, Irwin reappeared, switching off his police radio and noticed Willie for the first time.

"Yes?" asked Irwin.

"Hospital Radio," the clipboard brandished once more. "Is he okay to request a record?"

"Not really, he's helping us at the moment. You'd be better off coming back a bit later."

Willie cheekily peered through the small square glass pane in the door, "road accident is it?"

"No. He's just had a nasty fall, sir. So, if you could come back later?" Irwin strongly suggested, exerting a little bit of authority.

"Yes, yes, of course," said Willie, possibly overdoing the tone of humility. He turned slowly to walk back up the corridor, aware that the police officer was walking with more pace back to the ward, indicating the interview wasn't over. Surmising that the police interviewing would be continuing with a more senior officer, Willie Bolton thought it the best policy to hang around and see if he could glean any more information from his continued lurkings.

As he had successfully predicted, the interview with the injured man was moving into a second phase. Willie was sitting in a convenient waiting area when D.S. Craig Baxter entered the hospital main doors in a hurried manner, with the air of a man clearly Excited by something about to happen. Willie gave some careful thought to the next part of his plan.

In his hospital bed, Steve Quinn tried to move into a more comfortable position. A nurse had just come into the ward to check on the only other occupant, who was three beds away, at the other end of the room. She noticed Quinn's predicament and diverted to help him, glancing at the police officer sitting by the window away from the bed. "Have you not finished talking to him yet? He could do with some rest, you know," she seemed to admonish P.C. Irwin. She efficiently adjusted the pillows behind the frowning figure of Steve Quinn.

Quinn attempted a smile and asserted, as best he could, "it's okay, nurse, I need to give some information to the police. I think it may be very important. If I didn't, it would only prey on my mind. I wouldn't really rest"

The nurse gave a well-practised quizzical look towards P.C. Irwin, who was about to say something when D.S. Baxter walked through the swinging doorway. The nurse turned to see the handsome face of Craig Baxter at the end of the bed, "Oh, I see the cavalry has arrived." She gave a flash of her widened blue eyes which Baxter noticed with more than a cursory awareness, before she wandered off towards the other patient.

"Mister Quinn, is it?" asked Baxter, "Stephen Quinn?"

"Yes, but Steve will do. I never use Stephen."

"We received a message yesterday, about lunchtime, that you wished to report a crime. When we contacted the hospital, it turned out you were in the operating theatre. Your legs mainly, I understand. So we waited for this morning." Baxter explained. "I hope you now feel ready to talk. Constable Irwin here was sent to see you as we assumed the crime you were reporting was a domestic or traffic incident. He now tells me it is clearly more than that. From what P.C. Irwin has told me there may be a connection to another offence already under investigation."

Steve Quinn looked at both police officers and seemed to take a deep breath. "What I am about to tell you may be very difficult for you to believe, but I assure you it is the truth. The background is complex and will seem unbelievable, but the crime I wish to report is murder. More than one, definitely. I was shot at and had a fall which broke one leg and injured the other one. I am assuming that my attackers believed I died in the fall, or was killed by the bullet. I was incredibly lucky to get out of that mountain alive." At the mention of the last phrase, Baxter and Irwin exchanged knowing glances. Quinn spotted this. "Ah, you think I'm barmy, right? You don't believe me!"

"No, no, Mister Quinn….on the contrary….we *do* believe you. In fact we are going to listen to you very carefully. I also believe what you said about the background being complicated," he paused as he wrestled with which question to ask next. "We'll take however long it takes to hear your story, but briefly, to cut to the chase, in one respect, do you know who the attackers, your assailants, were in this main incident?"

"Well, I think I know a couple of names of the guys doing most of the shooting, but the big boss had put in an unexpected appearance about a week ago because something had gone wrong days before that. Things changed for the worst after his visit. He's a big businessman, I think he's quite well-known. I only saw him that one time, in the flesh."

"In the flesh?" queried Baxter with sudden alarm. Irwin threw a glance at Baxter and read his mind. "What do you mean, in the flesh?"

"Well, I'd seen him on the telly before!"

From outside the room came the clicking of heels, the only sound audible in the astonished silence within. Baxter stood up and looked straight at Quinn, who rather sheepishly seemed to sink into the pillow as if he had committed an act of obscenity. Irwin also stood up and the two police officers sent two friendly smiles at Steve Quinn. The man in the bed now seemed a little confused. Baxter looked at him, but spoke to Irwin. "Constable, do you still have those tapes?"

"Yes sir, I can get the stuff sorted out straight away."

Baxter felt a thrill of excitement course through his body. P.C. Jamie Malone's testimony was on the brink of being verified. He felt this instinctively. Continuing to look at the man in the bed, whose legs were under a protective wired cage under the sheets, Baxter grinned and said, "Steve, Steve...... we want you to watch some television!"

Quinn looked askance at this detective sergeant and wondered if *he* was the real barmy person in the room.

Two hours later, Detective Inspector Colin McNab gave a satisfied exhalation of air, as he replaced the phone receiver. Looking across to Craig Baxter he announced how extremely pleased the Yard was at this latest news which moved the case firmly forward. He had been assured that the new information they had obtained would be acted on by the end of the day.

31st August 1990.
Scotland Yard. 4.p.m.

Oscar Shackleton re-read the sheets of paper on his desk. He took a slim silver pen from his inside pocket and underlined something on one of the sheets. Checking some information on another sheet brought a brief satisfied nod and a thoughtful stroke of his beard. He looked across his desk to where D.I. Samuel Cummins sat, flicking through his own copy of the written material about to be put to explosive use. Their plan was to short circuit the upcoming interview and effect a positive outcome. The unusual nature of this ever-growing investigation had brought out the best in the team working on it. With so many challenges to face and so many unlikely ideas to follow, the process could have been expected to wear them down. But the more recent revelations and breakthroughs had been a great boost to the confidence of those officers busily pursuing an investigation which became increasingly captivating, but was also given a more personal and a more hardened edge because of the shooting of one of their own kind. This was an extra level of determination that was perceived, but couldn't be quantified. Here was the motivation which moved this growing team to their expected positive outcomes.

Both men were acutely aware of the critical importance of the next hour or so. Cummins had wanted to take a shorter route to their goal than Shackleton, but seniority won the day and a more softly-softly approach was now anticipated. In theory, there was a great risk involved with this particular strategy and the pros and cons of it had been discussed at length by the core officers of the team, but the chosen method had the confidence of all.

The phone rang. "Sir Henry Hughes has arrived, sir," said a voice, "and his legal representative, a Mister Marcus Armstrong," it added.

"Fine. Take them to the interview room at the end of the corridor, thank you."

Cummins grimaced at the desk, "so he *has* brought some legal assistance, sir."

"Hmmm," pondered Shackleton, "I wonder if that will make a difference to the outcome of the afternoon?"

Cummins held the paper sheets in his hand and rotated them back and forth, "I don't think so, sir."

"I think you're right, Cummins. I am trusting you on this one. Let's get on with it, then." They left the room.

The door opening into the interview room made a telltale squeak to announce the arrival of the police interview team. Two pairs of eyes shot a glance towards the officers from their seated positions on the further side of a solid, but plain-looking table. The tension already in the room which greeted Shackleton and Cummins was palpable. The effect this had on Cummins was noticeable; he almost had to fight off the beginnings of a grin.

Across the table the nervous grey eyes of Sir Henry Hughes seemed to peer through the walls in the hope of seeing what was on the other side. Cummins noticed this, and had a few mischievous thoughts about the nature of guilt. Hughes had the look of a gentleman, possibly even aristocracy, his usual urbane manner today however seemed somewhat masked with a rather furtive interest in his surroundings. Suave, neat and well- dressed, he was the epitome of a man used to a rich and elegant life-style. A vague demeanour of the matinee idol was almost discernible, but with more examination this impression became somewhat thin and the conclusion was more likely to be one of seediness. Cummins smiled mechanically at him; he was reinforced in his idea that he wouldn't like this man.

It was the other older man, who spoke first, "I am Marcus Armstrong, one of Sir Henry's legal team and I must express my client's outrage at the manner in which he has been treated. He is an important and busy man and we both feel in was unnecessary to have police officers waiting to meet him at the airport. Why the great hurry?"

Shackleton fielded this question in an understated, almost relaxed way, which seemed to disconcert Armstrong and Hughes. "Hardly a hurry. We'd been waiting three days. As Sir Henry was out of the country, we had no option." Shackleton was going to play this absolutely firmly, so emphasised, "three days, Mister Armstrong, so nothing to do with a 'hurry'." The tone of the last word was the sound of a gauntlet hitting the floor.

Hughes placed his elbows on the table and pressed the fingertips of both hands Together in an attempt to show considered calm, "if we can get on with any questions, then the sooner we can leave, right?"

Cummins, who was sitting directly across from Hughes leant forward and put his elbows on the table and mimicked the hand position of his opposite number and smiled, "that's the theory anyway." Hughes leaned back and folded his arms, resigned to the fact that things were not going to be as straightforward as he wished, and this was going to be a long haul. And not an easy one for him.

"Okay, then," started Cummins briskly, as if about to draw the tickets for a social club raffle, dispensing a subtle but clearly mocking smile towards Hughes," could you tell me what you know about Windsor Mews?"

The question was a bolt from the blue to Hughes and he wasn't really prepared for it, but forced an amused look, "I believe it's a housing development in Central London built, a number of years ago now, by a company I have a tenuous association with. I act as a financial consultant for them from time to time."

Cummins fired back, "how many houses in this development?"

"Goodness, I couldn't say for certain," Hughes replied. Cummins stared back, determined to get a fuller answer. "Er, about twelve, I think."

"Only one," Cummins sat back in his chair, keeping his eyes firmly on Sir Henry Hughes, "but a rather special one undoubtedly." Hughes actively avoided eye contact.

Marcus Armstrong felt compelled to speak. "Sir Henry can not be expected to know the detail of every scheme he has assisted with."

"Really," said Cummins, with a huge helping of surprise, aimed visibly at Armstrong. He turned his gaze back to Hughes adding, "you help in funding twelve houses and only one is produced? Someone is being misled here, surely. Tell me, Sir Henry, are you a very good financial consultant?"

Armstrong was incensed, "stop this sort of questioning now. I find your facetious tone insulting!" He had reddened with fury, but it was the level of discomfort he exhibited which Oscar Shackleton noted with a certain sense of satisfaction. He turned towards Armstrong with a cursory glance towards Hughes.

"Perhaps you feel my colleague is rather zealous in his questioning, Mister Armstrong? That maybe so, but I sense he could be on the right track. Progress is being made. It's important we get a clear, and truthful, picture." Cummins picked up clearly that Shackleton was pleased with the way things were going. The enigmatic, and slightly robust approach of Cummins had rattled both Armstrong and Hughes from the very beginning and there was no reason to change the game plan yet.

Cummins reiterated his point, "so having '*lost*' eleven houses, Sir Henry, would you say you are a successful financial consultant?"

Again, Armstrong was enraged, "this facetious tone again!"

Cummins stopped looking at Hughes and turned deliberately to face Armstrong. The policeman's confidence was like a kite. It was there for all to see. "Mister Armstrong," his tone was measured and hardened," I would not concern yourself about my tone being 'facetious'. In about one hour from now, you will have a lot more to worry about than that. The word 'facetious' will be the last thing on your mind."

For once, Armstrong was lost for words. Before that situation changed, Cummins pushed ahead; he was beginning to smell blood. "Enough about Windsor Mews, eh? As your legal representative indicates, you don't want to talk about that. We may come back to it later, who knows!" He leaned forward again and dispensed with his smiling attitude. "Something much more serious. The shooting of a police officer!"

"What, this is preposterous!" It was Armstrong again. "This farce has gone too far. My client agreed, reluctantly in the circumstances, to answer questions about his business Interests…and now you're bringing up nonsense about shootings!"

"A young police constable was shot while attempting to apprehend an armed man and we have reason to believe that Sir Henry may be able to shed some light on the incident." Cummins turned on his provocative stare once more on Hughes' now-sweating face. Hughes glanced at Armstrong, but it was clear than his advocate was looking as uncomfortable as himself. "So, what have you to say, Sir Henry?"

"There is nothing for me to say. I can tell you nothing about this alleged incident."

Cummins balked at the final phrase of Hughes' reply. "Alleged! Alleged! There was nothing alleged about the bullet taken out of the body of that young copper!" He had started with an overly dramatic response to effect fear in Hughes, but he had slipped into an honest rage about the shooting of Jamie Malone. He caught a glimpse of Shackleton who was visibly rapt by Cummins performance, but had time to nod support almost imperceptibly to his junior officer.

Cummins calmed down and pulled abstractedly at his shirt collar and then moved one of the sheets of paper, from the slim bundle he and Shackleton had been perusing to a position halfway between himself and Hughes. It was as if he was challenging Hughes to try and read it upside down. The policeman noticed that Hughes stared at the tantalising piece of paper. After a few seconds, Cummins snatched it and placed it to one side and stared with venom straight at Sir Henry Hughes. "We have two independent witnesses who place you at the scene of the crime. We have strong reasons to believe them."

With a raised hand, Hughes looked at Cummins and then Shackleton, "there's been a mistake here! This is absurd. Why would I be shooting a police officer?"

"That was to be my next question, Sir Henry. Why did you shoot the police officer?"

"I didn't. I can assure you. Your witnesses are mistaken." His attempt at a calming smile failed badly. It was clear that Hughes did not know which way to turn for the best.

Marcus Armstrong felt compelled to add to Sir Henry's denial. "Clearly there has been a mistake here. The witnesses have seen someone perhaps who resembles my client. That sort of thing has happened before, as well you know. I am concerned that there may be another agenda here which my client and I are not aware of. Or are we simply looking at a case of mistaken identity?"

Cummins leaned back in his chair and swapped a glance with Oscar Shackleton. He nodded thoughtfully like someone about to give way in an argument, and this time it was *he* who raised his hand. "I see, I see. What you seem to be implying here is the potential problem facing a jury when there's all that pressure in the courtroom."

The level of discomfort from Hughes and Armstrong at the mention of matters legal was visible. The body language of both men seemed to shout at the walls of the room. Cummins' instinct was preparing for a victory.

In an attempt to take the heat out of the confrontation, Marcus Armstrong gave a supercilious grin and slowly shook his head. "I think you're getting ahead of yourself Inspector Cummins. You don't really think this ridiculous business will actually get anywhere near a courtroom."

"Well, Mister Armstrong, our witnesses have maximum credibility I assure you. A jury will need to consider the credibility of any alibis your client produces, against the credibility of our witnesses." Cummins sat back once more, holding an expression on his face which he hoped suggested confidence rather than smugness.

Marcus Armstrong appeared to consciously attempt to compose himself. He was beginning to feel as though he was trapped in some excuse for a joke which he did not find funny in the least. The whirlwind approach of this police officer was certainly unusual, rather unorthodox, but of course, that was the problem for him, and his client. "This is a ludicrous interview. I don't know who your witnesses are but my client will be able to produce alibis for the time in question. He is a very busy man and is invariably in someone's company for the most of everyday, especially in recent weeks. Unless you have any more *sensible* questions, I think we should bring this nonsense to an end." He made to pick up the slim leather portfolio which had lain on the corner of the table previously unacknowledged.

The face of Sir Henry Hughes suggested that he was almost seeking leave to stand up, and exit with his advocate, but did not wish to appear too presumptuous.

Adopting a tone which indicated a more matter-of-fact attitude, Cummins suddenly asked, "these alibis, Sir Henry, could we perhaps see your appointments diary and take some names before you leave?" A way to take the pressure of himself seemed possible here. Some calmness was important now with maybe a little bit of indignation.

"Look, I was in a business meeting from ten in the morning; that didn't finish until about five o'clock. Before that I had a working breakfast with an estate manager. And after the main meeting I dined with some business friends, informally. I was probably alone for about an hour for the whole of the day." The edginess in Hughes' voice registered a particular note with Cummins. The policeman spoke rather robustly.

"Are we supposed to believe that all your days are like that, all the same?"

"No, of course not." Hughes was exasperated, clearly wishing he was somewhere else. Cummins returned to his fixed stare and put some pressure on his suspect.

"Your days are all like that or just that particular day, Sir Henry?"

"I have numerous alibis, inspector, all reliable and of sound character…."

"And they can cover the whole week can they?" interrupted Cummins.

"Yes!"

"Really?"

"Yes. From the Monday morning breakfast, throughout the meeting, including lunch I was with several other people……."

Cummins raised his voice, "and Tuesday? And Wednesday? And Thursday? And Friday?"

Hughes was angry now, "no! I'm talking about the Monday!"

The room was hit by a solid silence, until Cummins spoke, very softly. "Why?"

Marcus Armstrong paled. Hughes, anger subsiding into an annoyed confusion, queried, "what do you mean, why?"

The staring eyes of Samuel Cummins sparkled. "Why are you telling me about Monday?"

"You know why. This stupid shooting you're accusing me of!"

"Monday, eh? The shooting was on a Monday? Which Monday?" Cummins stopped, chiefly for effect. His gaze lessened and Hughes sensed that his opponent had another point to make. "You're telling me you *do* have alibis for the Monday?"

A very weak "yes" came in reply.

"So why the Monday? Nobody said anything about Monday. I said nothing about a Monday. Why did you talk about a Monday? What is special about the Monday, Sir Henry?" Cummins glanced over to Oscar Shackleton, who, in turn, had slipped his eyes in the direction of Marcus Armstrong. The solicitor had shrunk into a cocoon of quiet awkwardness, unable to say anything constructive which could rescue his flailing client. He could not imagine how this interview could have been any worse than it had just turned out.

"Well, D.I. Cummins, I think you've only got one more thing to say." Shackleton gave an approving nod in Cummins direction.

On cue, and with a huge amount of satisfaction, Cummins looked firmly at Sir Henry Hughes. "Sir Henry Seymour Hughes, I am arresting you for the attempted murder of P.C. James Malone on Monday 20th August 1990………."

⚶

Some time later, in an earnest conference with other members of the investigating team, Shackleton and Cummins drew attention to the potentially flimsy case they had against Hughes. The two detectives acknowledged that they had rode their luck in the afternoon's interview, but there was a lot of other evidence accumulating against Sir Henry, some of which they had chosen not to use, unless it had become necessary. The *two* independent witnesses had been a sleight-of-hand trick to put pressure on Hughes, and it had worked very well. Jamie Malone's testimony would definitely be attacked by Armstrong's team; probably on the grounds of how dark it was when the shooting took place and also Malone's account would be contradicted by the alibis provided by Hughes. The feeling was that alibis would be 'bought', but proving that would be very difficult, given Hughes' public profile, his power and his money. With David Carter's arrest now of lesser significance, Hughes' arrest was a breakthrough.

31ˢᵗ August 1990.
South London. 8.p.m.

The sudden sound of the telephone broke into the soft sunlit evening of George Ford. He wasn't too surprised when he heard and recognised the voice of Maurice Watson at the other end of the line. Daily, the overall picture of this whole messy business was becoming even more complicated in its lurid detail. But in a curious way it also became simpler, because of the differentiated nature of the open divisions exposed by the parallel plot of the treacherous Derek Martin and Sir Henry Hughes. Snippets of new information about underground incidents came to Ford's attention from other benign members of the organisation who had escaped, or avoided, trouble. Some of his more confident people had explored parts of the system, with great care, to try to build a clearer picture of the state of play, and help or rescue others in peril. The ongoing dilemma Ford continued to wrestle with was the decision he needed to make about whether or not he should come forward and assist the police with their investigations. He was sure that circumstances would arise which would force his hand sooner rather than later; he was already aware of a certain momentum, a certain inevitability, gathering pace.

As Ford listened to Maurice Watson's update, he gazed almost dreamily towards the western sky as it blushed its exit from the day. He caught the key reference to Henry Hughes instantly. "Custody?" he replied, unable to keep the surprise out of his voice. There was also some relief in there too.

"Detained? So he's out of the game....at least for the time being?" This was not only welcome news, it was the final persuasive push which brought an end to his dilemma; his own decision to reveal himself to the forces of law and order had just been made.

Maurice Watson was presenting an earnest proposition. "Call it a summit meeting if you wish. I know that sounds rather grand, but I mean it. For this to work, we need a coherent strategy. A free-for-all will not help us, the police. The Pickerings have already introduced the Met to one part of the system, and others are planned. We need to know the scale of the problem, from our network initially and then anything about Martin's network. Although we, as a group, know very little about that network, it's been shown that Hughes, in particular, had conned some people to carry out development work, and maintenance work. Some of it under duress. This Scottish base we didn't know existed is on a huge scale apparently. There was a group of men being coerced into working, when there was a sort of mutiny. But the dissenters hadn't banked on the firearms and all the violence. This was the situation which went pear-shaped for Hughes; that's why he went there, to sort it out, and presumably his people had lost a certain amount of control and it looks as though he became, probably reluctantly at first, involved in the actual violence. Despite what we have, I'm not convinced that Hughes will cooperate."

George Ford had listened attentively and was relieved to hear about Hughes' capture. "I don't suppose there's any news of Derek Martin's whereabouts?"

"No. That's one of the really big issues at the moment. But there is activity on a number of fronts. And I have some news about David Carter which I would prefer to discuss with Ken face to face."

Ford assented to the planned meeting, "five o' clock tomorrow, then."

1st September 1900.
Scottish Highlands. 9.a.m.

As he looked anxiously out of the car window, Willie Bolton bemoaned the fact that August really had made a statement about turning into September. The weather had taken an annoying turn for the worst, with glowering grey clouds obscuring the mountain tops and threatening rain, which looked likely to coincide with Willie's parking the car. The wide section of valley he was driving through was made up of walled-in fields and a constantly-rippling stream carrying white flecks of bubbled water down from the upper reaches of the towering mountains on both sides of Glen Druicht. Further up the valley and across to the far side were a few scattered small stone buildings, being the only obvious signs of human habitation. The undulations of the single-track road could be followed quite easily by picking out the clues of fences, stone walls and the occasional disorderly lines of hedges and the vertical poles showing the passing-places.

He reflected on the hectic few days he had had with this sensational story which was now bursting into the public domain. The good fortune of his information gathering had been matched with some highly interesting leads from his London colleague. While working separately on certain threads of gossip and speculation, the pair of reporters had found three well-known potential suspects, who had appeared on Question Time during the last few months. Despite the underlying feeling that the idea of a well-known person, possibly a household name, was involved in these mysterious criminal activities, there was a sense of unreality about it all. That did not mean it wasn't fascinating to speculate. When they had worked out, quite reasonably, that there were three suspects in the frame, the frisson of excitement and anticipation was almost too much to bear. One of their three was Sir Henry Hughes; this had caused them much angst because going to press too early and naming such a high-profile figure could seriously back-fire, if you weren't one hundred percent sure of your ground. Willie couldn't believe it when Tony had phoned from London to announce the arrest of Hughes. After experiencing a fair amount of disappointment on missing out on a major journalistic coup, Willie had given some thought to what could be 'salvaged' from their bit of the story. With a little more thought he realised it was *his* bit of the story. The idea which sprung to Willie's mind readily, that concerning the details of the crime under his very nose, was the fact that the mountain business was now being defined as real. In other words there *was* definitely something to investigate in his area of the country, and he was also aware that because of the story being in the public domain now, the police would be more generous with information. His own reasoning had suspected some form of cover-up, but he now realised why that situation had occurred. Even now, however, he was convinced that this business, which had linked the fatal shootings of two strangers in two separate events with the injuries to P.C. Malone and Steve Quinn, had a lot more secrets to reveal. It was this assertion which had brought him out in his car on a gloomy Saturday morning to at least make a general reconnaissance of the latest location in this Highland saga. Armed with information he had cheekily obtained from Steve Quinn while posing as a hospital radio broadcaster, and further information from Tommy McPhail and Alex McDougall courtesy of a dram or two in The Drover's Arms, Willie was about to continue his investigations 'in the field'.

Noticing an extended area of coarse grass running alongside the left-hand side of the road he pulled over to check the map he had shown to Tommy McPhail and Alex McDougall. The spot where the two men had encountered Steve Quinn was only further along the road. Now that Willie had reached this key point on his morning's journey he set his mind on the task ahead. He took in the view upwards and the steep slopes towards Ben Ochin sent a visual challenge to Willie Bolton. He wasn't one hundred percent sure what he was hoping to find; the information from Quinn had been vague about the precise location of the entrance to the mountain. The injured man had not taken much notice of the landscape when he was fleeing for his life. His concentration and physical efforts had been intent on negotiating his safe passage down to the refuge of the road. It was clear from Quinn's own recollections and the evidence from McPhail and McDougall that his mental state was far from lucid.

Willie Bolton climbed tentatively out of his car to be confronted by an abrupt drop in temperature. He had chosen to wear sturdy walking boots for his venture and, before setting off from the outskirts of Inverness, had made some other sensible preparations. He had added a fleece-lined waxed jacket, thick tartan wool scarf and a black woolly hat to complete his ensemble, and was now suitably equipped for rugged outdoor trekking.

Willie Bolton, in fact, was not used to rugged outdoor trekking, so within a hundred yards of the road, slightly dampened by the arriving rain, he was already at the point of reconsidering his decision to embark on what could be a foolhardy, if not dangerous venture. He appreciated the vast beauty of the valley and the general pleasantness of walking in the countryside, but moving upwards and experimenting with altitude was not in his usual weekend remit. Pushing on, he focused on the optimistic possibility of discovering something useful, maybe dramatic, perhaps sensational, linked to this current story. Surely that was the point of the exercise.

Lashing rain continued to attack him as he gradually progressed up the lower slopes of the rocky mountainside. The smell of the wet vegetation gave a curiously clean edge to the air and through the swish of the rain, he could make out the accompanying sound of fast-flowing water as it poured out of the hills. The path he was aiming to take would be alongside a tumbling waterfall. How far he needed to follow this route was unclear; the description from Steve Quinn was vague, but the cascade he was now nearing seemed to fit the picture communicated to Willie by the injured man. Exactly what it was that Willie expected to find he did not know. The one fact he had been told about the 'doorway' was that it had no view of the valley floor. In other words, it could not be seen from the roadway, the fields, or by anyone more than a few yards away. Thinking of the bigger picture, the idea of a 'somewhere' inside the mountain, Willie speculated about the entrance being a utilisation of a natural feature or was it wholly artificial, being constructed with the intention of being as invisible as possible from the outside. Trying to make sense of all these possibilities was an increasingly fruitless task. As the rain was now easing, the absurdity of Willie finding himself in these Spartan conditions subsided, and he thought back to the reality of Steve Quinn's injuries and his account of the shootings. And of course, the shooting of Jamie Malone reminded him of just how real it all was.

Willie Bolton adjusted his collar and flapped off the excess rain accumulated there. With his damp feet testifying to the sheer deluge his boots had endured, and the general lack of comfort he was experiencing, he might have considered turning back there and then. But his eye caught sight of something between two boulders, each the size and shape of slumbering sheep. It was the clear imprint of a boot; the sort detectives always hoped to find outside a window, the morning after a discovered burglary. On closer inspection he noticed there was evidence of scuffed marks of earth on nearby rocks. This, in itself, was hardly very exciting, but it told him that someone had been there very recently. Steve Quinn could have left the footprint four days earlier. Clearly, this was a strong possibility, which meant that Willie had successfully found the correct location. Or was it a print left by a less benign person, possibly armed and dangerous? Accepting the possibility of the latter idea reluctantly, the conclusion that this must be the sought-for location was reinforced.

As he scanned the immediate area, Willie particularly looked for likely vertical surfaces; Quinn's explanation of fleeing the mountain indicated leaving a doorway in the conventional manner. No climbing was involved. Thankfully, both the wind and the rain had eased significantly, allowing Willie to break out of his hunched posture and stand up straight. He stretched his shoulders and arms and instantly felt some cold rain trickle down his neck inside his clothing. How long would it be before he was dry again?

With a certain bluff confidence, Willie Bolton was beginning to see himself more in the role of detective rather than journalist. He found himself weighing up the evidence of information he had heard, and overheard, and used some common-sense deductions in an attempt to assess clues, perhaps even recognise clues. The footprint of the boot did seem quite pronounced; the print of a heavy man or the print of someone *landing* heavily? Had he been jumping from further up the slope. Would that fit in with Quinn's account of his escape? But Quinn had a broken leg and the other one was damaged. Maybe the print was the result of a hop? Willie speculated wildly, but did arrive at a decision; the maker of the footprint had come from further up the steep slope.

Now Willie was even more determined, so onwards and upwards he went. Within minutes he was facing a substantial mound which had the resemblance of a giant insect carapace.

Tufted coarse grasses grew over the mound shape, which was peppered by shards of lichen-covered stone and clumps of robust vegetation such as heather and gorse. Remnants of glacial shrapnel littered the area in front of the carapace-shaped mound and the whole area was drenched.

The foreground which Willie Bolton was now a part of looked perfectly natural, illustrating the bleakness of a Scottish mountain in a typical shroud of gloom. Somewhere nearby, unseen, was a way in, a way into the ground. Despite this recurring absurdity, Willie actively looked for anything which appeared out-of-place or unnatural. He walked to the lower edge of the mound and, although at first not quite believing his eyes, he observed an unnaturally-straight line in the protruding outcrop of rock and earth. In the split second it took him to realise what he was looking at, the hairs at the back of his neck bristled. The dark line indicated the edge of an opening. A few steps closer and he saw that it was a clear inch wide. A door left open! That was ridiculous, surely.

Willie needed to think. Very carefully. With a certain degree of calmness settling over him, after the rush of a racing heart a few seconds before, he reckoned the state of the door might not be as unlikely as he first thought. Quinn had been shot at and fallen over a railing in virtual darkness and he consequently believed that his attackers would assume he was dead somewhere below. They would not expect him to survive, so would have no particular reason to check any exits. Similarly, as he escaped through the doorway, Quinn was hardly likely to take time out to close the damned thing! So Willie's conclusion was that the doorway was left open by the fleeing Quinn four days earlier.

Willie now needed to think again. The argument, to enter a potentially dangerous place, unarmed, when the chances of people inside who were armed was high, was not a very convincing one. However, climbing for two hours through rain and wind, finding what you were looking for, and then turning back unrewarded, seemed stupid. He weighed up the two options and wondered if there was a third. He could not think of one, but momentarily wondered why the police themselves had not followed up this new information from Quinn. Were they preparing a full-blown operation of their own, perhaps?

Checking the edge of the dark line, Willie soon realised that the doorway, which had an outer surface of vegetation growing on an extensive layer of very fine mesh, rather resembling the effect of ivy growing on the walls of a house, *slid* back. Its utter invisibility was astonishing; it was a doorway brilliantly disguised as the side of a rocky and grassy mound. He carefully edged it open and was astounded by the relative absence of noise. Once inside, he fumbled for the pen torch from one of his zipped pockets; he had come at least partly prepared for exploration. Finding himself in a vestibule with rough shelving units on one side, and a number of ordinary doors along another, he was filled with a startling mixture of fear and excitement. He checked that the torch's wrist strap was securely attached to him and, with a conscious holding of his breath, switched on his own light source.

The shock that hit him was seeing, quite obviously, that one of the doors was open. All this gossip, all this speculation, all the tales, about 'inside the mountain' were right! And here he was!

Having established the veracity of that particular part of the story, he felt a pleasing wave of satisfaction. Surely, the discovery of this significant location was a clear coup for the reporter of the Inverness Courier. Couldn't he now leave, swiftly head back to his car, drive off to his editor and make a bit of a name for himself as a local hero? Yes, this was of course a possibility. While deliberating the pros and cons of whether to back off or push on, he became aware of a distant sound. It wasn't from outside! Despite the dark surroundings, he closed his eyes to help him concentrate on the exact nature of the sound he could hear. It was a clanging of some sort, definitely metallic in its resonant tone, with a hint of the echo about it, which suggested an element of distance. It would have been naive of Willie to think for one moment that it *wasn't* caused by a human presence.

1st September 1990.
South London. 5.p.m.

The front door was opened by Alan Pickering, "Maurice Watson?" he smiled, "George's in the kitchen with Lesley and Andrew. Everyone's here." He enthusiastically offered his hand to Watson, as they both stepped into the hallway of George Ford's home.

"You must be Alan Pickering," deduced Watson as he heartily shook the man's hand, before looking over Pickering's shoulder. "Is Ken in the kitchen too?"

"Ah, no. George said you wanted a word with him before we start."

"Yes, it's rather important." Watson followed Pickering into the conservatory.

Having exchanged an awkward, but knowing glance with Felicity Hood who made a diplomatic excuse to leave Ken Carter alone on the sofa, Maurice Watson found himself reluctantly ready to have his serious talk with Carter.

The anxious look on Carter's face indicated that he had probably gleaned from George Ford the subject matter of Watson's requested chat.

Watson knew exactly what he was going to say, what he meant to say. Whether it turned out the way he had planned, he would soon find out. He would sound like a policeman first and foremost, but he needed to create the impression that he was this man's friend. The two men had more in common than either fully realised. Watson had heard only good things about Ken Carter's role in the organisation, and he found himself in a position where he knew he would be respectful of that view.

"Mister Carter, I have discovered the whereabouts of your son, David…" he began.

"Is he alright? Is he safe?" Carter burst in.

"Yes, he's perfectly safe. We will do everything we can to help him," Watson noted the perplexed look which flashed onto Watson's face. "He's in police custody, in Bristol" He continued in measured tones, hoping it would be easier for Carter to process the dramatic information he was about to hear. "He is being held on a charge of murder, but I have interviewed him and I believe the charges will ultimately be reassessed. We do not believe he is a murderer." Watson paused for an expected response from Carter.

"Murder? David wouldn't murder anyone. I don't understand." Carter wanted to move his hands, but half-frozen in his attempts he merely succeeded in looking awkward.

"The person he is accused of killing had just murdered David's girlfriend."

"Jenny! Oh, God." Ken Carter's eyes filled with tears and he shook his head to rid himself of the thoughts and images which poisoned his brain. "He thought the world of her, so did Ellen and me." His half-sob stuttered into a bitter riposte, "if David knew this man had killed Jenny, then I *can* believe he killed him." He stared unashamedly into Maurice Watson's eyes.

Watson waited briefly, allowing some thinking time for both Carter and himself. "I can assure you, Ken," he felt more comfortable now using Carter's first name, "we will do all we can to verify his story, the circumstances, anything at all…." he began to tail off, then, more formally retrieved the thread of his explanation. "He will be held in custody for some time. We may be able to have him moved to somewhere closer to home. Some time early in this coming week he will be taking a team of police officers below ground to the scene of the original killings. According to David's story, there were five people who were killed by this man…he referred to them as executions. Once we find these bodies, your son's story will be looked on in a different light." Carter's face showed the strain of following this terrible tale. Rather self-consciously, Watson placed his hand on Carter's shoulder to reassure him, "I'm giving you the police line here, Ken. You must understand that they can only act on the evidence to hand, and at the moment it seems quite damning because he has admitted the killing. I believe your son's story, and so does my boss. D.I. Cummins. The Somerset boys don't know the full picture yet, so they have to treat him accordingly. So, the trip to Cheddar will be harrowing for David, I know, but it will make a huge difference to his position."

"Will we… Ellen and I..be able to see him?"

"I'll see if I can sort that for you," he smiled, hoping it didn't look too weak. There was a period of silence where Carter looked at Watson, as if to say thank you, but the words did not come; his mind was elsewhere. Watson understood. "I think it might be time for a glass of George's wine."

George Ford had adopted a resigned attitude to the collapse of his underground network. The debates which had emerged during the previous year about whether to 'go public' about their organisation had produced an accidental smoke-screen, a misleading impression of what was going on. The so-called militant element who espoused the complete secrecy argument turned out to be, almost exclusively, members of Derek Martin's criminal 'wing' of the organisation. Or, more truly, members of a completely different organisation! Any references to Trojan Horses had remained firmly apt. As the situation underground was now confused and complicated, any suggestion that the network could continue in it present form was clearly unrealistic. The deaths which they knew about caused those present to feel a mixture of anger, helplessness and guilt. The realisation that there would be more, was evident in their attitude to any decisions they were about to make.

When Ford had concluded his measured assessment of where the organisation was, there seemed little else to say. There was no dissent. The Pickerings, between them, had seen some of the bodies and been subject to an attack. They had been able to help the police already in locating three of the bodies. During the next few days, arrangements had been made for Alan and Lesley Pickering to visit all the underground locations they were familiar with in the company of a team of police officers. Maurice Watson had compared notes with the Pickering family regarding the range of London locations. Ken Carter had more specific problems to contend with and was understandably abstracted as he watched the clock. He was due to phone his wife Ellen, and elucidate the shock news about David. George and Felicity had agreed to contact Scotland Yard together to give whatever assistance they could. It was also agreed, that in the short term at least, Watson's membership of the organisation was still to remain secret.

There was a curious atmosphere within the group, an unexplainable refreshing of the spirit, a new and determined sense of purpose, with the prime aim of ridding the network of all evidence of the parasitic Martin and Hughes' faction. Just how far this group of people would be able to achieve such a positive outcome, from such an unprecedented position, remained to be seen. Maurice Watson certainly had some ideas of his own he wished to put into practice.

3rd September 1990.
Central London. 10.a.m.

D.C. Ben Clough had the distinct feeling that the ongoing investigations into Windsor Mews were becoming rather tedious. Since the discovery of the unusual nature of the street in question, extensive work had been carried out to reveal a network of hollow walls, secret passages and basement tunnels which linked every 'house' in this curiosity of a development. The rooms of the above-ground dwellings were exactly like the rooms in ordinary houses; they functioned perfectly normally. People could live in them. And probably had done, on a temporary basis. A small team of forensic officers had continued to exploit the abandoned evidence, and the behind-the-scenes aspects of Windsor Mews, in an attempt to discover the nature of the secret areas and how there may be possible access to the deeper system of underground locations which was clearly the main reason of their painstaking work. The actual rooms of the living quarters had not been given much priority, save the removal of a number of weapons found in storage in properties 8 and 8A. Essentially, it was felt that the 'cosmetic' nature of the domestic appearance of the mews was just that; a front to deceive people, a plausible diversion.

As a police officer was required to be present, in the event of someone turning up to access one of the properties or even to call there, Clough had resigned himself to a less-than-riveting experience. On his shifts, he had rarely been called upon to confront anyone; only the odd doorstep caller, but no-one trying to unlock a front door.

This morning he was inside 1 Windsor Mews, one of the end houses which, from an upstairs bedroom and from the downstairs lounge, one could view the whole of the street. As usual, there was no-one about other than an unmarked police van parked at the top end of the cul-de-sac. Half-abstractedly he wandered upstairs like a prospective house-buyer, making a visual note of room size, layout and what changes he would make if he was moving in with his girlfriend. The decor was not really to his liking, a little chintzy for his tastes. Probably not suited to his girlfriend's tastes either, he strongly suspected; it was a bit old-fashioned. On the landing, he noticed there was a rather large portrait of an aristocratic-looking gentleman, who no doubt would be a duke or an earl of somewhere or other. It was like a picture he had seen somewhere recently and, on a closer inspection, namely by lightly rubbing his hand over the surface of the actual paintwork, he realised it must be an original painting. It definitely wasn't a print. With a step back, he could take in the detail of the gilt-looking frame, suddenly recognising the style and then the pattern of the edging. The painting in front of him was a companion to another painting in one of the other rooms in another of the houses in Windsor Mews.

After making some brief notes about each painting he began some in-the-mind's- eye walk-throughs of more of the Windsor Mews' addresses. Identifying some other potential locations of works of art, he set out on a 'gallery walk' convinced he had unearthed a new aspect of this bizarre business of Windsor Mews. The simple idea of 'hiding' something stolen by having it on open view, but in an innocently expected place, like a painting on a wall, had been applied very cleverly by this gang of thieves!

Three hours later, the street was awash with police vehicles, and a variety of officers were swarming around like ants. D.C. Ben Clough felt very much the star of this new show which turned out to be a very cleverly organised, and very elaborate cache of stolen goods. The hawk-eyed Clough had been correct in his assumption that there were, on various walls in Windsor Mews, some extremely expensive original works of art, all of them apparently stolen. Having alerted his superiors, the pace of the investigation had suddenly exploded to life once more and D.I. Cummins had come along with a D.I. from the Flying Squad to join in the fun. A sheaf of documents and photographs were being used to match up many of the objects, that were being discovered with each passing minute, with those purloined from a series of unsolved high-profile robberies covering several years. Three hearths and fireplaces, in three separate houses, turned out to be constructed of ingots of gold bullion, thinly but cleverly disguised. In virtually all of the bedrooms, throughout the street, dressing tables and drawers were filled with stolen jewellery; easily overlooked as stolen, because the items in question were stored exactly where you would expect them to be in anyone's house.

D.I. Terry Holden from the Flying Squad was engrossed in his paperwork at one of the kitchen tables when Cummins entered with a small green velvet sack and placed it in the centre of the table. "Happy birthday," beamed Cummins, continuing a joke which had now survived for a couple of hours. "D.C. Clough sends his regards!"

Holden made a mock grunting sound, but smiled back at his tormentor. "Alright, alright....well done you. Well done your D.C. Clough!" He frowned at the velvet sack, "is that going to be what I think it is?"

"If you're thinking diamonds, then yes." Cummins opened the sack, just enough to show the tempting sparkle of a number of uncut diamonds.

"Yes, I might be able to guess where they've come from." He straightened up and put down the pen he was holding. "Seriously though, thanks again Sam. What we have here are the proceeds of a well-organised crime wave. Some of this stretches back years, probably before my time on the Squad. We're looking at bullion raids, jewellery thefts from shops and private houses. The paintings and sculptures and a whole range of valuable artefacts look as though they could be from galleries, museums or even private houses. This haul will certainly help our clear-up rate." Terry Holden stopped to bathe in the warm glow of professional satisfaction. He was picturing a positive report, good news in the newspapers and a massive boost to police morale. Then something else seemed to slip into his mind which took the edge off his apparent euphoria.

"This case of yours, Sam, this monster of an investigation… it's clearly not just about these robberies, I know. We aren't simply looking at a bunch of thieves are we? There have been a number of killings. Is that right?"

Cummins' grave face answered before he spoke, "yes."

The nod of agreement and understanding from Holden was a long way now from their joking of minutes before. "A number of these robberies were *armed* robberies. Two of them, at least, from what I've identified so far," he gave a sweep of his eyes and head, "involved fatalities. We're looking at the big boys with this one."

"I am not surprised these villains we have been pursuing for about a month now are the same ones you've been after for years," admitted Cummins.

"A month?" exclaimed Holden, "as long as that?"

"Strictly speaking, yes. Although we didn't realise it immediately. It started with a mysterious shooting, a fatality, in Scotland. Then there was one in Somerset. At the beginning they were both seen as local incidents. Anyway, when we joined up the dots, so to speak, it became clear that something pretty awful was going on. It's a national investigation."

"I had heard it was a big operation. Are Special Branch involved yet?" quizzed Holden, aware he was possibly playing devil's advocate in a murky game of police department competition.

"Special Branch!" said Cummins, almost despairingly.

Hands up in a surrender gesture, Holden gave an ironic grimace, "nothing official, just gossip. At the moment it's you and us. Organised crime, murders….. the gossip came from an idea that there have been incidents which involve plotting, coordinated killings and assassinations. That's moving in another direction. Arguably, that's a whisker away from terrorism!"

3rd September 1990.
Scotland Yard. 4.p.m.

Samuel Cummins was having a busy and eventful day. Perhaps the height of his satisfaction was just a little way off.

Taking advantage of the Windsor Mews revelations of earlier in the day, and the fact that D.C.S. Oscar Shackleton was highly pleased with the progress being made on a number of related matters concerning this extremely trying investigation, Cummins had an idea to put to his superior, regarding one of his most trusted officers, D.S. Maurice Watson. The imminent meeting along the corridor with two members of the 'original underground network' and Shackleton had provided an ideal opportunity for Cummins to ease the awkward and testing problem of Maurice Watson's dual status in this complex investigation. Although an unorthodox suggestion, Cummins was planning to suggest that Watson be unofficially given the vital role of liaison officer to the leading group of the network. The feedback about the David Carter situation had impressed Shackleton, even though he wasn't really aware of the fine detail of this 'success story'. Cummins was sure he could convince Shackleton that Watson was absolutely perfect for this unusual, but crucial, role. Given the unorthodox nature of the whole enquiry, such a suggestion would hardly be deemed inappropriate. With this in mind, he had already secured the confidence of Shackleton to allow himself and Watson to meet the two visitors in what was expected to be a crucial and dramatic discussion.

"Our two visitors have arrived, gentlemen," announced Shackleton, as he replaced the phone receiver into its cradle, "they are being brought up to the small committee room. I thought it better than using an interview room; after all, it isn't an interrogation"

"I understand the two people in question are a businessman and an academic?" asked Cummins, ostensibly to give the impression that he didn't actually know who these people were; a part of the bluff to protect his own knowledge of Watson's knowledge.

"Yes, this George Ford is a very successful businessman. He has a finger in lots of pots. It's curious, but he had a military background, then apparently espoused the peace movement in the fifties and helped found this network. The woman, Felicity Hood, has always been a peace campaigner, from a well-to-do family, bohemian type, feminist, a spectacular academic career. And now," he paused briefly, and gave a mock grin, "they are helping the police with their enquiries!"

Moments later, the three police officers arrived outside the committee room at the same time as a uniformed officer stepped out of the adjoining lift with George Ford and Felicity Hood. Shackleton offered his hand to George Ford, who was slightly surprised at the gesture. The Chief Superintendent stared intently at Ford, trying to imagine him as the same person wearing the mask and scarf in the recent video. Now he was wearing a neat business suit and exuded a rather reticent manner. The combination of George Ford with the feisty flowery-ness of Felicity Hood was a striking one, presenting, on the surface, a quite unlikely pair. He could not stop himself from comparing them to Sir Henry Hughes.

Hand shakes and introductions over, the five occupants of the committee room sat in a state of strange tension; there was no precedent for the discussion which was about to take place. Oscar Shackleton reiterated that all those present had seen Ford's video so knew the background to his organisation.

He was now keen for a major input of further information to aid their investigations. With a glance towards Felicity Hood with his steel grey eyes, George Ford settled in his chair and began to speak.

"Felicity and I are here today to give you as much help as we possibly can. I do, however, need to impress upon you an important proviso. You must take our word on two things. One, we have not, to our knowledge committed any crimes. Two, what we have chosen to tell you will be that information which we genuinely consider will be of use to you. We reiterate, Mister Shackleton, that all of us in this room are on the same side. Much of the information we could give you concerning our network and its personnel will be of no help to you. Accepting that will save a lot of time." He stopped and gauged the expressions of the three men opposite him and gave a wry, but friendly smile. "Of course, that may sound less than cooperative to your ears, but I earnestly assure you that what I have said is absolutely true."

Felicity Hood repeated the expression on George Ford's face, "More positively, we are more than willing to show you areas of our network which may be of use to you. Sadly, some of these locations are places where we could expect to find victims of more shootings. Remember, we are dealing with *two* underground networks. Ours," she deftly indicated Ford and herself, "which we know very well, has been infiltrated by the enemy in some places. These we can gain entry to and we will help you to this end. The other network, the creation of Henry Hughes and others, is not known to us personally, but we know that some of our people have been coerced, in recent times, and tricked on other previous occasions to work on the other network in the belief it was legitimate. This is something we will be working on. We do now have a list of these other locations, but we suspect it may be just the tip of the iceberg. The Windsor Mews complex for instance, we knew nothing about. Not even that it existed. When Andrew Pickering was escaping from the underground area, he stumbled on this exit by accident. He had no idea where he was or where he would come out topside..on the surface. He was incredibly lucky."

Ford, who had been listening to Felicity Hood with lowered eyes, now looked across at the three men, "Alan and Lesley Pickering have already embarked on a process of helping you at certain locations; they are familiar with a number of London locations. The Windsor Mews experience shows us that some of our own locations have add-ons, so to speak, which we know nothing about. The Pickerings will continue to help of course, but the two of us can show you more locations which could be of use. We wish to start on this as soon as possible." He was looking straight at Oscar Shackleton.

The Chief Superintendent viewed this couple, this unlikely couple, who had volunteered to help him in one of the most complex investigations of his career, and was reminded of Cummins' suggestion about using Maurice Watson as a communication link between these 'network' people and the police. He arrived at a decision. "If you don't mind, I would like to suggest that D.S. Watson here operate in a liaison capacity with your..er, organisation. Any new information which comes your way can be channelled through him, and the arrangements for these underground visits can be coordinated in the same manner. Issues concerning the deployment of police officers may be informed by further intelligence obtained. Needless to say, we will expect honest assessments from you regarding the relative safety of these individual underground operations. Public safety and the safety of my officers is paramount." He stood up, leaned across the table and offered his hand for the second time, saying, "thank you very much for coming in today. This has been most helpful. I shall leave you with Inspector Cummins and D.S. Watson so you can arrange the first visits underground." With that said he left the room. Samuel Cummins was rather surprised at what he saw as Shackleton's early departure from the discussion. The interpretation he chose to put on his superior's actions was that the old man was perfectly happy to leave the business in hand to his efficient, professional colleagues, namely Cummins and Watson. With Shackleton gone, Watson moved the chairs so the two couples faced each other across the table.

George Ford, after exchanging a knowing glance with Felicity Hood, spoke first. He stared squarely at D.I. Cummins "We understand that you're aware of Maurice's own unique position. We are grateful for your candour and hope you don't feel compromised in any way, inspector."

"Thank you for that, Mister Ford," replied Cummins, "I appreciate what you say and I agree with the view that Maurice's position should be protected. I also agree with your contention that we are, all of us, on the same side."

"So," began George Ford, "to the business in hand." He looked at each person in turn, "tomorrow, I propose we visit Richmond!"

3rd September 1990. Inverness. 4.p.m.

The remaining thick ginger curls of Jock Murray's hair flapped above his coat collar in the gusty wind of the afternoon, as he crossed the car-park towards the main entrance of Raigmore Hospital. As the editor of the Inverness Courier, he had a rather paternal attitude to his staff and had been increasingly concerned, throughout the day, about the whereabouts of his chief reporter and protégé, Willie Bolton. He knew Willie could be a bit of a maverick sometimes and had had a few scrapes in his time, but he was a promising reporter, was generally honest and was rarely missing from his work. The first few phone calls Murray had made had eliminated any likely causes for Willie's absence. After a more tense telephone conversation with D.S. Craig Baxter, it had been decided that the two men meet at the hospital. The main reason for this was to do with some previous sightings there of Willie, and the eventual realisation that the reporter's 'snooping around' had clearly become linked with the current police investigation involving Messrs Malone and Quinn.

Baxter was sitting in the reception area, flicking through the pages of his notebook. When the bulky figure of Jock Murray stepped through the doorway, Baxter stood up and approached the worried-looking man. "Any news?" he asked tentatively.

"No," replied Murray, "the Saturday morning sighting by his neighbour is still the last time anyone has seen him. He went off in his car, the blue Escort. It seems fairly clear that he was following up some lead he'd picked up about this mountain story. As I said on the phone, I think we should talk to this Quinn bloke."

"Well, I reckon that would be a good starting point. Willie had managed to talk to Quinn, apparently when he was posing as someone from the hospital radio," began Baxter. This made Murray smile for the first time, "he's a clever reporter, sergeant, he knows where the stories are."

"Hmmm," speculated Baxter, "let's hope he hasn't bitten off more than he can chew. This *is* a good story, Jock, but it's also a dangerous one!"

"Aye, that's what's worrying me."

The two men proceeded along the wide corridor to the casualty ward, where Steve Quinn was out of bed practising his walking-with-crutches skills. He seemed in a buoyant mood when Baxter and Murray approached, "oh, hello..not another interview," he said with mock sternness.

"Do you remember talking to the guy from hospital radio about your experience on the mountain?" asked Baxter.

"Ah, the reporter you mean! The nurse told me later he was from the local paper. A bit sneaky really." He smiled with a hint that he might just have admired such a course of action from his erstwhile interrogator. "Yes I remember giving him some of the details, those I could recall. He was interested in the two men who brought me into the hospital, McPhail and McDougall. I even mentioned their names when I gave my record request to him. Remember, I thought he was from hospital radio!"

Ten minutes later, Baxter called the station on his police radio, from the hospital car-park. "Has there been a patrol car out at Glen Druicht today?" He scanned the cloud- swept sky as he waited for a reply. "Yes, anything, but particularly a blue Ford Escort car." The concern on Baxter's face was beginning to match that of Jock Murray's. The grating rasp of the radio reply broke the subdued quietness between the two men. Baxter switched off the radio, leaned into the car and replaced it in its pouch by the dashboard. He then straightened up and faced Jock Murray, "has your boy tried to play the hero before, Jock?"

"You mean you think he's gone to trace Quinn's footsteps?" Murray said with more than touch of anxiety.

"It seems so. His car has been abandoned on the Glen Druicht road. He hasn't been seen by anybody up there, but a conservation warden saw the car by the side of the road about tea-time on Saturday, and it's still there."

"Don't you have your own men checking out Quinn's story?" asked Murray, clearly a little annoyed by the idea that police action may have been a little tardy.

Almost as if he was slightly embarrassed by this thinly-veiled accusation, Baxter responded cautiously. "This whole investigation has been a bit awkward, from the very beginning, as you know. The decision to keep information from the public, in the initial stages, was taken elsewhere. The Jamie Malone shooting, then the Henry Hughes link, it's all outside the usual pattern of policing up here, out of our experience I suppose. What we do know now, from Steve Quinn, is that there are multiple entrances and exits into the mountain. The one that Quinn came out of, we think may just be a minor one. We really don't know. There *is* a vehicular entrance; that was the one which Quinn entered by." He stopped as if he felt he had said too much to a member of the press. Murray looked at him with a little more sympathy than he had previously.

"So the entrance, exit, whatever, Willie Bolton has gone for, is not a priority?"

"Come on Jock, it's not that," Baxter was exasperated, "could you do a feature on police manpower?" He was showing a bitter edge. "Shock horror, lack of resources, read all about it! Police chase their own tail!"

Murray half laughed, "okay, point taken. But where does that leave my man, poor Willie Bolton?"

"He's a missing person now, so we'll be able to move on that. We'll get the chopper up again." He gave a cursory glance at the sky. Was that an over optimistic suggestion? Was it premature? The wind still blew erratically, changing direction it seemed constantly. Were there enough daylight hours left to make a helicopter search worthwhile? Or would it be wiser to leave it until the next day when the wind may also have abated? Baxter continued to ponder the sky and its covering of moving clouds.

"I hope that happens sooner rather than later, eh?" responded Jock Murray.

4th September 1990.
Richmond-upon-Thames. 9.a.m.

With an uncanny synchronicity, the two cars approached the old rectory, from opposite directions at the same time. One came from the west, winking its indicator light before turning into the small car park area, while the other vehicle briefly waited on the other side of the road and followed the first car into the adjoining space. Into the morning freshness stepped D.I. Samuel Cummins, D.S. Maurice Watson, George Ford and Felicity Hood. Loosely assembled by an arched gateway, the group exchanged greetings before turning their attention to the large Victorian building which had once served as the rectory for the nearby church. It was surrounded by mature bushes and expanses of lawn divided by flagstone pathways which led to different parts of the house. As they walked with a steady purpose towards the stone porch-way at the front of the building, they could have been mistaken for an ecclesiastical delegation from a past era on some sort of earnest ecumenical mission. Their thoughts were focused on more earthly concerns. There was a strong awareness of the fact that they were embarked on an activity which was clearly intended to prevent any further loss of human lives which had resulted from the recent horrors below ground.

St. Giles' rectory was a solid stone building which had been sold off, by the Church Commissioners at a time of failing church functioning, some time ago. Now, an impressive private house, its original external features had been well preserved and meticulously maintained by the current occupants, Mister and Mrs Connor, good friends of George Ford and Felicity Hood. Belying its quaint outward appearance, the rectory was one of the more sophisticated examples of the underground network's access points. Within a few minutes, today's guests had entered the homely dwelling. Ford and Felicity Hood had introduced Watson and Cummins to the Connors and it was obvious that Ford had prepared the ground for today's underground visit. Cummins, particularly, was aware of a distinct solemnity, almost a reverence about the business in hand, about the manner in which he was going to be introduced to this intriguing underground world. The wary eyes of Connor gave a lucid clue to the significance of the approaching moment, this historic point in time. Cummins reminded himself that this network had come into being over thirty years ago and now, at the culmination of a few weeks of disaster, it was now about to be revealed.

As an 'old school' guardian of the underground portal, Nigel Connor was very conscious of the fact that D.I. Samuel Cummins was the first person, who was not a member of the organisation, he had ever admitted to the network. The added fact that the entry point was from his own beloved rectory was a monumental moment in his life. His separate gazes at all the people present seemed to show a mentality from a different place; this was something he could hardly believe was actually happening. It was against all his instincts. For almost twenty years, he had lived in this wonderful house with the proud responsibility of looking after one of the organisation's oldest 'entry points', and today, this ordinary, run-of-the-mill day, he was creating history. He turned a look of almost resigned helplessness towards his wife, Rose, who gave him a reassuring smile in return and looked towards George Ford. "We really never thought it would turn out like this," the expression was almost dead-pan, "but we appreciate exactly where we are now." She turned towards Cummins, "I do hope you'll be able to stop Derek Martin and his vile lot!"

"We intend to. With Henry Hughes in custody we are hoping to make swift progress on several fronts. Its *his* underground network we need to expose," volunteered Cummins. A general assent of nods and thin smiles acknowledged his words.

Rose Connor was to stay behind, while Nigel accompanied the investigatory party underground. His proprietary attitude towards the tunnels, and other parts of the network, was not going to change overnight. He would act as guide and custodian for the hours they were to spend below ground. George Ford acknowledged this tacitly and was pleased to witness this level of dedication from one of his long-standing 'compatriots'. Any suggestion of sentimentality seemed to be out of place and out of touch with what was going on around them. Only a professional and efficient application to the job in hand would suffice.

The actual entrance to the underground system was, predictably, located in the basement. An impressive wall-mounted wine storage unit revealed itself to be an even more impressive moveable wall, which hinged open very cleverly, barely making a noise, and leaving Samuel Cummins not only in awe, but prompting an idea he needed to perhaps apply to a particular feature he recalled at Windsor Mews. He insisted that Nigel Connor showed him the mechanism and detail of the operating procedure, before moving on to the next stage of their underground journey. The first 'revealed' area, the vestibule, was almost always an 'empty area' as George Ford and Felicity Hood pointed out. The vestibule they were standing in now demonstrated this fact. Originally, Cummins was reminded by Ford, the whole underground system was structured in zones and was designed to give as much protection as deemed possible in the dire event of a nuclear conflagration or similar catastrophe. Despite the happy events of the previous year when the Berlin Wall came down and the air over Eastern Europe was filled with glasnost, there were still plenty of people whose optimism was relatively guarded. Ford made the suggestion to Cummins and Watson that the alternative, rogue network may not have the same level of protection, presuming it had been constructed with other things in mind! The security systems would undoubtedly be just as robust however, they both reckoned.

The second chamber was significantly larger than the vestibule, with lockers, wall units for storage, some solid-looking free-standing shelving and changing cubicles, each one bedecked with various sizes of boots, safety helmets and the ubiquitous blue overalls used by people working below ground carrying out maintenance work and other related activities. There was a familiarity about much of the physical trappings of the network for Maurice Watson; he had spent a considerable amount of time below ground, especially in his earlier years in the organisation. This particular section of the network under the neat streets of Richmond however, was new to him. His obvious fascination mainly revolved around the endless comparisons he made to other underground areas he knew well. For Samuel Cummins, the nature of his own fascination was very different. To him the whole experience was a complete eye-opener! He had so many questions he wanted to ask, but felt he could all too easily slip into interrogation mode and spoil the camaraderie within this rather earnest group of explorers. He indulged himself with pangs of guilt when he found himself speculating on the likelihood of all he was seeing below ground being the result wholly of non-criminal activity. It was difficult for him to switch off his natural suspicions of a clandestine network of tunnels and secret areas not having a criminal context. The cynicism halted when he caught sight of Maurice Watson. "How safe is all this?" Cummins asked of no-one in particular.

"Very safe, to be perfectly honest, Mister Cummins." It was Nigel Connor who answered, almost with an air of pride about him. "Accidents are very few and far between. We do have medical facilities…you'll see those a little later…so we are prepared for most things."

Cummins noticed an acute exchange of glances between Felicity Hood and George Ford, and seconds later a reciprocal glance with Connor, who closed his eyes in the manner of someone who has just committed a social *faux pas*. When the positions of eye contact settled down, it was Felicity Hood who made the final move, taking her eyes from Ford to Cummins. His policeman's brain told him he had 'stumbled' on something.

Felicity Hood simply said, "George?" Everyone looked at George.

The slightly bowed head of George Ford lifted to face Cummins and then Watson, who appeared to be oblivious to the subtle silent exchanges which had just taken place. There was now a new silence as George Ford was waiting to speak, but seemed to need time to compose himself. The faraway look on his face was not what Cummins was expecting. Aware now of something significant about to be said, Watson glanced at each person in turn, and then George Ford spoke.

"Elsa, my wife, died here..not far from where we are now, five years ago. It was an accident. There were no witnesses. She was working on her own and she apparently fell from one of the platforms near the central office, further in, where we had added a system of new tunnels to a natural cave formation. We don't know how it happened. It was such a terrible business, recovering her body from the floor of the cave. She was committed to the group, but I have always wrestled with the guilt. Would she have been here if I hadn't been involved in this…" he waved his hand half-heartedly, "grand idea?"

"Elsa was as committed to the idea as any one of us. You know that, George." Felicity Hood came to rescue him. He nodded absently and started to move forward.

"I'll show you where it happened." George Ford's outstretched arm indicated the way ahead. His movement now resembling someone in a trance.

It was the turn of Maurice Watson and Samuel Cummins to exchange an intrigued glance. They continued now, deeper into the system of tunnels, the incline of the floor dropping more noticeably. Through well-lit passages they steadily trekked until there was a noticeable change in the air temperature and the clear sense that now there was some air movement. They were approaching a cave where the volume of air rose quite dramatically and any feelings of claustrophobia would surely be alleviated. The sudden sound and echo of Ford's and Connor's footsteps rattling on metal, told Watson and Cummins that the tunnel they were in was about to run out. The solid rock and concrete floor they had covered from the start of their expedition gave way now to an industrial rigid steel mesh walkway which clung, on the right- hand side, to the wall of a cave. Probably sixty feet from top to bottom, the vault of the cave curved in a broad convex arc out of sight, giving the impression of vast space ahead, and around the next corner.

The expressions of wonder on the faces of Watson and Cummins as they gazed into the depths of the cave, were not shared by Ford, who kept his haunted eyes firmly on the metal walkway ahead as the party progressed to the first bend. Once he had reached that point he slowed down and disappeared from sight momentarily as a bulge of the rock wall interrupted the straightness of the raised steel platform. The solid mesh flooring widened now and when all five of the party had turned the first corner they were met by a tidy collection of rooms, very office-like in appearance, with glass windows and doors. The incongruity of this brought an unexpected smile to Samuel Cummins. The curiously unexpected sight in front of him resembled the upper internal offices found in some large manufacturing warehouses or vast engineering factories, where managers could step out of the office and survey the whole array of machinery, oversee the various processes in operation, the to-ing and fro-ing of activity and supervise and monitor the workers from the iron-railed gantry above the busy work areas.

Indeed, these *were* offices. Nigel Connor opened three separate doors and, playing the role of a strange underground host, informed the others that he would put the kettle on while George and Felicity gave some further explanation about the organisation's usual day-to-day dealings, and the investigations continued. Watson took a brief look in each of the opened rooms, then returned to the first room where the others had taken a chair each and brought them to the rectangular wooden table which was end-on against the wall. The clearly-subdued George Ford was obviously content to let Felicity Hood take the lead on explaining the pertinent details about the workings of the organisation for the benefit of the forces of law and order, in the shape of D.I. Samuel Cummins.

Felicity Hood loosened the scarf inside her sturdy waxed jacket and pulled the zip down a few inches, clearly more at home with the higher temperature inside the office. "I suppose this may seem like the proverbial guided tour so far, but, as we indicated at our meeting yesterday, we want to focus on information which may be of real use to you." She stood up and gave a smile towards Nigel Connor, "as well as making a lovely cup of tea, Nigel is a most efficient administrator. He is meticulous. And after talking to him over the last couple of days, allowing him time to check some of our records; some of our Nigel's most meticulous records, we may have discovered a piece of good fortune." Cups of tea poured, Felicity carried two to the table placing them in front of Watson and Cummins.

"What sort of records are we talking about?" asked Cummins. Watson had an idea about what was coming next. He grinned towards Nigel Connor, who spoke with a sudden enthusiasm, now clearly intent on helping these previously-regarded interlopers.

"Each entry and exit of personnel to the network, the physical underground network, is recorded. The monitoring is primarily to do with safety more than security. The security of the network has rarely been a problem. Well up until now that is. At any one time, it is important to know who's in or out, as well as their location within the system in case of some problem, emergency etc." Was he trying to avoid using the word 'accident'? "These records are kept for future reference to check such things as who was involved with supplies, maintenance, training, meetings and such like. As far as possible, we tried to operate a 'buddy' system, so no-one was ever working in the network alone."

Cummins was listening intently, but felt he hadn't reached the crock of gold yet. Felicity Hood seemed to read his mind. "So," she began, "we checked the 'attendance records', for want of a better expression, to monitor the recent visits of our erstwhile villains, Derek Martin, Henry Hughes and some of their other cronies." The level of self- satisfaction Felicity Hood was demonstrating was telling Samuel Cummins that she clearly had something useful up her sleeve, something useful to reveal. He gave her a silent theatrical smile which she noted with grace before she added, "it seems he left a substantial amount of paperwork here, personal documentation we think, a few weeks ago, and hasn't been back since."

"And here it is!" announced Nigel Connor, placing a large bundle of manila folders on to the table, "we are fairly certain that some of the information in here refers to parts of the network which aren't ours. Towns, areas of the country where we have no sections or even plans for any. There is clear evidence that Hughes and Martin were using some of our own members of the network, those with particular expertise and skills in construction, mining and maintenance, to develop their own underground projects. We've heard anecdotal evidence of that sort of thing happening from several members in recent days. Night-time visits to uncertain locations have been mentioned, where transport was arranged to move people in and out, without them knowing exactly where they had been working. At the time, the people doing this work would have no reason to suspect there was anything wrong with the requests or the placements. They would not expect to be deceived. We strongly believe that when some suspicions were raised, some weeks ago, that was when the violence started and the killings." Connor stopped abruptly as he had suddenly become aware of the words he was using.

"Your Scottish problem," said Felicity Hood, more grave in her manner now, "is referenced here. The location I mean. It appears to be a massive project and one which we knew absolutely nothing about. We have nothing that far North!" She opened a folder with a strip of card, acting as a bookmark, slipped into the middle of some loose sheets of paper, and handed the whole thing to Cummins. "Read it for yourself, inspector."

"I certainly will," he agreed, looking at the paperwork in his hand," I'll take a closer look at the detail later. Do you have any other gems for me?"

"Quite possibly. There seems to be an awful lot of material in these folders which has nothing to do with our organisation. It appears to concern Sir Henry's companies. His business interests are wide and many," explained Felicity Hood with a sarcastic gesture, "I'm sure some of them have a semblance of legitimacy. I'm definitely not an expert, but I suspect there's enough information here, evidence really, which will help your ongoing case against him." The earnest look on Felicity Hood's face seemed to prompt something in Cummins' thoughts. He turned to Watson.

"Watson, could you check with Mister Ford and Mister Connor for any other folders which might relate to any other villains below stairs! A list of possible suspects would be useful. Those close to this Derek Martin or Henry Hughes need to be at the top of the list."

Ford and Connor indicated the room next door where the bulk of the old filing cabinets were kept. Connor grabbed a clipboard and pen from a hook by the door and earnestly set off to peruse his archive of information. His earlier reservation about this visit was rapidly evaporating and being replaced by a strong sense of resolve. Watson too seemed more fired up now and followed Connor out enthusiastically; he felt real progress was being made. George Ford had moved away from his mood of abstraction and headed for the second office with a less morose demeanour and the beginnings of his own new resolve.

With the three men now out of the room, Cummins peered intently through the glass panel to check they were out of view and out of earshot, then turned to face Felicity Hood. She seemed slightly alarmed by his proximity. He spoke in a half whisper, which seemed to rasp in her ears," this death of George's wife. How certain are you it was an accident?"

Felicity was stunned. "Well…we don't know what happened. As George said earlier.. she fell presumably.. it was about thirty feet, perhaps more. She had gone to one of these offices, I think to do some admin work, filing and such like. She was working alone and…."

Cummins interrupted. "Do you have the 'attendance records' from that day, the exact day? Shouldn't she have been with a 'buddy'?"

"Yes, Nigel keeps everything. He'll be able to sort them out for you…"

"Good. We need to know who Elsa's 'buddy' was on that day, if she had one. There may be other details we can gather concerning this incident. We need this information." Cummins saw the look on Felicity's face."But not when George is around. We don't want to upset him." Cummins had recognised a suspicious death which had gone un-investigated for some time, and the policeman's brain in Cummins' skull was moving into a higher gear and scenting blood.

4th September 1990.
Scottish Highlands. 9.a.m.

D.S. Craig Baxter pulled up the zipper of his waterproof jacket and peered up the mountainside at the swathes of heather and assorted ferns which provided a pleasant backdrop to a police operation which was systematically moving into 'major' mode. Swinging high above the peak of the mountain was the insect swooping of a police helicopter. A handful of police officers were donning their own waterproofs, checking footwear and assembling the pieces of equipment required for a search party over hostile terrain. This particular operation was more than a straightforward search for a missing person. It was a search for a 'missing' place too, and it was likely to be an encounter with person or persons unknown, who were expected to be armed and dangerous. D.I. Colin McNab had issued clear and detailed instructions to his men so the thinking at the present time was that their prime objectives would be realised *inside* the mountain rather than *on* the mountain.

"Okay, Craig, you get the walk in the countryside," said McNab as he checked his wristwatch, "I have a flight to catch." He moved off towards the flat stretch of tarmac at the end of the line of police vehicles and waited for the approaching helicopter. As part of the assault on the mountain, four armed officers had been assigned to accompany McNab to the summit area, in an attempt to secure any area which might include an entrance to any location controlled by gunmen. In his briefing earlier in the day, McNab had gravely reminded his team that two confirmed murders, two attempted murders and reports of perhaps at least three other murders was a scenario which threatened to rewrite the statistics for their local police region.

From the police helicopter, McNab and another officer scanned the landscape with their binoculars for some clue to the whereabouts of Willie Bolton, or something unusual which might indicate an entrance to the mountain. The landscape seemed to spin around below them, and tricks of gravity and balance gave an extra element of confusion to their whereabouts. The now-distant figures of Baxter and the other officers were left behind to attend to their own systematic searching, as they progressed slowly up the mountainside.

Almost miraculously, McNab spotted the darkened gape of an opening which was set into the front of a mound-shaped formation in the terrain, only a few hundred yards from the near peak of Ben Ochin. Trying to shout above the noise of the rotor blades, McNab instructed the pilot to touch down some distance away, where he and his armed team could be landed safely and giving them space and time to affect an authoritative presence around a probable crime scene. Once the landing was achieved, the helicopter curved upwards and off to the west, to check out something which had been noticed on the initial flight approach half-an-hour earlier. There was a likelihood that the vehicular entrance to the mountain, mentioned by Steve Quinn, had been observed from above.

Less than ten minutes after returning to *terra firma*, McNab was directing his four officers in the virtual silence of the mountain. The gape in the doorway, which Willie Bolton had entered three days earlier, was wide; like Quinn before him, Bolton had not given priority to closing the door. So there it was. Right before McNab's eyes, a door into the mountain; the second one he had witnessed. His memory of the first adventure now tempered and tainted by the unfortunate experience of young Jamie Malone. He knew it was important that the deployment of his four armed officers gave paramount importance to their safety. The fact that the doorway was open could of course indicate a trap. McNab thought this to be highly unlikely, believing that Quinn's experience seemed to show that because he hadn't been followed and 'finished off' by the gunmen was probably due to his assailants' belief that he was already dead. McNab's mind was racing. He speculated towards the positive then the negative. Was the fact that the door was open mean Willie Bolton had *not* been discovered? Surely, if a stranger had been found inside, all the exits from the mountain would have been checked and secured? The idea of leaving a doorway open, as a trap, was clearly absurd. A softly-softly approach to the entrance seemed to be the best policy and this was what McNab signalled to his men. Watching his men taking their positions around the area in front of the entrance, McNab was impressed by the military-like efficiency of the team; a firm reminder and a welcome reassurance about his own safety. The indulgent drift of his thoughts briefly touched on his intended impending retirement, beginning to occupy his mind.

A sudden and swift movement from one of his men brought him back instantly to his sense of duty. The officer closest to the left-hand side of the doorway signalled that something was happening, something in the region of the opening. The other three officers took up guarded, almost invisible positions, leaving McNab to slip, as quickly as he could, behind an outcrop of rock and out of sight of the entrance. He waited tensely, not being able to see the entrance himself, so relying primarily on the armed officers around him.

A blue-overalled figure wearing a workman's hard-hat had stepped silently out of the doorway carrying a dark duffle bag which seemed to be filled to bursting point. In an almost-theatrical over-cautious manner, resembling tip-toeing, the figure continued to move furtively towards the rocky outcrop which obscured McNab from the man's sight. With a short deft swing, the figure tossed the laden bag behind a rock and turned away, as if to return to the open doorway. With a sudden leap, McNab grabbed the man from behind, one arm tightly under the armpit and across his chest, the other arm across the lower face covering his mouth, so preventing him from calling out. McNab tightened his grip firmly while the armed officer nearest to McNab instantly trained his weapon on the restrained man. The other officers didn't move an inch, their own weapons still aimed at the entrance.

McNab swung the helpless man to the ground. It had been a long time since D.I. McNab had indulged in the sharp end of police practice and felt invigorated by his sudden apprehension of a suspect. Capitalising on the swiftness and skill of his successful assault, he roughly turned the grunting man onto his back and, as he thrust his forearm across the prone man's chest, he looked sternly downwards and found himself looking into the eyes of a fearful Willie Bolton.

5th September 1990.
Somerset. 11.a.m.

A fine drizzle filled the air around the car park as the intense police activity continued to attract attention from both bewildered locals and curious tourists. The movement of officers between vehicles and the public cave, at the lower end of the Cheddar Gorge opposite, continued to fascinate the onlookers with its apparent sense of random purposefulness. But it was all highly coordinated, and each person in the cog of this forensic machine knew exactly what he or she was doing. For several hours now, the car park had been commandeered by the police and the area was now a designated crime scene, albeit the actual crime scene was below ground and away from public gaze. The thin strands of blue and white security tape bearing witness to police authority and providing a psychological barrier for the largely timid spirits of the public. Uniformed officers, plain-clothed detectives and white-overalled forensic officers strode around like costumed players in a tragedy. And the tragedy in question was very grim.

As Detective Chief Inspector John Gates watched from the doorway of a police incident van, he found himself harassed by a mixture of emotions. The seven body bags extracted from the cave was an appalling total. If it was a total. Such a body count was beyond his personal experience and he was filled with sympathy for the people he hadn't even met; the family and friends of the deceased. However 'hardened' he liked to think he was, some criminal acts simply pushed a person past the limits of their imagination and stretched their emotional endurance. Events seemed to be unreal, but you knew just how real they were. The feeling that the present investigation was emerging from a gloomy cloud of mystery was scant compensation for how he was feeling about the horrific evidence brought to his attention. The results so far had heightened his anger towards the perpetrators of such cold-blooded killings. The previous two weeks had been two of the strangest weeks of his career. The initial reports of the Cheddar murder, the ensuing man hunt and the subsequent arrest of David Carter had seemed relatively straightforward at the time, but when the revelations emerged about the details of the killings in the caves, the whole business had been turned upside down. Given the evidence of the last two hours, Gates' perception of David Carter had utterly changed. Was there a real possibility that the killing in the car park may have prevented further killings underground? Had David Carter relinquished the reluctant role of villain to assume the mantle of a hero? Gates was sometimes glad he was a policeman and not a member of a jury. He knew where his own sympathies lay. Killers came in all shapes and sizes. Their motives, as individuals acting alone, were generally made clear at an early stage. Some, in their own way, were victims fighting back desperately, and would never kill again; their objectives had been achieved. Spontaneous retaliations, spur-of-the-moment outbursts, reaching an emotional breaking-point, were all causes of homicide. Then there were the disturbed types, perhaps being ruled by strange internal obsessions, the psychopaths who defied reason and who killed, as far as the public were concerned, randomly. The current killings below ground were different. They had been the actions of people who were free from the risk of being observed. Their victims were captives, out of sight, away from the protection of society's prying judgements; like the invisible casualties of war.

Gates' mental abstractions came to an end when he spotted D.S. Frank Harvey crossing the road towards him. The expression on his face was testimony to how the last few hours had affected him. Like Gates, Harvey had not encountered killings on such a scale before. It was unprecedented and each member of his police team was of the same view. The difficulty of retrieving the bodies had made the task even more onerous and traumatic, and there was a discernible shift in morale. What sort of criminal were they dealing with here?

The underground search for bodies had transformed the case against David Carter, and now there was effectively a new 'active' case again, aimed at finding an unknown killer or killers. Although Carter had eliminated the killer of Jenny Shaw, his girlfriend, and three other friends, there were question marks about the probability that more than this one particular deceased killer had been responsible for the total number of victims. Carter himself had always maintained there were several assailants involved in the terror inside the caves. He had described it as a war where one side had most of the weapons; more bluntly, it had been a massacre.

"Sir?" Harvey intoned as he approached Gates.

"How's it going? Or should I not ask?" returned Gates, questioning reluctantly, more out of a dutiful habit rather than a genuine query where he may be subjected to further unpleasant information reaching his ears.

"The leader of the pothole and cavers' group has halted any further exploration for today. The increasing rain means the potential build-up of water could bring a risk of the party getting stranded. The water levels that far into the system can often cause the inner chambers and tunnels to become cut off from safety," reported Harvey. He took off his hard hat and wiped his forehead with the back of his wrist, and turned back to stare at the cliff face as if he was deciding whether it warranted a look of admiration, or contempt. He thought about what was beneath that particular glowering rock edifice.

A gem of natural beauty, a hidden tourist attraction and now a killing field.

"Right," Gates responded automatically. "Any more evidence….of any kind?"

"Well, there's a lot of evidence of this organisation and their network. The system itself is a mixture of natural caves and tunnels, which is to be expected. But Carter has shown us examples of the man-made additions. It does seem absolutely clear that these people had genuinely prepared many underground areas for shelter and survival in the event of a nuclear attack. Resources, supplies, equipment…it's mind-boggling to be honest." Harvey caught the expression on Gates' face, then smiled rather sheepishly and looked at the ground. "Of course, none of this is actually indicative of criminal activity necessarily. But, what seems clear to me, sir, is David Carter's story. I have found no reason to disbelieve him. The bodies were where he described. We were able to locate them immediately. All shot, from close range it looks like. Jenny Shaw was the first body we retrieved. Carter was visibly upset, but pulled himself round and has been remarkably helpful considering the circumstances. There is still a lot of anger, beneath the surface. He is containing his rage. On *that* day he killed the gunman his rage could *not* be contained." Harvey's earnest tone subsided as he looked straight at Gates. "Sorry, sir, I'm beginning to sound like a defence lawyer."

"Indeed you are," said Gates, placing an avuncular hand on Harvey's shoulder.

"Anyway, sir, there was no further evidence of the presence of the assailants; Carter said they would have disappeared into the system, and probably out of the system some time ago. Given the number of personnel Carter was aware of, at that location when he was working there with his girlfriend, he does not think there will be any other bodies to find."

"Where is Carter now?" asked Gates.

"With his parents, Ken and Ellen, sir. We've made arrangements for further discussions. Ken Carter is one of the founder members of the network and has a wealth of information about the locations which, as he describes it, have been infiltrated by this criminal group. There's a solicitor coming up from London to help David Carter with a release from custody. I know it's unusual, rather unorthodox, but continuing to hold him in the circumstances is probably not necessary, although there may be possible issues regarding his safety. At the moment we really have the wrong person in custody!"

"Yes, I agree. It's a bit of a bugger. We'll have to see what the legal people come up with," stated Gates, now checking his watch. "I need to get back to Bristol as I'm expecting a call from Scotland Yard about this underground business. There has been talk about other agencies becoming involved. We may have to convene some sort of meeting. The picture…er… the jigsaw gets bigger by the day!"

5th September 1990.
Inverness. 2.p.m.

"Jock Murray is utterly overjoyed," announced a buoyant D.S. Baxter, "they've got a genuine scoop. He thinks he's really hit the big time. He had no problems with the reporting restrictions. The details he isn't allowed to use are not that important to the main story, to be honest. It's the human angle he's more interested in. And with Willie Bolton's role in the whole affair, well…enough said!"

Sitting back in his chair, D.I. McNab looked over to his enthusiastic sergeant with a quiet pleasure. After the traumas and worries of the last few weeks, it was a wonderful experience to wallow in a wave of satisfaction, brought about by the sensational outcome of the day before. His imminent phone conversation with his opposite number at Scotland Yard, Detective Inspector Samuel Cummins, would be a welcome new source of personal and professional satisfaction, as well as receiving the latest update on the progress of 'the strange case of the underground business'. A business which had now been identified as a massive criminal conspiracy on a national scale. It had become a lot clearer than before, and was also spectacularly real.

The jangling of the telephone brought instant smiles to both men. Baxter took a seat as McNab reached forward to pick up the receiver. "Ah good afternoon D.I. Cummins…. oh yes, Samuel. It would appear that we have secured the mountain!" He paused while some response and laughter came over the line. He grinned, "yes, that does sound unusual, but it does describe the situation as it is. We have apprehended five men and confiscated a large number of weapons. We'll have more details later after they've been checked by our forensic people. Explosives were also found. Sadly, we recovered six bodies I'm afraid, so the five suspects will all be charged with murder. The man Quinn, it seems, was luckier than we thought. These people don't exactly take prisoners. We reckon Quinn's escape was truly miraculous." He paused to allow comments and questions from Cummins, before continuing. "Yes, I suppose Bolton was lucky too, but to be fair he used his initiative. He found the opening into the mountain quite easily; it was the same one Quinn escaped through. Once inside, Bolton found a place to hide and disguised himself in a set of those blue overalls they all seem to wear. On the off chance he might have been spotted, he thought it might help him to look like one of them, at least from a distance. As it happened, that situation never arose. It was really quite incredible how he managed to get close enough to eavesdrop on some of their meaty conversations, including a great deal of talk about Sir Henry Hughes' involvement and role in the whole organisation, but specifically his role in recent events up here. It appears to be one of their major projects. Bolton worked out quite quickly that there were only those five of Hughes' men present, looking after the installation inside the mountain. Because of this recent business, which has been a great shambles from their point of view, the day-to-day organisation of the place had gone haywire. There had been some sort of lockdown after a challenge from some of the men who had been drafted in to work reluctantly. There had been suspicions from some of the maintenance team that the project under Ben Ochin was not a kosher project. The resulting 'revolt' had brought about a vicious backlash and a purge of the objectors. Hence the two victims we found on the mountain. So once we encountered Bolton and he told us of the depleted number of men left it was clear that we could infiltrate the underground areas and arrest the suspects relatively easily. We are happy to report there were no casualties on either side." McNab felt as if he had come to the end of his report, and listened to the buoyant voice of Samuel Cummins as he was congratulated by his distant English colleague.

"After the recent difficulties we've had, I'm pleased about the outcome," McNab continued. "I was wondering if our experience is reflected in the other enquiries? There are things we hear on the grapevine, mainly to do with the discovery of other bodies. Is there a clearer idea what all this is about? It's hard to believe all this has stemmed from our finding the body of Alfred Craddock!"

As McNab listened to the latest update of information conveyed by Samuel Cummins about the progress being made, and underlining how important the Scottish revelations were, there was a quiet tap at the door which opened slowly. It was P.C. Ronnie Irwin.

Speaking *sotto voce* to Baxter and performing an impromptu mime, he managed to indicate that Willie Bolton had arrived to talk with them. It was clear that McNab had followed Irwin's 'cabaret' and gave a thumbs-up gesture to the other two officers. Irwin interpreted this as assenting to Bolton's entrance to the office and off he went to fetch him. Shortly after Irwin had left the room, McNab finished the phone call.

"This is an ugly business, Baxter. The existing body count is the wrong side of thirty with the expectation of more, with each passing day." The resigned shaking of McNab's head coincided with the slight jaw-dropping movement of D.S. Baxter, whose eyes also responded to the horror of this appalling update as he abstractedly replied with a rather helpless, "Hell!"

"It seems very likely that a meeting will be convened in the next day or two to pool the growing mass of information and intelligence from across the country. The involvement of other agencies is probably on the cards. The Home Office will coordinate the meeting with the likelihood of some committee or other emerging to deal with the ongoing investigation. It's organised crime on a completely new scale, even though the deaths, the assassinations, smack of terrorism. We now know that many armed robberies committed over recent years are linked to this network. Well. Henry Hughes' version of the network, anyway." McNab seemed to be stunned by his own words, as if finding it hard to believe that some of this major organised crime was happening on his patch. Craig Baxter watched him closely. He was beginning to anticipate something, and he quite liked the idea. The reference to Henry Hughes prompted Baxter to enquire further.

"So Henry Hughes *is* heavily involved with this national picture. Not just 'our' part of the operation?"

"Up to his neck! But his legal team are pushing to have him bailed. The Yard are feeling the pressure on that score, because of his profile, his public profile. That's one of the main reasons why we have to be extremely careful of the intelligence we have on him. There must be nothing to compromise the case against him. Steve Quinn's information, and even Willie Bolton's, would be hammered by a half-decent barrister as hearsay, circumstantial and all the rest of it!" McNab's indignation was clearly showing. "Jamie Malone is key to the success of a conviction as it stands." He paused and looked directly at Baxter and took a deep breath before continuing. "I have been earnestly advised that the possibility of a further attempt on Malone's life must not be ruled out."

Baxter was aghast, "surely not! They wouldn't try that, would they?"

"I know that may sound absurd. It does seem madness, but I am not prepared to take a chance with Malone's life. Some suggestions have been made about moving him to a safer haven. We need to discuss these with him, but be firm about outcomes. There's no need for him to be a hero second time around!"

The door opened, and McNab continued his expressed ideas in a seamless flow of words. "Talking of heroes, hello Willie!" Willie Bolton stepped further into the room, smiled and nodded at Craig Baxter, before acknowledging the larger-than-life presence of Colin McNab.

"Hello, Inspector McNab. You're not going to wrestle he to the ground again, are you?"

"Not today, Willie. I think I'm getting a bit old for that caper, to be honest."

Willie Bolton had a certain sheepishness about him, as he flicked a glance at the floor. "I want to thank you again, Inspector. And apologise again I suppose. Going off into the mountain like that....perhaps wasn't the wisest thing I've done."

McNab's look of seriousness could have been *mock* seriousness. It was difficult to tell. "It turned out well in the end; I can't deny that. But we don't really recommend the public to investigate crimes on their own. Perhaps the gods were with us on this one. The truth is, the information you gave us was invaluable, and, as you already know, not all of it can hit the public domain yet, especially the stuff concerning Sir Henry Hughes."

"Yes, I understand that," replied Bolton quietly, with more than a tinge of disappointment apparent in his tone. McNab sympathetically picked up on this.

"The thing is, when the court business emerges, and hits the media and your role becomes obvious, you'll have one hell of a story to tell. You just need to be patient. There'll be more to come, I can assure you of that."

Baxter, who seemed to have had a fixed smile throughout this exchange, decided to add his own friendly contributions to Willie Bolton's ego. "Anyway, Willie, how are you feeling today after your assault yesterday and your three day incarceration?"

"Fine really," came the relaxed reply," I was checked over at the hospital. I seem to be more healthy than I thought I was! And I've had a decent meal. Hot food, lovely! Not being able to have a proper cooked meal for three days was the worst part of it. I had to survive on the bits and pieces I could find underground. The living quarters were my best bet. The kitchen area was too tricky, too dangerous I reckoned. But in their quarters I could nick a few odds and ends from those murdering bastards; biscuits, some cold meat, chocolate, crisps, stuff like that. It was like a really crap picnic lasting three days!"

6th September 1990.
Manchester. 6.a.m.

The early morning chill was gradually losing its effect on the few people who were drifting into the day, and going about their ordinary Thursday business. Shadows played across the rooftops and the brickwork of old warehouses and apartment buildings, along both sides of the modest River Medlock, as it pursued its almost secret course through the city of Manchester. The redbrick citadel of the Palace Hotel, its central tower an edifice of confidence overseeing the new day, stood resolute in the growing sunlight, a study in gravitas.

The sudden yell that cracked the air was completely unexpected. It seemed to come from behind a block of tall, solid buildings by one of the short bridges, which at varying intervals spanned the narrow river. The second yell was louder, its harshness echoing from the walls of nearby buildings. The immediate effect on passers-by was negligible. A cursory glance to each side, by a couple of men, briskly walking past the stone and metal wall of a bridge, was the only response visible. The subsequent yells merged, the tone being one of alarm, and it became apparent that it was a group of voices, rather than an individual one, trying to attract attention. And soon, the shouting became a strange cacophony of jeers, and screams, and random calls of 'help' and 'police'. And now it became difficult to avoid the urgency of the commotion. The careful articulation of those crucial words 'help' and 'police' brought the first active response from an old newsvendor operating by the bridge, who soon realised the noise came from the river itself. Peering cautiously over the parapet he noticed a small crowd of figures, emerging steadily from underneath the huge grey monolith of a grubby warehouse. Mouth slightly agape now, the newspaper seller thought he should go for help. Bursting into a small cafe a few yards up the road, he shouted to the bemused proprietor to phone the police, as there was a disturbance on the river! This done, he dashed back to his newspapers. Moments later, as he was about to take another look at the incident, a clear shot rang out. Flinching instinctively, he ducked down behind the parapet, taking the Lord's name in vain, in the process. By the side of the bridge was a trellis-work of metal bars which he was able to peer through tentatively, and safely, in an attempt to find out what was going on.

Since he'd last observed the crowd, it had grown. Quite considerably. There must have been about thirty people now, some milling around, but others grappling with a lone figure and dragging him vigorously towards the wall on the opposite side of the shallow river. A number of people had separated from the main body of the crowd and appeared to be putting their efforts into raising the lone figure above their heads as if in the process of throwing him somewhere. From his safe position by the parapet, the newsvendor watched the scene turn ugly. Now there was something like the hysteria of the lynch mob about the raw actions of this posse, and the resulting atmosphere curdled the early morning air, and it seemed the victim of the crowd's attention was screaming; screaming for his life!

Believing that something awful was about to happen, the vendor ventured a shout towards the crowd. Almost instantly, someone in the crowd shouted to the rest of his cohorts and pointed at the bridge. "Call the police!" came the curiously reassuring cry.

Now feeling more confident in the light of the reply, the vendor returned, "we have!" He stood up and moved more clearly into the view of the crowd, "what's wrong? What's happening?" By now, there was a lessening of the noise from the crowd and a more subdued mood was obvious. Two men were now holding the previously-screaming man by the arms as his legs trailed in the murkiness of the shallow water, his limpness caused by the fatigue of his exertions in trying to escape the mob. The two men looked as if they could be preparing to lift him onto a cross for the purposes of crucifixion. One of the two men called up to the bridge.

"This man is a murderer and we intend to hand him over to the police!"

"Right," replied the vendor, stunned completely by the conversation he was now a part of, "I think the police should be here soon." His assurance seemed to be welcomed by the people of the crowd below. The growing confidence and calming effect of the change in atmosphere helped the vendor with his curiosity. "Was that a gunshot I heard?"

"Yes," answered the man below, "it was the bastard's last bullet. It went off while we were struggling with him at the entrance to the tunnel"

The baffled vendor did not fully understand the reference to a tunnel, but was still intrigued by this sensational beginning to his workday. There seemed to be more order in the people below him and some were making their way to some steps which led to a long raised walkway from the fire exit of the adjoining hotel. As he continued to watch this strange scene unfold before his eyes, he noticed that virtually everyone in this mysterious group was wearing dark blue overalls.

7th September 1990.
Scotland Yard. 9.a.m.

The two coffee cups were picked up simultaneously, and the measured sips indicated how hot the drinks were. Samuel Cummins and Maurice Watson had been planning something slightly unorthodox and had reached a potential impasse regarding the transparency of their actions. There was no argument between the two men, just a genuine doubt about one element of their course of action. Should they come clean about Watson's membership of the network?

"I think it's fair to say that the nature of the division in the network has clearly revealed that the difference between the two sides is absolutely clear. There is the benign side to the organisation, the original grouping, the one I joined. Then we have Hughes' lot, the criminal organisation. I don't see any grey areas. The experiences of the Carters and the Pickerings show that we're dealing with victims and villains." Maurice Watson was presenting a straightforward assessment of the situation and he therefore felt there was a well-reasoned case for accepting that most members of the network were not security risks, did not pose a danger to anyone, and were not a threat to the general public.

Cummins agreed. "So it might be time to tell someone else," he smiled at Watson, "further up the food chain, about your secret?"

"Yes I do," asserted Watson, "I truly believe that our current plan, for me to go undercover, will more likely gain

Shackleton's approval if he knows I have the advantage of useful insider knowledge."

Cummins considered the pros and cons of this contention, but in reality he had agreed with everything Watson had said. He believed in Maurice Watson and thought the ideas they had been sharing over the past couple of days were good ones; maybe slightly unorthodox, maybe slightly risky, but well thought-out and should be put into practice. He also believed in Oscar Shackleton and expected the 'old man' to look favourably on their plans. Not before giving them close scrutiny and making a stern analysis. "Right. We'll put our plan forward to him after this meeting." He consulted his watch. "There are a number of developments and updates we'll be hearing about, so we can add one of our own, at the end!"

With another almost-synchronised final swig of their respective coffees, the two men stood up from the table and set off down the corridor for the latest instalment of D.C.S. Oscar Shackleton's underground updates.

Inside the operations room, the atmosphere was noticeably less formal than usual, and the members of the team had some idea of the content of the talk because of the individual contributions passed on already in the shape of brief reports on the progress made since the previous meetings. It seemed that the familiarity of these updates had taken the edge of the formal mystique of the subject matter because everyone on the team was involved with a range of enquiries. The individual inputs, of course, helped the morale of the team, because they contributed to the overall picture of the investigation, but the enthusiasm for knowing 'the big picture' was a crucial element of team and individual motivation. Ownership of the growing amount of knowledge and intelligence was now a communal entity. The 'actors' had now assembled for the director's overview.

The general murmurings and mutterings subsided when Shackleton, with calm confidence, walked through the door. The heightened expectation which pervaded the room was a result of all those present anticipating their leader standing out in front of the team and joining up the dots.

"Good morning, ladies and gentlemen, let's make a brisk start to what could be a very busy day. Although you all have your own areas of enquiry at the moment, it is more important than ever before to keep you fully conversant with the operation in its entirety. Before bringing you up to speed on the newer incidents, I need to inform you of moves, at a higher level, which may....or may not..." his emphasised hesitation here was clearly, and consciously, dramatic," affect how this investigation might continue. Obviously, the Home Office have been increasingly alarmed, as we have been, about the magnitude of the criminal activity we have uncovered. The media, as you know, have limited detailed information about this current operation; it is largely focusing on the continued custody of Sir Henry Hughes. This has been a bone of contention with his legal lobby, for this last week, but we now have even more intelligence regarding his central role in the criminal underground network and further investigations into this man's involvement are ongoing. Much of the information concerning this point has emanated from what we have learnt about this Scottish project he is allegedly involved with." He paused, to allow those present to facially express their responses to, and enjoy, his ironic use of the word 'allegedly. Noting the consensus within the room, he gave a satisfied nod.

"Further incidents!" He announced this like a subheading for anyone who might have been taking notes. "In Manchester, yesterday morning, we had a large group, thirty- two to be precise, of witnesses who came forward with a murder suspect. These people, who are part of Ford's grouping, had been trapped underground, hiding from their captors for several days. It is understood that at least four individuals have been killed…all of these bodies have already been retrieved and are now being examined. A spokesperson for the group is of the opinion, as are others who were there, that a number of other bodies are likely to be below ground. This particular location is part of the original network and was taken over by this man, Derek Martin, and his henchmen some time ago. Several of the people who escaped had been subjects of missing persons enquiries; parents of children who had left offspring with family or friends, while they were ostensibly away on holidays, but in fact working underground. We have someone investigating a number of similar disappearances across the country, which we now believe could be connected to this underground network phenomenon." A small sea of concerned frowns gazed back at Shackleton as these simple but worrying revelations were presented.

"Back to Manchester!" He needed to move on. "The tunnel system in question is an extension and development linked to the old Picc-Vic abandoned railway system built many years ago. We had previously been notified of its existence by Ford, but we were unaware, as were Ford and his friends, that it had been infiltrated by criminal elements. So, we have another suspect in custody and the underground location in Manchester is being explored as I speak. From interviewing the escapees….survivors…from this incident, it is looking increasingly likely, that not only are there two distinct networks underground, but also there is more and more evidence that the criminal element have built other secret additions to Ford's network and that there may be links, physical links, between the two systems, but only known to the criminal membership."

Shackleton paused to take a few sips of chilled water before continuing. "In Chislehurst Caves yesterday afternoon, there was a shooting incident in one of the inner galleries where the public have access. I understand that the situation was similar to the Manchester incident in that it resulted in the gunman being apprehended by members of the network, and then being handed over to the police. There are no reports, at this point, of any deaths, but once again this was a location we were aware of and it had been infiltrated by others. It appears that many of the underground locations are experiencing similar situations. A small number of gunmen are taking control, or attempting to take control, of these underground systems, but are finding it problematical in keeping a much larger number of people hostage. These apparent 'breakouts' have been reported across the country in a range of places such as Nottingham, Newcastle and Glasgow where Ford's original operations were linked to known public tunnel systems. Many of these tunnel systems had been abandoned, then taken over with newer additions built by Ford's people. Some sections were cleverly 'grafted on' to something already in existence."

Shackleton's audience absorbed the scale of this massive venture once again. It was like a war, with new information coming in from different fronts. Had someone been given the task of keeping a tally of the body count? There had been a tendency, in their offices and in the canteen, for team members to exchange mental sums on the subject each day. It seemed now to be a rather fatuous task as the figures changed so quickly and, the realisation of this, may begin to cause damage to the morale of the team.

"A couple of final points. Closer to home, we have unearthed a significant entrance into the Windsor Mews location. Following a hunch from someone on the team," Shackleton avoided looking at Cummins, and Cummins kept his eyes resolutely blank, "an entire wall in one of the basements turned out to be the prime gateway to the system. I should remind you that Windsor Mews is the nearest 'enemy' venue. Ford and his people were not aware of its existence. We have mounted a twenty-four hour watch on this location… as some of you already know!" Those present who had been drafted in to Windsor Mews knew what Shackleton was alluding to. His acknowledging smile slowly slipped away and his usual gravity returned.

"The importance of confidentiality is vital on any investigation, for all the obvious reasons. I could sincerely apologise to each one of you for suggesting that you really need reminding of the fact. However, it is very likely that an undercover operation of some sort will be instigated in the next twenty-four hours. Nothing must risk the safety of a single operative, whether from our team, or from some other agency. The best of luck with your ongoing endeavours. Thank you." He stood and surveyed the people in front of him, as they quietly dispersed and headed towards their own purposeful tasks.

Cummins and Watson remained in their seats until the other team members had disappeared towards other rooms, other offices. Cummins spoke first. "That matter I mentioned earlier, sir? I think this might be the time to broach it in more detail. If you have time now, of course."

There was a discernible sparkle in Shackleton's eye when he turned to face his junior colleague. "I have put some time aside for this conversation, Cummins. Watson. I think we should reassemble in my office immediately!" And he lead the way out of the room, striding purposefully, with the two men following in his slipstream.

One minute later they arrived at Shackleton's office and sat down in the offered chairs. "I am anticipating a 'plan', a suggested plan that is, from the pair of you. I shall listen sympathetically, but may have to defer any decision until later tomorrow, because of this meeting with the other agencies. These bods from the Home Office are going to be there, so goodness knows where we'll end up! I need you to understand that from the outset." The expectation shown by Shackleton came as a slight shock to Cummns.

"We understand perfectly, sir." Cummins agreed, and nodded. As he turned his head slightly, he caught the movement of Watson's head, also nodding.

"Good, good. Fire away!" Shackleton leaned forward to indicate his interest.

Cummins looked directly at Shackleton, "in a nutshell, I would like Watson here to work undercover on a specific operation targeting Derek Martin." The combination of Shackleton's raised eyebrows and his somewhat quirky smile made it difficult for Cummins to judge the response. He maintained his level of verve, and continued. "We've come by a lot of information gleaned from our visit to the Richmond location, when we went there with Ford and the others. There appears to be a considerable amount of new evidence about the criminal network's locations. To have someone inside one of these locations would give us an excellent opportunity to bring Derek Martin to justice."

"And Watson," Shackleton glanced at the subject of the conversation, "would be, presumably the obvious choice for this mission." The border between irony and sarcasm in his tone had been breached. Cummins had heard the subtlety, prompting his next line of his tactical presentation.

"Well sir, that brings me to my next point. Watson is a member of the network, and therefore best placed to infiltrate the other side of the organisation." Cummins let the enormity of this statement sink in, before continuing. But Shackleton, rather than giving out expressions of surprise, simply nodded sagely and came back with his rejoinder.

"So that's what the magic touch was in Bristol!" He seemed pleased with himself.

"Sir?" Queried Cummins, feeling as if he had utterly lost the initiative in the conversation now.

Shackleton slipped into the explanation mode of the seasoned detective in an Agatha Christie drawing room denouement. "When the erstwhile silent suspect being held in Bristol magically emerged as David Carter, I had wondered what it was which made him change his mind about revealing who he was, and then begin to cooperate with us. Chief Inspector Gates was very impressed by 'the magic touch' the pair of you exerted that day. I thought there had to be a personal connection of some sort; Gates had told me about the 'secret' circumstances of the interview. So that's what it was." It seemed he had concluded his deliberations, until he finished by looking straight at Cummins and saying, "And you knew about Watson's position?"

The sense of accusation in the question wasn't exactly clear. Cummins was unsure whether he was actually being accused directly over this apparent subterfuge. "Yes sir, I knew. Watson had confided in me and I took the decision, personally and professionally, to trust him and use the fact to our advantage, in the course of our investigations." Samuel Cummins paused with authority and dignity. He was standing his ground.

Shackleton spoke. "As will I, Cummins, as will I!"

The pleasant shock of agreement was greeted warmly by the two police officers. This approach to their superior had achieved more than they had initially expected. It appeared that Shackleton was a more 'creative' detective than either of them realised. He confessed in their subsequent discussions that he would have done exactly as Watson had done, and exactly what Cummins had done. The plan for some form of undercover operation was clearly the way forward. It was eminently sensible and all three of them were in agreement that the principle would be broached at tomorrow's high-powered meeting as a strong contender for the 'next step'. The finer detail would be the subject of intense planning over the next forty-eight hours.

Towards the end of their discourse, Shackleton asked a question about probable location. There were implications for back-up, resources, communication.....

"The Yorkshire Dales, sir!" volunteered Watson, with enthusiasm.

"Oh, very nice," exclaimed Shackleton, as if he were sharing holiday destinations, but clearly confused by the suddenness and the content of the reply.

"We recovered some documents belonging to Sir Henry Hughes which, at first glance, implied there was 'a new facility' about twenty miles south-west of Richmond. This location was not one known to George Ford and his people. The information did not make real sense at first; there were points about the location; its nature and strategic value for instance which did not fit. We were at a loss about what to make of it when I made the suggestion we were looking at the wrong Richmond!"

Shackleton grinned, almost smugly, at both men, "Richmond, in the north of Yorkshire, eh?"

"And suddenly, it all made sense. We think, from the information we have, this is a significant site for Martin's operation. My hunch…my considered opinion… is that we're looking at a farm, at least on the outside, but what lies beneath is anyone's guess."

8th September 1990.
Scotland Yard. 10.a.m.

Saturdays, for several weeks now, had become part and parcel of the working week for many of the staff working on this complicated investigation, which had been dubbed 'Operation Axel' by several members of the team. Someone had pointed out that Axel was a central character in the Jules Verne fantasy story 'A Journey to the Centre of the Earth'. Whether this impromptu naming had been regarded as clever, apt or corny had not particularly mattered, but it had actually become a useful shorthand for the subject in question. So, it had stuck, unofficially. Although someone had noticed that D.I. Roger Melville had been heard using the epithet on more than one occasion.

So, this Saturday seemed to be simply yet another addition to the new pattern of work inside the organisation, another day for taking the investigation forward. The presence of representatives from other agencies, including Home Office officials, added an extra frisson to the morning's scheduled meeting and speculation was rife about the various possibilities about where the proceedings would go.

After the formalities and introductions had been made, the Home Office minister focused the minds of all those present on the recent thinking from the corridors of power, concerning the ongoing underground criminal activity of a group of murderous villains.

Walter Bingham, the minister, a rather slight figure with a sickly and pallid look about him, was outlining the wishes of the cabinet, and the Home Secretary specifically, regarding the 'preferred way forward' and which issues had been identified as priorities. It had emerged that there was a certain amount of discomfort about the continued custody of Sir Henry Hughes. The first subtle response to this raised topic was a slight leaning back in the chair from a number of senior police officers. Those officers present, who had been on the case from the very beginning, bristled at the veiled suggestion hanging in the air. D.I. Roger Melville was the first one to slowly fold his arms. Whether this latent sign of dissidence and implied challenge was observed by the gentlemen from the Home Office wasn't clear, but the Scotland Yard people were clearly of one mind.

"We understand that there is some *circumstantial* evidence, mainly in the form of documents, which may implicate Sir Henry in possible untoward business dealings and maybe even suggestions that there is the possibility of money laundering. Such activity is often difficult to prove and demands intense scrutiny over a long period of time. Should this really be a priority when more and more killings are being unearthed? Surely this line of enquiry, into Sir Henry's business interests, is an unnecessary distraction when you are engaged in hunting down murderers." D.C.S. Oscar Shackleton wasn't sure whether Bingham's final point was a question or simply an observation. It wasn't a major concern; he knew where he and his team stood as regards their prime suspect. He made the firm decision to clarify their position from the outset. Although complex and far-reaching, the case in hand needed to be carried out by a high-powered police team, and aided where appropriate by other agencies who would ostensibly report to the police leadership. In his own mind, he was of the firm opinion that anyone arrested, as part of this major operation, should be treated as murder suspects, until proved otherwise.

"If I infer correctly, from those remarks minister, that Sir Henry Hughes be given bail, I would wish to express my complete opposition to that course of action." The movement of people's heads as they looked towards Shackleton was almost audible. The minister blanched, and the expression on his face resembled the look of a man trying to hide the fact he had been kicked in the shin. At first there was a silence as those present took their time to assimilate the change in atmosphere.

Walter Bingham unsuccessfully tried to smile. "I'm sure you feel strongly about having someone in custody over this business, but we need to look at the evidence, as well as the nature of the suspect. There has been a lot of pressure from Sir Henry's legal team and, with his high profile and his links to government contracts, it has become an acute embarrassment. The evidence against him on the more serious charges is rather tentative, and it has been vigorously suggested to us that legal action may be taken in respect of a case of wrongful arrest. And this could surface at any moment!"

A few murmurs could be discerned around the table and pairs of eyes locked on other pairs of eyes, questioning, challenging, wondering. A sense that 'sparks may begin to fly' was a nuance in the air above the table. Dry mouths prompted two of Shackleton's team to reach for the water jug and pour out modest drinks for themselves and silently offer the jugs to other members of this tense conference. A red-faced, almost trembling Home Office official reached for a nearby jug of his own as he anticipated a troublesome journey back to the office at the end of the meeting.

Oscar Shackleton was not to be railroaded, or diverted from his preferred plan of action. His swift glances towards D.I. Cummins and D.I. Melville were like portents of solidarity. He briefly looked down at the table before, very consciously, looking straight at Walter Bingham. For a few seconds he hoped he was not going to over-dramatise his position. "I think it would be helpful if this knotty issue of Hughes could be dealt with first, minister." The nascent challenge was heavily implied by the use of Hughes surname only. The status of the suspect in question gave a clue to Shackleton's attitude. Aware of this, Bingham wasn't too sure how to approach the apparent dissent. Start firmly, but reasonably, when embarking on negotiations, was his general premise.

"I think it likely that the Home Secretary will recommend to the court that Sir Henry be granted bail. Unless there is a substantial amount of new hard evidence against him over the next few hours!"

Unexpectedly, Shackleton stood up and calmly asked, "what about the huge embarrassment?"

Bingham appeared disorientated by the reply, especially as it was given from a standing position. He felt he was missing something. He was confused in his reply. "Well, the embarrassment will abate quite quickly once Sir Henry is out of custody, I would expect." He had answered Shackleton's question and there was no real problem to worry about now.

Shackleton had continued standing, and now he placed his fingertips firmly and deliberately on the table. "I was referring to the embarrassment caused by my resignation, minister." A few gasps escaped from one side of the table, and shocked facial expressions were shared by these same individuals. Their looks towards each other were replaced by looks to the other side of the table, gauging the response to this apparent bombshell The air in the room had been shuffled and most eyes now came to rest on Walter Bingham.

"Don't be absurd, chief superintendent....this has nothing to do with resignations. It is madness to suggest that. I suggest you sit down and we continue this discussion in a professional manner!" Bingham looked away, still smarting from the outrageous idea which had just been thrown at him. Shackleton remained standing, so Bingham picked up the cudgels once more. "For goodness sake, man, you're a professional police officer!"

"Then you should acknowledge that fact and understand that my job is to catch criminals. When I have one in custody, who is a danger to the public, I expect to be able to continue with my job and protect the public!"

"Mr Shackleton, we do not believe Sir Henry is a danger to the public. Bail would not be a problem. Your threat to resign over the matter is both fatuous and absurd. This is not getting us anywhere!" Bingham was visibly rattled and was now uncertain where this meeting would go next. His erstwhile instructions from the Home Secretary were looking somewhat tattered and the meeting had not really 'got off the ground'.

"Hughes will be convicted of heinous crimes in due course. That is a matter for a jury to decide. I have no doubt at all concerning that outcome. We intend to continue with our investigations to that end. And we will succeed." Shackleton grew in stature from his oratorical posture. It was abundantly clear to all in the room, regardless of their view of him, that here was a man who would not be prevented from voicing his heartfelt stance on the most burning issue of his day. A mixture of loosening jaws and faint smiles filled the room. With a conscious fresh breath, he moved in for his main critical point. "If this man is bailed, he will have time to fabricate alibis, intimidate witnesses, destroy evidence and manipulate circumstances for his own benefit. If he deems it necessary he will flee the country and live on his ill-gotten gains. There are people, as we speak, who are potential witnesses and victims of his criminal actions, who will be in greater peril if he is at large. He would kill, or have others kill for him, in attempts to evade justice. To bail this man? That is the absurdity here." The attack on Bingham's central idea was almost complete. The other repercussions were now waiting to be explained. "If it transpires, in the next few hours which lie ahead, that

I need to resign, I feel obliged to tell you how that action would proceed." Bingham's face was a picture of horror and anger. "I would first call for Hughes' legal representative to be present with his client. Hughes would then be charged with murder, and conspiracy to murder. This done, I would then give out a press release to that effect, and then give my full reasons, to the media, for resigning from my job as chief superintendent and specifically from my role in leading this particular investigation. At that point I would leave it up to the Home Secretary to gauge the level of embarrassment caused and leave him to ponder the effects on the public and what he tought he would do about it."

The atmosphere in the room defied description. The scribes recording the detail of the meeting had been writing furiously, not knowing if anything they had recorded would be able to escape confidentiality or security codes, and allowed to stand, but duty-bound to continue the task in hand. Who would speak next? Who would respond? These were the obvious questions which spun around inside their heads and settled nervously, tentatively, waiting, inside their ballpoint pens!

Walter Bingham desperately tried to convince himself that he had not lost his argument, but was finding this theory a difficult one to uphold. Shackleton's undoubted passion was unassailable and there was probably no hiding place now for the Home Office's favoured position. Perhaps, and it may be the last throw of the dice, he could call Shackleton's bluff. "If you really feel as strongly as that, Mister Shackleton, then any resignation offered would be considered for acceptance. I would pass on your intention to a higher authority!" The ensuing silent pause did not last very long.

"And mine, minister." This was Roger Melville.

"Mine also, minister." Samuel Cummins was now standing, joining the two figures of Shackleton and Melville. Bingham baulked and gave an almost hysterical, very unconvincing laugh. "This is utterly ludicrous, what is going on here?"

In answer to his question, two other senior police officers stood up, not needing to voice their opinion or give an offer of resignation. The new mood in the room was quite unequivocal. Whatever decision the Home Office minister came to in the next few vital minutes, would have an instant effect on his life and reputation in politics, the public's view of the government he belonged to, their perception of police power, their attitude to the status of people accused of great crimes, and a hundred and one other things, no doubt, once the Great British Public had read between the lines!

Almost forgotten, and feeling now very forgotten, was an official from a branch of the security services, who had been enlisted on today's panel initially as an observer, but with the remit as a possible participant. He sat, transfixed by the apparent stand-off between the two sides of an argument he had never realised existed when he sat down comfortably twenty minutes earlier at the table in front of him. The impromptu notes he had been taking had come to a shuddering halt. This was something he could not record and give justice to. Part of him wished he wasn't here, but the other part was insanely fascinated by the scenario he was witnessing. He was enthralled, and was now clearly of the opinion that this investigation had higher levels of commitment from those already involved, and was therefore something worthwhile. Something he could get his teeth into. Something unprecedented had just taken place, and he had been a witness.

The proverbial atmospheres which require a knife to cut them seemed to diminish in reputation and power inside the tense room, inside Scotland Yard, on this Saturday morning. Walter Bingham had to do something, so he retreated. Looking around the standing figures at the table, he was reminded of the Western movies of his childhood, when there was a tense and thrilling standoff between men with guns. Who would move first?

His false smile heralded his decision. "It is patently clear to me that the issue of Sir Henry Hughes' proposed release on bail is not an action without repercussions. I shall inform the Home Secretary of the *mood* of the meeting. At this point in time I, personally can do little else. I shall advise that the idea of bail be deferred, until further notice, on the strong recommendation of the senior members of the investigation team. However, I do urge that a more concerted effort be made to establish more rigorous evidence against Sir Henry as I have no doubts that appeals from that quarter will be forthcoming."

Taking their lead from Shackleton, the four other officers who had been standing, sat down in their chairs and waited for Shackleton's verbal response.

"Thank you, minister. I appreciate the difficult position you may find yourself in, it is, I'm sure, an awkward one. My fear was that the investigation could be seriously compromised if Hughes was freed. He is clearly one of the leaders of this criminal group, and the brutal ruthlessness which has been unleashed on innocent people has, most likely, been carried out under his orders. The same is true of Derek Martin, a far more elusive figure in this dark business. Later in this meeting I wish to discuss the details and nature of a proposed undercover operation which we are confident should bear fruit in our pursuit of Martin and his cohorts. Although the total scale of this criminal organisation is unknown, there is no doubt about the leadership. Having Hughes in custody is a major coup for us. I reiterate once more the importance of holding him so that we can bring him to justice as soon as is legally possible."

The meeting, now that the heat had been released, was able to continue in a more conventional manner and with a degree of fluidity more suited to agreement. There were positive decisions made regarding the use of army reserve personnel in the exploration of identified underground areas. Some members of Special Branch would be utilised where deemed appropriate, as the scale of the criminal activity blurred the usual demarcations of the agency's parameters. The over-riding feeling that the rulebooks about differing jurisdictions, and the traditional roles of the various agencies, had been re-written was the source of much conversation. As it stood, at the end of the meeting, Shackleton was pleased that the inter-departmental jealousies which frequently arose in these situations, had not emerged. Even this bonus indicated the uniqueness of the case. No-one had been here before.

9th September 1990.
Yorkshire. 10.a.m.

Inside the Land Rover, nourished by a Harrogate Hotel breakfast, Maurice Watson was on his way to a destination of which he knew virtually nothing. The cryptic clues found in Henry Hughes' documents had proved extremely helpful, but the information which had been gleaned from them was hardly cast in tablets of stone. The location indicated by the information from the Richmond documents had been fine-tuned by a protracted series of telephone communications with the local police. Watson's guess that the outward manifestation of the facility would be a farm was only partly correct. Historically correct, in fact. What had been a farm once was now a rural resort, having a mixture of modern facilities, various outbuildings and areas for camping and caravanning. This detailed intelligence had come from a local bobby in Pateley Bridge, only a few miles away. He had identified the place from the description cobbled together by Watson and others.

The rugged, but beautiful, landscape Watson was driving through lay under the late summer sunshine, an innocent facade giving no clue to what might be lying beneath. Dry stone walls snaked their way along the sides of valley roads, and the upper reaches of the fells were patched with the shadows of clouds drifting across the hillsides. Strands of darker vegetation defined the edges of fields where distant sheep stuck, silently and still, like small pieces of white-grey fluff.

A colourful array of tents came into view, set back from the undulating road on which Watson was travelling. The grouping of these amorphous triangles, along the edge of a farm roadway, indicated the presence of parties of campers and holiday-makers. More discreet was a double-row of caravans at right-angles to a large, very substantial building which was clearly not an original farm structure. The surprisingly low-key signage welcoming visitors to Ingdale Country Resort could only be read by people travelling on the opposite side of the road. The cynical smile on Watson's face as he drove past the gateway, was his response to the strong impression that the resort did not want to attract too much attention. This reinforced the idea that he felt this 'resort' was indeed a suspicious rural enterprise.

Now that he had located his destination, he needed to ascertain to what extent the premises succeeded in portraying itself in the role of tourist attraction. He, himself, was about to portray a role of his own. It had been a few years since Watson, as a rookie detective constable, had used a disguise professionally. It had been as part of a raid on a drug-dealing operation which turned out very well for him. Today's get-up was not dissimilar to the previous disguise; thick wig, headgear and shades. He was going to make an overt approach to the Ingdale Country Resort as a speculative fell-walker checking out the future suitability for a possible holiday. A perfectly plausible idea for many people choosing a walking break in such wonderful surroundings. Once he had parked the Land Rover in the pub car park in the nearest village, he donned his full outfit and simply set off walking as so many other people did here every day of the summer. There was little about his appearance to make him look out of place. He would enjoy the walk, back along the valley where he had just driven.

The pleasant morning sunshine meant his wearing of sunglasses would not draw attention to himself, and would not arouse suspicion when he turned up at the resort. The earlier clouds had drifted away, so he expected the sunshine would accompany him all the way to Ingdale. The modest backpack he was carrying contained nothing particularly suspect, other than a set of dark blue overalls, *de rigueur* in the workplace of today's underground world. These, in effect, would become his second disguise of the day, but that was the part of the plan where improvisation may be called for.

When he was within sight of the cluster of buildings, which made up the Ingdale Country Resort, he stopped by the side of the road and stepped over the ditch and leant against the stone wall. Feeling like a spy, he took out of the side pocket of the rucksack a pair of binoculars. The ironic gesture was not lost on him as he slipped into the role of naturalist, not spy! He scanned the horizon of fell tops and, with a stroke of stunning luck spotted a buzzard circling high above the fields. Following its movements through the binoculars, he was fortunate that the bird's flight path brought it down towards the cluster of buildings. A smooth sweep of the binoculars, then a few seconds focusing on the various buildings would not arouse any suspicion. Watson wondered, vainly, if anyone was watching him. He thought it unlikely, but continued in his role of bird watcher. By a miraculous coincidence, a great slice of luck, the bird he was observing glided over the main building of the Ingdale Resort. Watson panned the flight of the bird over the dark rooftops and, in a slightly sinister piece of symbolism, the buzzard was attacked by two carrion crows which seemed to appear from one of the nearby gable ends.

The aerial battle allowed Watson to follow a lot of the birds' movements, but also he had ample opportunity to survey the buildings and their environs. The sound of the two crows' cawing carried to the road where he was leaning against the wall. He was excited, and genuinely enthralled now by the action in the air above the resort. The buzzard, losing patience with the marauding crows, spun and twisted in the air, superbly exposing its talons to its assailants. Chastised and croaking, the crows gave up the conflict and flapped off. The buzzard soared upwards to freedom.

Leaving the pair of binoculars hanging around his neck, Watson replaced the protective caps over the lenses and resumed his walk towards the entrance of the resort. The most significant thing he had noticed about the resort was the curious absence of people. In reality of course this absence was *not* curious, it simply confirmed he was at the right place. As he approached the gateway, he pondered on how authentic and sincere the greeting would be on his arrival at the reception. The farm track which led from the main road to the cluster of buildings was imprinted with the patterns of man-size heavy duty tractor tyres. Although partially surfaced with an asphalt covering, the access driveway was a hotch-potch of materials; tarmac, concrete slabs, hardcore and impacted earth. Not an obvious choice for a working holiday resort!

Down the driveway walked Maurice Watson, on his way to investigate the nature of this unlikely collection of buildings, tents and caravans. Before he reached the brick reception building, a structure the size of a large residential garage with a simple sign indicating 'Reception' and an arrow pointing towards the door, he noticed a camera. This was part of a closed-circuit television system, aimed towards the roadway and covering the driveway and access to the central compound. So, he thought, someone may have been watching him for the last five minutes. Taking in his surroundings, the observation that worried him the most was the fact that there seemed little pretence that this site actually *was* a resort. Clearly, the people who ran this facility did not expect any great scrutiny of their location.

Adjusting his sunglasses, he entered the door to 'Reception'. On cue, a tall, pale- looking man stepped out of the back office, having obviously seen Watson's approach on the CCTV. A manufactured smile was switched on instantly and a, "hello, can I help you?" came from the other side of the counter. Watson half-turned, indicating the premises with a general wave of his hand.

"Yes. I was walking by and saw your sign. I just wanted to enquire about your rates. It seems a good place for a family break; we all enjoy trekking and looking at the wildlife…the whole family…I'm on a lone walk this weekend. Spotted a buzzard overhead ten minutes ago…..watched it having a scrap with some crows…" He rattled on, in the very convincing role of 'keen outdoor type'. "So, do you have a leaflet, or anything I can take back?" He considered what sort of answer he would receive to his question. What sort of excuse would be forthcoming?

"Oh dear, sir," the explanation began, "I'm afraid the resort has just recently changed management and the new brochures have been ordered, but won't be available for a couple of weeks. We're somewhat in a state of turmoil. If you could leave your details…name and address…we'll happily send you a brochure when they arrive."

Clever, thought Watson, very plausible. "That's okay. Right." The man produced a cheap notepad for Watson to write his details. The name he gave was false and the address was based on a friend's address in Birmingham; he just changed the door number. Handing it back he mused, "I'll just have a little butcher's before I press on. Cheers!" The look on the man's face flickered with a brief shock which he managed to conceal quite quickly, but it spoke volumes to Maurice Watson. The man's fixed smile continued.

"There's not a lot to see at the moment. We have some maintenance work in progress, so be careful please." He paused, before adding, with a misplaced sense of occasion, "have a nice day." Watson smiled weakly in return, and left the reception block.

Realising that he had a few minutes 'grace' so he could legitimately look around in a cursory manner before arousing suspicion, he took advantage of this time by simply walking in a vague circle around the central compound area, making mental notes on where doorways were, the positions of CCTV cameras, and any other vital details of the premises which may be of use when he returned later. As he was about to make his final turn of his farmyard promenade, he caught a glimpse of a figure which gave Watson his one hundred percentage confirmation that he really was on to something. The figure he had seen, dashing surreptitiously from a large outbuilding to the nearest caravan was wearing dark blue overalls.

9th September 1990.
Central London. 10.a.m.

The operation at Windsor Mews was well established now and the constant monitoring had reached the point where little new information was being elicited. The various inventories of stolen goods had been completed and the exploration of the underground approaches to the premises had been successful. Although some linked tunnels had been explained by the Pickerings, and other members of the network who had either escaped or avoided the recent disasters, there could not be the complete certainty that all had been revealed. Although the Windsor Mews project belonged to Hughes' 'alternative' network, it did have physical links to the original network, but to what extent had not yet been determined.

A fortuitous call to the car, which D.I. Samuel Cummins was travelling in, about a new suspect taken into custody, was a pleasing aspect of his Sunday morning. Detained at Windsor Mews, the suspect had asked about Cummins by name. Intrigued, and only ten minutes away, Cummins announced that he was on his way.

Climbing out of the police car, nine minutes later, Samuel Cummins advanced expectantly towards No. 8 Windsor Mews, the adopted address for this part of the investigation. He strode through the door to be greeted by two constables and a familiar, but often elusive figure. "Tommy Best, you old sod, what on earth are you doing in such fashionable surroundings?" He sounded as if he was almost pleased to see him.

"Hello, Mister Cummins. I wanted to talk to you. I want to confess, see!" Tommy was in his early fifties with a slight, but agile frame. With grey sideburns, he could have been a preserved teddy boy, although his quiff was sadly thinning. An awkward smile revealed bad teeth, and he cut a rather pathetic figure as he stood between the two officers and facing Samuel Cummins.

"Confess, Tommy? What have you got to confess about?" Before Best had a chance to respond, Cummins held a halting hand out towards him, but addressed the police officers. "Where did he come from?"

When the officer spoke, it was almost with a sense of disbelief," he turned up in one of the tunnels, sir, waving a white flag…well, a handkerchief actually."

"A white flag, Tommy! Have you been in a war, then?"

"Bloody seems like it, Mister Cummins." He spoke with a voice that was resigned, but also relieved. "You know me, Mister Cummins. I like the sparklers and stuff. I ain't used to the violence, the fisty-cuffs, the bleedin' guns…that's not me, Mister Cummins, never have been involved in that caper. I've been scared… out of me depth, see."

"Well, Tommy, what is it you're confessing to?"

"Anything you like, theft and burglary, yeah?"

"You'll need to be more specific, we need details."

"Look, Mister Cummins, I want to come clean.. make a deal, like…."

"A deal, Tommy?"

"I can tell you a lot about this underground stuff. I got caught up in it years ago. Was a good idea at the time. I thought! Then things kicked off a few weeks ago. Then the shootings, the killings started…I had nothing to do with that. I was up to me neck in the robberies. I'll confess to those. But I ain't getting done for the bad stuff!"

"It seems we've got a lot to talk about, Tommy. And you look as if you could do with a square meal!" Cummins now *was* pleased to see Thomas Best. In the past, Best had been a reliable source of information about big robberies he himself hadn't been involved in, and he was a keen observer of gangland feuds and related violence, which somehow he had always managed to avoid himself. On that score, Cummins felt he would be able to glean much useful information about the state of play below ground. It was obvious that reading between the lines, Thomas Best also felt the need for some police protection. Cummins speculated about the probability of other petty crooks and 'career criminals', who eschewed violence, being in a similar position to Best. These were certainly curious times, and new alliances and allegiances could not be ruled out!

In the car, on the way to the station, Cummins was given a flavour of Best's knowledge of this criminal network he'd been lured into. The detective's ears pricked up when the names of Henry Hughes *and* Derek Martin were mentioned in close proximity. Before the end of the day, Cummins had enough detailed information to pass to Oscar Shackleton about Henry Hughes. More information which could be waved under the noses, and slammed on the desks, of the Home Office. There was also some peripheral information coming to light about the nature and physical features of how underground travelling took place throughout the 'Trojan' network, which rang a particular accord with Cummins and became anything *but* peripheral!

9th September 1900.
Yorkshire. 5.p.m.

The sun had started to slip away and there were shadows. Maurice Watson was intending to take advantage of the shadows. His 'assault' on Ingdale Country Resort was a calculated gamble. There were some very clear risks and he was under no illusions that he may be confronted by some awkward moments. If he thought about his task too much he would soon realise that there was a risk of being killed. As a positive-thinking person, he chose to dispel those worries and gave more emphasis to what could be achieved, and began to focus on whatever intelligence could be gained by his imminent infiltration.

His approach to the resort on this second occasion, was by way of the woodland and fields which surrounded the buildings, rather than by the driveway of his earlier visit. About a hundred and fifty yards from the 'caravan side' of the resort was a small area of woodland, where he could hide and shelter under the rustlings of yellowing beech leaves and change into the obligatory blue overalls. Once decked out in his new outfit, he packed his clothes and hid the rucksack in a cleft of a dry stone wall. He then checked his torch and a small pair of binoculars; the larger bird-watching ones he'd used during the day would be too burdensome for the mission ahead. He also carried a bogus bunch of keys. There was a 'culture of keys' below ground; everyone carried them. To be found without any keys at all would automatically look suspicious. He was ready for his adventure.

He set out along the blind side of an adjacent stone wall, the side that could not be viewed readily from the resort buildings. Wary that his approach from this new direction would be regarded as dubious, it was important to remain unobserved. In his own mind he believed it was highly unlikely that there was anything like a constant monitoring of the resort. It would probably not be deemed necessary in normal circumstances. But Watson would take no chances, so he adopted a strange crouching gait to keep his head below the top of the wall, as he progressed down the slope of the steady incline towards the Ingdale Country Resort.

From a safe observation point, where a rowan tree grew tight against a low wall as it engaged in the long and pointless process of breaching a stone wall, Watson was able to make some decisions about his means of entry to the underground location. The mass of intelligence that had come his way about the nature of the technology used by Hughes and Martin had brought him to the conclusion that the criminal element he was up against had not developed anything of their own. This did not surprise him at all. The two networks, the two organisations, were in existence for completely different reasons, and they had very different motivations. Growing in confidence about his own ability to survive, but more importantly, his ability to achieve some advantage from this daring operation, Watson carefully climbed over the half-broken wall, and strode casually towards the nearest building.

The building he had chosen was the biggest structure on the whole site. It was the one nearest to the two rows of caravans, where Watson had observed the dashing figure of the man in overalls during his morning's visit. A shrewd guess that the door at the corner of this structure would be open, was Watson's first calculated gamble. His first throw of the die. A six! It opened easily and quietly, and Watson slipped inside. There was no-one about, but his priority was to find cover; a hiding place. The size of a very large barn, the building he was now in seemed to be a storage area for vehicles and heavy equipment. Almost a third of the width of the building was given over to a huge inspection pit, as if it had been constructed for giant vehicles, clearly on a scale beyond normal commercial size. In the shadows of this barn-like structure, the smugness of Watson's smile was hidden. He knew what this was.

A visual check of the hydraulic jacks, the oil-smooth tubular columns, clean and shining in the leftover daylight coming through the skylights, confirmed that this, in essence *was* an inspection pit, of sorts. This would be the vehicular entrance to the main underground area. Earthmoving machinery, drilling equipment and a range of other diggers, tractors, and any other ancillary vehicles required, would be lowered through the 'inspection pit' and into the tunnel. The size of this would roughly resemble the opening to a conventional road tunnel. This was one of the features, of this 'rogue location', he had come to verify. Operation Axel. All the trappings of 'Journey to the Centre of the Earth'. Watson stopped his boyish daydream. It was time to focus, time to stay smart.

In the absence of any sign of personnel, the prime problem for Watson being seen by someone, even with his blue overalls, was an ever-present risk. With a hundred people wandering around in the same overalls, he would have no difficulty remaining 'secret'. The hundred people he wished for weren't here. Rather than skulk around in the shadows like a worried rat, he felt he needed to actively explore the premises and see what he could learn. Almost as soon as he had made that decision, he heard the approaching sound of a heavy vehicle. It sounded like a truck of some sort.

A second gamble with the same door. He slipped back to the doorway, and gently opened the door marginally. He had a clear view of a large covered truck idling in the compound with half a dozen men in attendance. They were preparing to unload the vehicle. The engine stopped with a shudder and the last breath of exhaust was heard. Someone shouted a general instruction to wait until the heavy covers were drawn back and after a few seconds, Watson heard something he had difficulty believing.

"Mister Martin will be here soon, lads. Okay?" A voice from the cab rang out.

There was a discernible stirring among the men present as this piece of news was acknowledged. From his observation point, Maurice Watson allowed his brain to race. If ever there was a need to think fast, this was it! Was this good news or bad news? The unexpected opportunity to observe Derek Martin was surely a potential bonus he must take advantage of. This could turn out to be crucial to the operation, even though this possibility had not been envisioned. Watson's priority now was to find an opportunity to eavesdrop on whatever it was that Derek Martin had come here to say; he certainly wasn't here for a camping holiday. The police officer's focus now was on finding a place to hide, where surveillance could be carried out successfully. But where?

Believing that all the available personnel were now outside, helping to unload the truck, Watson embarked on a whistle-stop reconnaissance of the building, in the hope of discovering enough about the layout of the place to make life easier and safer for him over the next several hours, if necessary. Along the far wall, beyond the assorted vehicles, was a raised walkway, leading to a metal door which Watson surmised was one of the entrances to the underground area. His swift and silent movements brought him to this point within a minute. He listened carefully. He heard nothing to suggest there was anyone on the other side. Holding his breath, he very carefully tried the door handle. The door was not locked. His luck was holding out. Unrealistically, he thought. It couldn't last forever.

Once inside, he found himself facing a narrow corridor with several adjoining rooms. It reminded him of the open gantry area below ground at Richmond, only here there was less space. He wondered whether this set of rooms functioned as offices. The nearest of these had its door open, which Watson peered into. The only window in the room invited him to observe the outside compound from a new angle. He could clearly see the truck and the busy activity around it. As he watched the general bustle around the truck, he caught sight of the incongruous beams of two sets of headlights, prematurely switched on for the early approach of dusk. This will be Derek Martin, deduced Watson.

Hearing the two cars pull up at the front of the building, it seemed very likely, to Watson from his position inside this particular building, that he could expect visitors. This barn was the most obvious destination for Martin's party, so finding a suitable hiding place, preferably where he could eavesdrop, became an instant priority for Watson. The open vault where the vehicles were would not be site chosen by Derek Martin to talk to his troops; it would need to be more intimate, more controlled.

Stepping into the corridor, he heard someone approaching from further inside the building. The sound seemed to come from the other side of a doorway where the corridor stopped He guessed the person in question was on the other side of this door, and judging by the sound of the footsteps, there was a longer extension to the corridor Watson was now occupying. And someone was about to make an entrance. Watson took the initiative and grabbed the door handle, just as somebody pulled the door inwards, revealing, as Watson had expected, a further, and wider corridor.

"Mister Martin's here! I'm with Martin. Is everything ready?" Watson bluffed dramatically. He made to continue into the new corridor space, feigning a level of tense agitation indicative of hurriedness. Immediately in front of him was a confused-looking, overcalled man standing as if transfixed, and completely taken aback by this sudden intrusion from someone he didn't recognise. Watson's brusque manner had removed any chance of a challenge, and it was clear that this transfixed man was of the opinion that the stranger before him was indeed a member of Derek Martin's party, and was not standing on ceremony!

"Oh, er..yes. The big room at the end!" He pointed to a vague spot further along the wider corridor behind him, where he had just come from.

"Good, good. That's fine!" Watson enthused, and vanished down the corridor in the direction of 'the big room'.

As he tried to picture, in his own mind's eye, the nature of this anticipated room, Watson had struck on an instant plan which was utterly reliant on his knowledge of other underground installations he had visited. It involved his experience and memory of the planning, construction and placing of the ventilation system.

Checking that there were no new 'strangers' around, he glanced into the big room, which was set up as a modest, minimalist, meeting area. He identified the position and type of ventilation grilles along the internal wall. These installations were primarily for the benefit of those working and living below ground, rather than for the inhabitants of the surface buildings. It was the smaller room next door that Watson now focused on. He knew that the grilles themselves were relatively easy to remove, and silently sneaking into this adjacent room he prepared his hiding place.

The square grilles were held in place by the mere pressure of the sprung metal edges. In the event of the ventilation shafts and tunnels being used as emergency escape routes, the grilles were designed to simply be pushed or kicked out, allowing egress from the wall space. Watson had quickly realised that the behind-the-wall tunnel would run along the inside wall of the meeting room, so that was where he would ensconce himself for the next hour or so. Any escape plan at the moment would have to wait.

The slight movement of air as it eased through the ventilation spaces had a curious relaxing effect on Maurice Watson. As long as he remained silent he would be unheard and unobserved, but more importantly, he desperately hoped to find out vital information from the mouth of Derek Martin.

It wasn't very long before voices emerged from along the corridor, as Martin's party swept towards the room. Derek Martin's voice was audible above the rest. He sounded angry and agitated. His entrance to the meeting room was more a burst of energy than an introduction to discourse. Watson had seen him only once before, several years earlier, when he was regarded as a respectable figure in the network. Interestingly, his entrance on that occasion had been benign, friendly and pleasant. It seemed a life away.

Watchful and wary, Watson peered through the grille at Derek Martin. A tall, well-built giant of a man, he exuded power, and his closely-cropped hair gave him the menacing presence of an uncompromising door-steward. He circled the room, like a lion in a cage, gauging the parameters of the new space he was occupying, taking in the 'lie of the land' as he made possession of the room. Momentarily, he stood by the table as if to sit down at the nearest chair, before stepping away and sitting at another chair, almost as if claiming unquestionable rights over that particular piece of furniture.

For a few moments, Watson tensed as he noticed the confused man, he had briefly encountered earlier, make a tentative remark to Martin. Was he mentioning the stranger? With a wave of his arm, Martin snapped a remark about leaving two men outside the front of the building. It appeared the man was satisfied with Martin's explanatory reply, so the man's continued confusion kept Watson in his own continued confidence.

Derek Martin coughed. The other men in the room stopped their low murmured conversations and found seats or leaned awkwardly against other items of furniture. One tall, slim figure, dressed completely in black, and wearing the line of a scar across his face, sat on the edge of a table, exuding a visible aura of threat. He was clearly one of Martin's henchmen and certainly looked the part. Martin gave a glowering sweep of the room with his dark eyes. "Okay." This was his signal to start.

"Right, we've had some problems of late, and I'll come to those in a minute." The challenge and authority in his tone meant that no-one visibly responded to this apparent bad news. Martin saw this in their faces, and carried on with his briefing. "But firstly, I want to remind you that this facility, where we are now, is secure. We have no reason to believe that Ford's lot or the police, or anyone else, knows about the Ingdale site. We have other sites which remain secret and this is an important strength to remember. Some of our surface operations may need to be put to one side for a while, but that's all it is. We are still in business. The discovery of our Northern Scotland operation has been a bad blow. And Sir Henry being held is our main worry. We can't do a lot about that. We don't think he'll compromise our operations, he's got too much to lose. His legals should take care of that. I can't see him cutting a deal with the Yard either. Another big blow was Windsor Mews. Now that *did* look bad, at one point, but we don't think the police have sussed out the links we've made between the London sites, particularly the fast North-South rail link. That's one of our gems, as a lot of you will know. Those of you who have used these links will still be able to do so. You'll still be able to vanish when you're up in town!" This time there was an audible response of agreement and satisfaction to Martin's information. He was pleased with the reaction of his audience and gave a curt nod of the head before continuing. "I'm annoyed about what's happened; make no mistake about that! But we reckon that only about forty percent of our underground sites have been compromised. Over the next few weeks some of you will be travelling to other sites to help us block off some of our links to Ford's network. This will secure some of our own areas. We'll be busy, yes! But it will be worth it. Over the coming months we will have a network which will be ours, and ours alone. Remember, this is safe and secure and so is Barnet. And our sites in Nottingham, Newcastle, North Wales and Derbyshire. And plenty of 'attached' sites. We've taken a blow to the chin and we might have a black eye, but we are not lying on the deck!" Martin finished with a stiff right-handed fist gesture into the palm of his left hand, creating the impression of acute wrath as he raged and rallied his men as if facing a fight to the death. His pugilist's ego seemed to have the desired effect on his partisan audience.

In his ventilated eyrie, Watson was assessing the new information he had picked up from Martin's diatribe. 'Barnet' was significant and so was the reference to the 'fast rail link'. Here was intelligence he needed to pass to Scotland Yard as soon as possible. The time had arrived when he needed to consider an escape route. Was he likely to hear any further useful information? Was he going to risk moving through the ventilation system while there were still people within hearing distance? Something else bothered him about Derek Martin's party, which might prove troublesome if he didn't make an exit soon.

His unobserved grimace indicated his concern. The irony of his erstwhile disguise had suddenly hit him. The blue overalls had been chosen as a plausible cover in the event of him being observed, or meeting someone on site. His brief encounter with the confused man clearly utilised this premise and it appeared to be successful. However, when Watson thought about it, he realised how lucky he was that the man was not too bright. Watson's assertion that he was with Derek

Martin's group did not actually ring true, with hindsight. No-one who came with Martin was wearing overalls! Why would they? They had all just arrived by car and were all wearing dark suits. Thankfully, it seemed, this discrepancy in attire had not yet worked its way through the confused man's thick skull. But as soon as it did, it would be realised very quickly that there was a stranger somewhere on site. That fact would have serious repercussions for any escape plan Watson may come up with. A new sense of urgency gripped him as he weighed up the pros and cons about exits and their probable whereabouts. While Martin's current party were still within the main building, Watson realised, he could still take advantage of his 'disguise'. The two men left outside, the two men who had come with Martin, would *not* be alerted by a man on site in blue overalls. So, a quick exit of the building was Watson's new instant priority.

Martin had broken the tense informality of his performance and brought the main business of the day to an end. There was now a relatively relaxed atmosphere, as smaller groupings emerged and drifted into their own discussions about 'other operations' and talk of visits to other locations. Inside his ventilation void, Watson hoped that the general hubbub of conversation below would mask any small sounds he might make on his slow, sliding progress back along the space towards the grille he would chose to exit by. He had estimated that there was a possibility of a way out, on to the roof. From there he would have to make the next part of his escape, on the hoof. Literally.

His torturous journey, sliding carefully on his stomach, along the metal tunnel, was interrupted when he heard Martin's voice close by. Watson froze and stopped moving completely as he urged his ears to stretch for more information. Martin had wandered out of the meeting room with one of his compatriots.

"Look, I need a word with someone, but I'll be out the front in ten minutes. Have a smoke, Jerry, have a smoke." Watson heard the sound of Martin, presumably, slapping someone on the back. Two sets of footsteps were heard, moving in opposite directions along the corridor.

Given that this part of the building was empty of people now, Watson was able to pick up speed in his exertions and within a few minutes he had reached a point where he could stand up and allow his body to re-adapt to a vertical position. The flimsy nature of fabrication at this end of the ventilation system made it surprisingly easy for Watson to move a couple of panels and find himself in the fresh air of a Yorkshire evening.

As he breathed in triumphantly and gazed at the darkening sky, he was curiously thankful for Derek Martin's and Henry Hughes' ideas about their underground sites. The ventilation system Watson had just crawled through was a conventional one, and that fact had made it straightforward for Watson to eavesdrop, travel through and escape from. In George Ford's systems they would be far more complex, because they were constructed with Armageddon in mind, which meant they were not as 'open' as the Ingdale example. Watson suddenly felt a light relief of tension and needed to quickly focus again as he remembered he wasn't 'out of the woods' yet.

Scampering as silently as possible across the roof of the barn-sized building, Watson arrived at a point where it was feasible to climb down to the ground. He tried to recall the positions of the security lights he had noticed earlier. A sudden choice came to mind. Several feet from the side of the building was a substantial pile of neatly packed wooden planks and posts, which rose to a height closer to the level of the roof. This route would divide the drop to the ground into smaller parts. Getting off the roof in one drop would mean jumping and risking an injury or hanging over the guttering and dropping. He decided the wood structure looked stable enough. So, seconds later, he leapt from the edge of the roof to the top of the wood pile. As he landed there was a sharp crack and a small wooden post was dislodged from the pile and slipped away from the wood pile on the side away from the building. Two things happened simultaneously.

The first was a startled response from someone at the corner of the building who had obviously heard the sound of the wood falling. The second thing was the appearance of a large dog fox which had been lurking near the pile of wood. Man and fox faced each other. "Bloody fox!" grunted the voice of the man in black who had sat on the table in the meeting. A casual and confident stare came from the fox. It then turned away and slyly slipped away into the dusk to continue its hunt.

On top of the wood pile lay a prone Maurice Watson, actively controlling his breath and listening intently to the two men only yards away. The exclamation about the fox was for the benefit of Derek Martin, who had been standing by the man in black at the corner of the barn, when the fox made its appearance. A wisp of smoke identified the man in black as the 'Jerry' from Martin's brief conversation ten minutes earlier.

"So, you reckon there may be a problem with Hughes, then?" enquired Jerry.

"I don't really know, to be honest. He's made a bloody mess of some things recently and I'm not sure how reliable he is in keeping his mouth shut," argued Martin.

"We could take him out, of course," came the reply.

"Take him out? He's in police custody, Jerry. How would you do that?"

"Come on, Derek, you know. Swift and silent. No noise. It's worth a try, eh?"

Jerry's mouth pulled on his cigarette as Martin wandered away from him, clearly considering this interesting proposal. The blue-grey smoke hung in the cooling air and Jerry seemed to enjoy watching Martin in his contemplations. Derek

Martin held his chin in a ponderous manner and slowly turned towards the man in black again. "I see what you mean. Your trusty cross-bow."

Above this overheard conspiracy, Maurice Watson realised in an instant that he was listening to the assassin who tried to kill Andrew Pickering.

9th September 1990.
Central London. 6.p.m.

After a hectic and dramatic day tied up with the business of Operation Axel, it was a welcome respite to be relaxing on a long sofa, cosseted by an abundance of velvet-soft cushions. Such was the envious position of Samuel Cummins as he slumped on the soft furnishings of Felicity Hood's Bloomsbury apartment. His eyes wandered over the array of framed prints and photographs which adorned every wall in the room. His fascination prompted an ocean of questions, but Samuel Cummins had asked enough questions today. Some questions would be inevitable in his conversation with Felicity Hood, but the calm and cultured haven he was now luxuriating in would sugar the pill of any idea of interrogation. Carrying a tray of tea and biscuits, Felicity entered from her kitchen.

"It's good of you, Inspector Cummins, to keep us informed of the progress being made with this business. It is truly appreciated. I know I speak for the others. Particularly George." She smiled at Cummins and poured tea into two china cups.

"Well, we've gained an awful lot of information today about the links between the two networks, mainly regarding the London locations. There are numerous threads of investigation at the moment, but one of them, specifically, concerns George, which I am eager to pursue." Cummins' tone was subdued, almost apologetic as if he was excusing himself for intruding into areas of sensitivity.

Felicity asked, "something George has done?"

"No, no….on the contrary. It's about Elsa, his wife."

"Elsa? But that was five years ago. It was quite dreadful. I know you spoke, er, asked about it when we visited Richmond. I believe you asked some questions of the Connors too."

"I need to be blunt, Ms Hood, I'm sorry," Cummins started. Felicity sat up with a straight back quite suddenly.

"You think she was murdered, don't you?"

"I'm afraid I do," said Cummins and took a full mouthful of tea.

Felicity Hood stared at the tea-tray and breathed heavily. She looked up, her eyes moist and her face slightly contorting into one of those terrible expressions which could become a smile, or presage a burst of weeping. She fought it well, and composed herself, before responding. "It does not surprise me, inspector, I always felt it highly unlikely that Elsa could have fallen over those rails. The idea of an accident was absurd. But there was nothing real to suggest anyone else's presence. It simply remained a horrible mystery."

"And there was no way, in the circumstances, that the police could be involved."

"Exactly," replied Felicity, "it seems rather pathetic to suggest it was regrettable; it hardly does the incident justice. It certainly gives no justice to poor Elsa."

Cummins finished his cup of tea, replaced the cup on the saucer neatly, and looked searchingly towards Felicity Hood. "I have a theory which is gradually taking shape, but I need a few facts and ideas to be confirmed. I could be wrong, but I don't think so."

"Right," nodded Felicity, "I'll do all I can to help."

"Are you aware of a high-speed rail link between the London locations? For example Barnet to Richmond?"

Felicity Hood blinked. "Goodness, no. High-speed, you say. No." She seemed somewhat confused, but recovered and spoke further. "Now, as for rail links we do have, in various locations, some monorail systems. They were developed by extending some track and utilising stock and equipment which we purchased many years ago from a holiday camp, of all places. It was about to be scrapped, when the resort was due revamp. It had been used as an outdoor, overhead system, but we put it underground! It was rather successful, to be frank, but could definitely not be described as high-speed! And as for your reference to Barnet, no. We have no site in that part of London, nothing at all in fact, north of Edgware."

"Well, that is interesting, because earlier today we spoke, in great depth and detail to someone who is very familiar with the rail link and knows much about the Barnet location too," explained Cummins.

"Ah," said Felicity, realising where this was going," this person presumably is one of 'them', one of Martin's and Hughes' lot?"

It was Cummins' turn to say, "exactly!"

"So do I deduce that this fast link to Richmond is pertinent to Elsa's death?"

"It's certainly looking like it. Our main problem, which may be insurmountable, is trying to establish facts and find evidence that are anything but circumstantial. With no body and no forensics, proving anything criminal could be virtually impossible."

Felicity Hood poured out a second cup of tea for each of them. She gazed at the walls of her living room, as if lost in thought momentarily, considering and appreciating her own taste in decoration. Then she sighed. "You probably think we are just a group of naive and eccentric old peaceniks. Well, maybe, maybe. But we started out young. I was twenty-two years old, my life and career ahead of me, filled with ambitious plans, and I really thought all of that was being put in jeopardy because of the ugly stuff that was happening around the world. George, Derek Martin, Ken and Ellen Carter were there at the beginning. Our project was bold, it was big and it was successful for such a long time. The bond between us all was wonderful. Derek's betrayal has come as a tremendous shock to us. And especially as we now know the betrayal was a long time ago. The ethos, the philosophy we had was fine. Wherever you visited or worked below ground, you knew that everyone you met was a friend, a colleague, a kindred spirit. Elsa's death was seen as an appalling accident. It could have been nothing else. Why would foul play ever be suspected? That belonged to the other world, the world we tried to escape from."

Cummins looked at Felicity Hood. "An ideal? That's everyone's dream, isn't it? The ideals may vary from person to person, they can be very different. While it lasted, Martin's and Hughes' world must have seemed ideal to them. Criminals being able to just vanish, become invisible. They must have thought it was perfect." Cummins spoke thoughtfully. Although Felicity had described a world of hers as being over, he couldn't be fully certain the world of Martin and Hughes had quite ended yet!

"Hmmm, I see what you mean. Secrecy. Everyone craves that, in some form or other. It can be the classic 'double-edged sword' as some people tritely say," condemned Felicity Hood. "Perhaps it is as simple as that!"

Cummins drained the last of his tea and stood up. "I should be off now. Thank you for the tea. I hope we'll be able to give you some better news soon, Ms Hood."

"Felicity, please," she admonished and insisted. And smiled.

"Thank you, Felicity," he returned, as he moved towards the door.

In the hallway, before she opened her front door, Felicity seemed to believe that an explanation was due. "We thought there was always a chance that it would work. An ideal society, I suppose. Some delusions are very strong, but we were mistaken. We were just another religion."

9th September 1990. Yorkshire. 7.p.m.

Aware of the coarseness of the rough timber he was lying on, Watson was feeling stiff and uncomfortable and beginning to believe he would be stuck in his present position for some time yet. Not realising that they had a 'captive' audience, Derek Martin and the crossbow assassin Jerry talked at some length about the recent events within their criminal network. One major theme that was apparent from their idle chatter, was the problem they had with Sir Henry Hughes inability to organise his affairs, and how he had become a real liability to their organisation. The two men seemed to catalogue Hughes' major and minor botch-ups over the years, with their respective stories spiralling into hyperbole.

"His bloody organisation could be awful," complained Martin, "he was used to a P.A. for his legit businesses, you see, and he had little to do himself really. But when it came to us…well, he would leave sensitive stuff, financial stuff, lying around, here and there. That office he used in Richmond…. that was nearly a complete bloody disaster! He was bloody rubbish. Five years ago he nearly blew it. Again it was more papers…that bloody Ford woman…sticking her nose into our plans. Couldn't believe how stupid he'd been. He apologised. Started to use Tommy Best, my old driver, to fetch and carry for him." And Martin's moaning went on and on, until Jerry decided to intervene with a, "so, are we set on the right solution to the problem? Are we going to take him out?"

"I don't know. It seems risky. Opportunities are few and far between. When would you be able to even attempt it? You'd be on your own, Jerry. Would you need anyone else?"

"Just a reliable driver, possibly. That's if I was going to do it from a motor. Like last time. Hopefully the bastard won't be as lucky as the Pickering lad was. Jammy sod!" Jerry was clearly still embittered about the failed attempt on Andrew Pickering's life.

The men fell silent and Watson waited for a clue as to their next move. Dusk had taken a gentle hold of the evening and the air was still very pleasant. Despite this, Watson thought longingly about the near future, when he could be on his way out of this particular tight spot. He concluded that the safe and comfortable bedroom, which waited for him in the village pub a couple of miles away, was the place he'd rather be.

When the voices started again, it was clear that the two men had moved further from the wood pile and seemed to be returning to the barn. A careful raising of his head gave Watson a brief view of the two menacing figures as they disappeared around the corner of the building.

It was time for Watson's next move. He made a swift exit from the timber stack and climbed cautiously over the stone wall. The sound of the truck's engine fired into life again and a couple of shouts rang out, echoing from the darkening walls of the buildings. Whatever had been brought in, had now been delivered. For Watson to attempt a further exploration of the site, in the hope of discovering what the cargo in the truck was, would be a very risky task. He had enough information to advise his colleagues on a future raid on these premises. Leaving the location of his very fortunate and very rewarding mission, Watson looked ahead to the rest of his evening.

Once clear of the resort, he would be able to reach the pub safely within an hour or so. His planned highlight of the day would be to order a tasty Yorkshire supper, a pint of real ale and make an important phone call to Samuel Cummins on schedule at nine o' clock.

12th September 1990.
Scotland Yard. 10.a.m.

Oscar Shackleton was reading a newspaper intently. The subject of the article was Sir Henry Hughes. The comment and speculation from the political pundits, the business columnists and the crime reporters was rife. Some of the information contained in the various pieces he had read was accurate, despite the fact that much of the truth, at the moment, was solely in the possession of the police. More information was coming in by the hour. As far as it was possible to feel pleased with the positive progress of something as desperately dangerous as Operation Axel, Shackleton felt that there had been a number of clear positive events in the past few days. Two consecutive days had passed without a change in the body count. That had been a great relief to him, and to the rest of his team. He folded the paper and was placing it on top of a side table when the door opened. His two D.I.s, Samuel Cummins and Roger Melville came in, closely followed by the lively figure of D.S. Maurice Watson.

"Good morning, gentlemen. I hope your extra-curricular activities have proved worthwhile and that you are ready to inform the next stage of this investigation."

Samuel Cummins indicated Maurice Watson with a clear look of pride on his face, and brought Shackleton up to date with the detail of the latest developments. "Watson has unearthed some very pertinent information about Derek Martin and this, coupled with more information from an old acquaintance of mine….an informant shall we say, it seems more than likely that we have identified a murder, which was previously unknown to the police, from five years ago!"

Shackleton's eyebrows lifted and he looked at the three men. "Yes? And whose murder would that be?"

"The victim was Elsa Ford, and the suspect is Derek Martin. We do have some problems with pursuing this particular murder, because of the time elapsed, but we have a number of ideas under consideration, which may mean we can resolve it in other ways. On the subject of a crime we are aware of, the attempt killing of Andrew Pickering, we seem to have a prime suspect. A character called Jerry Russell. Watson heard his first name mentioned in an overheard conversation involving this man and Derek Martin, and the surname was supplied by my informant. Russell is an elusive character and specialises in weapons other than firearms; he has a penchant for various blades, but his specialism is the crossbow."

Shackleton held his hand up and looked directly at Maurice Watson. "You clearly managed to come away from Yorkshire with a lot of useful information. Did you pick up anything about any future activities or was it all regarding previous crimes?"

Watson replied with his customary eagerness, "yes, sir. I overheard the suggestion that Russell would make an attempt on Sir Henry Hughes' life. Martin and Russell agreed that Hughes may not be relied upon as far as not revealing evidence to the police. There were no clear details of a specific plan, it was more a statement of intent really. But Jerry Russell would be working alone if it's going to be carried out. He mentioned he may need a driver. It seems to me, sir, they could use the same M.O. as the attack on young Andrew Pickering."

"Thank you, Watson. Good work." Shackleton stood up and stretched his legs by moving towards the window. "How realistic is an attack on Henry Hughes? Being on remand makes him pretty safe I would have thought."

"His new hearing is tomorrow, sir, at the City of Westminster Magistrates' Court. I think that would be the only opportunity Russell, or anyone else, could try to take a shot at him!" offered Roger Melville.

"Damn and blast," exclaimed Shackleton, "we'll need to review our manning of his court appearance. Any harm to him while he's in police custody, due to a charge of the attempted murder of a police officer, will be jumped on immediately by the press!" Shackleton wrote a brief note as an *aide memoire* for his later instructions regarding Hughes' protection. He sat down again, almost sulkily, and retrieved something from earlier in the conversation. "Tell me more about this Elsa Ford killing. Five years ago and it was never reported?"

Samuel Cummins opened the small notebook he had been holding and recalled the information he had collected. "Elsa Ford's body was found underground at Richmond in the early evening of June 4th 1985. It appeared she had fallen from a platform, over a set of safety railings, thirty-odd feet. No-one witnessed this apparent accident. There was no reason to suspect foul play. At that time the membership of Ford's network had no knowledge of the rogue network carrying out their regular crimes. So, no-one at the time suspected that criminals had access to the underground areas. Recent events have brought to light evidence that might explain why and how the murder took place. The theory, and it is only a theory, but a pretty solid one in my opinion, is that Derek Martin caught Elsa Ford looking at incriminating documents, belonging to Henry Hughes, about the 'rogue' alternative network. Martin simply pushed her from the platform thus keeping the secret of his own network…for, as it happens, a further five years. At the time the rogue network had recently completed a fast underground miniature railway, a monorail system, which Ford's lot we unaware of but we now know was used by Martin on that very day! My informant was working as Martin's driver at the time….and….more pertinently as a sort of 'buddy' where people going underground, are paired up for safety reasons. The actual rail link runs from Barnet, one of the prime rogue locations, across London, more or less north to south, to Richmond. The timings given by my informant and the records held at the Richmond location match perfectly. Although the murder itself was not planned in advance, Elsa Ford was unbelievably unlucky in the circumstances. And Martin himself was unbelievably *lucky* to use the rail link on that particular occasion when he went to recover some documents belonging to Henry Hughes which he had left at Richmond."

"Your informant, D.I. Cummins," assessed Shackleton, "appears to be a rather invaluable resource. Do we need to give him protection, too?"

"Actually, sir, not yet. We are certain that Martin's lot do not know that 'our man' is in custody. He gave himself up at the Windsor Mews site. I've known him for several years. He's a petty criminal, out of his depth, and he has been frightened by the sudden violent turn of events in recent weeks and he wanted out. We intend to use him to pass a message on, designed to give Martin an opportunity of incriminating himself. This bogus message will be sent to Martin within the next twenty-four hours." Cummins paused and noticed that Shackleton was earnestly hanging on every word and was nodding with clear encouragement.

"Do I ask how this is to be achieved?" questioned Shackleton, hungry for further information.

"To be blunt, sir, we're setting a trap for Martin. He is very aware of Hughes' weakness for leaving paper work, documentation, incriminating material, in places where it may be discovered. The plan is to tap into Martin's concerns on this issue and bring him out into the open....er, figuratively speaking, sir. We are very confident that the apprehension of Derek Martin will be a major blow to the organisation. In fact, we would expect the whole network to implode completely, once the news of Martin's capture is made public. The remnants of his people would realise that their 'leader' is out of the picture. All the organisation of the major crimes has been done by Martin and Hughes; without them, the organisation would be rudderless."

"Very good, Cummins, very good. I only need to do two things now," Shackleton said with an ironic smugness, delivered for comic effect, "I sincerely thank you all for your endeavours and the accumulation of such intelligence. And, I wish you the best of luck with your scheme to bring Martin and his cronies to justice." He paused. "Are there any questions you wish to ask me?"

13th September 1900.
Central London. 10.a.m.

Taxis negotiated the traffic, and delivered smartly-dressed passengers to meetings, and trysts of all sorts, at addresses along Cheapside and Cornhill. Tired tube-travellers spilled out onto the pavements outside Bank station, as the overhead grey clouds trudged by, vaguely threatening the city with rain. Big red buses, partnered in twos and threes, crawled between stops and coughed and pushed their warm and toxic diesel fumes into the roadways around the City of Westminster Magistrates' Court.

The presence of television camera crews and a jostling battalion of keen press photographers convinced many of the passers-by that there may be something of note happening nearby, something worthy of their attention. A cordon of police officers, with ancillary court officials in attendance, and assisting with the organisation of keeping the entrance to the building clear, was further evidence that an imminent arrival, involving an element of public interest, was taking place. Soon, a few people walking by slowed their pace and stopped, half bemused with the obvious expectation within the melee of press personnel. A casual curiosity prompted some bystanders to take more notice. Some faces looked up the road, towards the end of Threadneedle Street, eyes stretching earnestly to see any tell-tale approach of the appropriate vehicles. Others peered in the opposite direction, their anticipation directed at any activity on Queen Victoria Street.

A procession of traffic slowed to a halt, as a group of uniformed police officers signalled their instructions, and a group of three official vehicles drove swiftly into view, moving up the middle of the road, blue lights flashing through the morning air. Pulling up by the pavement, after crossing the street in front of the second line of halted traffic, the first police vehicle mounted the edge of the pathway, where the space had been cleared of bystanders. Two officers climbed out of this car and turned to face the second vehicle, a prison service van containing Sir Henry Hughes and his escorts. The back doors of the prison vehicle opened and Hughes emerged, wearing a smart light grey suit and white shirt, and handcuffed to a prison officer. A theatrically restrained surge from the press reporters and cameramen was held in check by a short line of stout police officers as Hughes, and his stern partner, moved across the pavement towards the entrance of the magistrates' court.

There was a brief moment when someone, from the sidelines of the reporters' section of the crowd, called out to Hughes by name, and he instinctively looked up towards them. The vague smile of recognition which crossed his grim face was instantly interrupted by a horrific change of expression, and a wild explosion of blood bursting from Henry Hughes' neck. Three or four screams rang out, as Hughes twisted and writhed downwards and hit the ground with a dull thud, blood continuing to gush out of a gaping wound. Pandemonium broke out as police, press and public agendas erupted into a frenzy of confusion. Screams, shouts and sudden sirens split the London air, and the prone Sir Henry Hughes gasped his last contorted breath, and expired on the pavement in a growing stain of his own blood.

On the rooftop of an impressive-looking block of offices on Poultry, overlooking the slaughter on Queen Victoria Street, Jerry Russell efficiently packed away his trusted crossbow into a slim black executive-style case. He wrapped the secured item with a sheet of rough sacking and placed two elastic cords tightly around this incriminating parcel and carried it calmly to the edge of the rooftop at the back of the building. Calmly and very carefully he manoeuvred himself towards the corner and looked down to a quiet narrow street. Six storeys below his feet was a parked pick-up van. With a clinical accuracy he tossed the sack parcel from the roof and watched it spin slightly in its descent, keeping its horizontal orientation, and land flatly, seconds later, with a brief burst of dust in the open back of the waiting van.

The figure of a man suddenly emerged from the shadows of Grocers' Hall Court and threw a second sack over the package. He slipped into the vehicle, started the engine, pulled out carefully into the busy road, and drove off along Cheapside.

Above the streets of London, the black-clad Jerry Russell opened the rooftop exit door just as he became aware of the sound of a police helicopter, churning through the air towards the City location. The aircraft circled and tilted towards adjoining rooftops. The eyes inside would be feverishly searching for any sign of suspicious movement Safely into the upper storage area of the office block, Russell briskly walked down the echoing stairwell, down to the ground floor. Out through a side door into the noisy siren-ridden atmosphere of Bank, Russell strode purposefully past the crowds accumulating around Bank tube station. The busy morning buzz was now a low background accompaniment to the newer and louder cacophonies of the continued frenzy and mayhem around the magistrates' court.

Confident and anonymous, Russell made his way along Moorgate towards the tube station there. From here he would take the Northern Line tube train back to High Barnet, having had another successful day 'at the office'.

13th September 1990.
Richmond-upon-Thames. 11.a.m.

Some distance below the pleasant and peaceful streets of Richmond, inside an innocuous storage room, a wall panel, the width of a double door, slid open to reveal the curved roof of a small-scale, and largely secret, underground railway. What passed as a platform was a narrow walkway which was now open to the inside of the storage room. Three men stepped into this small room, having just alighted from a streamlined and one- time-futuristic-looking monorail train.

One of the men moved forward across the space of the storage room, and flicked a hidden switch above the main door and waited. The door at the back, where they had just entered, closed silently and the railway tunnel disappeared. Next to the first switch was a second switch which was now activated to allow the main door to open. A second man stepped into a broad, dimly-lit corridor and was followed by the first man. Looking both ways, they carefully ascertained that no-one else was around.

Into the corridor strode a bold Derek Martin. Once the door to the storage room was closed, the three men proceeded swiftly along the broad hallway, adjusting the dim lighting at intervals as they continued on their way. Within a few minutes they arrived at a point where the pathway they were travelling along reached a junction. Here they found a number of doorways indicating a series of separate rooms for accommodation, and others for other ancillary activities. It was quite clear that there was nobody in the vicinity, but

Martin's accomplices checked each room in turn. When this task was complete, Martin turned to one of the men.

"Okay, Benny, you stay here. I can't see you'll have anything to do, but I want you to stay sharp. No-one else comes this way. Got it?"

"Yes, Mister Martin," replied the obedient Benny.

As Martin and the other man continued on their way along the main corridor, Benny slipped into the nearest room and extracted a chair. He pulled it outside into the broad hallway and made himself comfortable as he sat down facing the junction, intent on guarding this crucial underground thoroughfare.

The area of the tunnel system Martin and his henchman had now moved into was governed by a staggered series of illuminating lamps. For purposes of saving energy from their own generators, each section of the network was lit independently so when people were moving through the system, as they were now, the section ahead was switched on and then the section behind was switched off. Their progress so far had taken them five switchovers, when they arrived at an area that opened outwards and upwards into the echoing vault of a large cavern. The vast space was used to store huge water tanks, heavy machinery to help the whole underground system function, and for general storage of an array of old and new equipment. It was also the location of Elsa Ford's death.

Mysterious shadows seemed to permanently haunt this cathedral of a space. Even though the lighting didn't move, the shapes cast across the walls, and sometimes distant ceiling, of this largely natural edifice, inspired the imagination into pictures of all sorts. Stare long enough and you could be in heaven, or you could be in hell.

Derek Martin stood looking into the chasm before him, one hand on the safety railing, the other pointing vaguely ahead for the benefit of his second henchman. "Gary, I want you to keep going that way, right. There'll be three light switchovers before you reach the next junction area…a bit like the one where we left Benny. Same thing. Don't let anyone through. Give me half an hour, then come back."

Like Benny before him, Gary obediently did as he was told. "Will do, Mister Martin." And he set off past the office area where Derek Martin was left to carry out his document retrieval work, as urgently suggested by the recent message he believed had come from Sir Henry Hughes. He needed to find the relevant papers, and either destroy them, if it became necessary, or simply hide them somewhere else. Somewhere else, in their own network. The message itself had cleverly been put together by Felicity Hood, Samuel Cummins and Maurice Watson using the criminal conduit of Tommy Best as the line of communication.

Back in one of the offices, Derek Martin was quickly, but fairly methodically, flicking through banks of files in the nearest filing cabinet. Any he thought might be pertinent, he placed on the long table where he could sit and peruse them with greater care later. He surprised himself at how readily he could recognise Henry Hughes's handwriting on the tabs of the relevant folders. At one point, in a moment of slight alarm, he came across a folder of his own which he had not realised was missing. Had Hughes borrowed it? He wondered about the sort of evidence he was unearthing here which could be used against him! He accepted that Hughes' 'goose had been cooked' as far as any court case was concerned. He then wondered if Jerry Russell had attempted to get rid of Hughes after all. It would need to be something pretty spectacular, pretty audacious, Martin thought, if a plan was to succeed. It was no real concern of his now. His own contingency plans had been 'put on standby' and he would be in a safe haven soon waiting for the metaphorical dust to settle before beginning the next wave of robberies. As far as the practicalities were concerned, he reckoned that his own surviving network would more than suffice for the foreseeable future. With Henry Hughes in prison, or in the ground, he himself would be the lone figurehead and he had enough nous to be able to run the whole show without the dubious help of the unreliable Hughes.

While Derek Martin was engaged in his vital admin work, Benny, his first stalwart guard had suddenly heard a sound and stood up from his chair.

A jolly whistling tune carried itself towards Benny. Somewhat confused by this, Benny was uncertain what to do. Clearly someone was approaching. Should he take out his gun? Or wait to judge the situation as it enfolded? It may be quite innocent. Leaving his gun concealed he stepped towards the tunnel where the tuneful melody grew clearer and louder.

A figure in blue overalls, carrying a large toolbox, appeared. "Oh, hullo, I didn't realise there was anyone down today!" the figure exclaimed. The man was wearing a dark woolly hat and safety goggles. He then nodded at Benny's absence of blue overalls, "not working? Jammy bugger, huh?"

"Where you going?" asked Benny, as politely as his uncertainty allowed.

"Nowhere!" the man laughed, "I've arrived. I'm replenishing some supplies, light bulbs and other bits and pieces. I'm not going in any further. I just want to be in there." His second nod was at the room behind Benny. "We won't be too long."

"We?" Benny worried at the word.

"Yeah, of course. Buddies?" the man didn't try to hide the patronising tone of his voice, as if he believed Benny was a child on his first sojourn below ground. With a brusque stride, the maintenance man entered the room, just as another sound came to Benny's ears. As Benny turned he was confronted by another man. He wore blue overalls, with a dark blue woolly hat and safety goggles. The first of the maintenance men spoke again, "alright there, Fred?"

Benny now felt outnumbered by this sudden appearance of a workforce. Warily he looked from one man to the other, twisting his head backwards and forwards before he spotted yet another man emerging from the tunnel. At the point he was about to exclaim something on the lines of 'what are you doing?', Benny was pushed, unceremoniously into the room and held firmly by the arms, turned quickly and forced to the floor where, within a few seconds, he had his left cheek squashed firmly on the floorboards with his hands handcuffed behind his back. Dragged upwards, he was pushed robustly into a chair and the whistling worker stood before him. Benny was held by the other two men.

Feeling slightly breathless from his exertions, Maurice Watson lifted up his safety goggles and removed them, along with his woolly hat, and stood, grinning at Benny. "So, Benny, you're under arrest! One of these nice police officers will read you your rights in a moment. You could make things a little easier for yourself if you can tell me something. Off the record, of course." Benny looked beaten. He also felt beaten. The police had never been encountered below ground in all his experience. This was new. This was different. This was the end.

"Who's with Martin?

"Just me and Gary." His voice sounded beaten.

"Okay lads, read him his rights and take him straight off to the station." Watson pondered for a brief moment before deciding to replace his hat and goggles. A fourth police officer had arrived as Benny was bundled into the room, so Watson had a fresh man to take up the guard position, previously occupied by the obedient Benny. The two officers and their charge headed off, back along the tunnel. The new officer took his seat and Watson strode off cautiously, but with confidence, along the path taken earlier by Derek Martin.

The level of obedience exhibited by Derek Martin's henchmen was possibly admirable in a simplistic sort of juvenile way. For them personally, it had over the years, provided plenty of dividends, a certain amount of loose kudos and a sort of visceral satisfaction. Gary, maintaining an obedient sentry role for Derek Martin, was just checking his watch to ascertain how much of the half-hour was left, before he was allowed back along the tunnel, when he was suddenly aware of voices. They were further along the tunnel, away from where Derek Martin was. Should he turn back early to warn Martin? Or should he investigate what was ahead?

The voices continued in quick bursts of conversations and there were now loud scraping noises he couldn't account for. It sounded like people working. Gary moved in the direction of the sounds, and after only a few short yards he saw three figures of men dragging heavy toolboxes along the tunnel floor. With wire brushes they appeared to be cleaning stretches of pipework. Clearly intent on their work, they were wearing the usual overalls with the headgear and goggles to protect their eyes. Gradually, they were moving in his direction. What was Gary to do?

Before he could come to any considered conclusion, one of the men looked up from his scraping, noticed him and waved a gloved hand towards him, acknowledging his presence. The man faced Gary, smiling. "I didn't think there was anyone else down today. I see you aren't working. Have you seen any more chalked pipes?"

"Chalked pipes?" Gary hadn't the faintest idea what the man was referring to.

"Yes. The inspection squad have indicated the pipes which need cleaning with chalk marks. Are there any more further along there? It'll save us time if we know!"

Gary spoke with a hint of confusion in his voice, "no, I haven't seen any chalk on the pipes. Not this way." He swept his arm loosely towards his section of the tunnel, vainly hoping the gesture and his answer would halt this maintenance party in its tracks. It didn't. The friendly man stepped forward and the other two stopped working, but held on to their brushes.

"I'll just check the next few yards. We needn't do a lot more this side of lunch, eh lads." The man followed the path of the pipe-way and shuffled passed Gary, who was simply hoping these men would finish what they were doing and disappear. "Not a lot to do really!" The man turned to face Gary directly and gave a big beaming smile. In the moment that Gary wondered about this apparently over-friendly attitude, he was grabbed roughly from behind, pulled backwards and dragged to the ground. Like Benny before him, he was rolled onto his front, head held against the cold concrete of the tunnel floor and then handcuffed with his hands behind his back.

Pinioned on the ground, the next sound Gary heard was Samuel Cummins' voice as the detective inspector spoke to his men. "Good work, lads. Let's get rid of him." He knelt down to speak into Gary's free ear. "You're well and truly nicked, okay? You can help yourself a lot if you tell me how many of you are here with Derek Martin."

Realising there was no real chance of anything positive coming out of the situation he found himself in, Gary mumbled, "three of us. Just the three of us came here."

The two police officers hauled Gary away to the outside world, where a police van was waiting for him under the overcast sky of Greater London. With a pleasing sense of satisfaction and confidence, Cummins was happy to acknowledge that the intelligence he had received about Derek Martin's party of three had been absolutely correct. With a clear feeling that the matter in hand was surely about to come to fruition, Cummins pushed up his goggles and continued on his way to meet with Derek Martin.

The man in question was reaching the end of his rummaging around the folders left by Henry Hughes. He had recognised some documents dealing with Hughes' money laundering activities and others referring to links with his legitimate companies. Reports and information about offshore accounts, lists of transactions, many of which were of dubious accuracy or honesty, a whole range of stuff which needed to be spirited away. Some of it could be destroyed, some of it retained for purposes of extortion or blackmail at some later date no doubt. Martin glanced around at the table. The number of folders was more modest than he had thought earlier. He pulled open the bottom drawer of a filing cabinet to take out two large bags which would more than suffice for the baggage waiting on the table. Just as he lifted the bags, the room was plunged into complete and utter darkness.

"Shit!" was the only thing Martin could say.

He fumbled in his pocket for a small pen torch. Click. The only light anywhere was beaming from his own hand. He tried to remember where the appropriate light switch was and realised this would only be useful if the switch was working. Why had the lights gone out? A failure? Then the switch would be no good. Someone switched them off? Where were they, then? He switched his torch off. Total black darkness. Nothing. Not even a single security light, not even a single small red indicator light of any description. This was it then, a total blackout which could only be achieved below ground. Where he was now. His torch came back on and he set to with the folders and started to fill the two bags. Gary should be back in a couple of minutes, thought Martin, after checking his wristwatch. The nearest section of tunnel lighting would come on with Gary's approach, or at least the beam of his accomplice's torch.

The time, between a sudden burst of bright light close to his face and a severe thump in the back, was something Martin had difficulty registering. He had a second to make a grab for his gun, but it was knocked out of his hand and clattered to the floor. In the next instant the full section of lights blazed on and Martin was aware of two figures on either side of him. With a swift and agile action which belied his stature he had leapt across the open hallway and grasped a long pole, about six feet long and sporting a metal hook at its business end. The pole was one of a number of similar accessories designed to reach over the edges of platforms, and placed at intervals along the walkways. They were frequently used to pull lights and other apparatus within reach of people standing on the existing platforms. It made a useful weapon in the absence of anything else, more deadly, being available. Martin swept the pole in a wide arc wildly, keeping at bay Detective Inspector Samuel Cummins on one side, and Detective Sergeant Maurice Watson on the other. The standoff was punctuated by three pairs of flashing eyes, as the parties sized the others up. And it seemed simultaneously that Martin and Watson noticed the position of the dropped gun. Slicing the air with the vicious hook, Martin stepped toward the gun, while aiming the weapon at Watson's upper body. Understanding Martin's intent, Watson jumped forward in a sliding tackle motion, which his PE instructor at Hendon would have been proud of, and kicked the gun over the edge of the platform. It clanged and chinked its way against the rocky terrain before clattering to a halt on the concrete floor thirty feet below. The swinging hook caught Watson a nasty blow on the shoulder and tore through his jacket and gashing his body. Watson stayed on the floor and Martin swung the pole in the opposite direction now, threatening Cummins. Moving even closer in towards Martin, Samuel Cummins was taking a risk. He eased his way to one side, nearer the metal safety railings, hopefully making himself less of a target. Martin quickly looked at both men, in a double-take movement of his head, assessing which of the two to focus on and suddenly froze and looked beyond Cummins' shoulder. The inspector realised that someone was behind him.

Facing Derek Martin with a revolver in his hand was George Ford.

This was a new standoff. Martin held a firm grip on the pole, but took a couple of steps back. Clutching his upper arm, Watson retreated to the wall near the office doorway. Cummins had twisted round quickly as was shocked to see that it was George Ford who was standing behind him. George Ford had not been party to this Richmond operation. Neither Cummins nor Watson had expected him to be there. But here he was.

The gun aimed at Martin was telling its own story. Cummins did not want Ford to do something he might regret later. "George, we've got him, he can't get out." Cummins had spoken softly, trying to reassure Ford that they were in command. It had ended in their favour. Cummins spoke to Martin this time, his voice harder, without sympathy. "We've got men at both tunnels, both ways out. You really can't get away."

George Ford walked steadily forward, his revolver pointing straight at Derek Martin. "You killed Elsa, didn't you, Derek?" Ford's anger was thinly restrained.

"George, George," Martin's tone was almost mocking, "she was interfering. She stuck her nose into our business and she found out too much. She wasn't going to say nothing, was she? She had to go, George. The nosey bitch had to go. We got more than five extra years, five more good years. Before all this bloody lot." He waved the pole in the general direction of the policemen.

George held his ground. The muscles in his jaw and neck tightened as he listened to Martin's venom about his beloved wife. He kept his eyes fixed on Martin's face.

Martin knew he was caught, but he wanted so much to goad George Ford. He mocked the man with the gun. "You won't do it, George, you just won't do it. You're a bloody pacifist, remember!" Martin struck out, to no-one in particular, with the pole, sweeping the wide arc under the bright lights of the cavernous void. He started to shout, ranting towards George

Ford. "All this, George, all this. Your stupid dream, your new world, a new society, your big secret. George Ford, the man of peace! You won't pull that trigger, you won't shoot me. You know you won't!"

Samuel Cummins moved closer to George Ford. "You don't need to use the gun, George. Don't listen to his rubbish, his poison, don't listen. You're a bigger and better man than he will ever be. You've come out on top, George. It's over for him, Martin has lost, his network is all but ended."

"Thank you for that, Inspector Cummins. Your plan has worked well, your team has succeeded. However, I have some unfinished business with Mister Martin." Ford turned towards Martin again and gave a wry tight smile. "You do have a chance of getting away, Derek. You know there's a way out down there." He nodded towards the bottom of the dark cave, "one of our emergency routes; I'm sure you remember."

Martin did remember and he suddenly ceased on the idea that perhaps he could actually achieve an escape. He was convinced that George Ford would not shoot him. Was it going to be worth the chance? He feigned fear and backed towards the railings. George Ford advanced further and was now only ten yards from Derek Martin. And still the gun was pointing straight at him.

Unexpectedly, Martin climbed onto the metal railings and stood, one leg either side of the top rail and reaching sideways to the rock wall which pushed out into the centre of the cavern.

"What's going on? What are you doing, George?" asked Cummins, alarmed.

"He's taking his chance, inspector. I'm giving him a chance. I know that's more than he gave Elsa. He's taking his chance to get away. He's making his bid for freedom." Ford moved against the railings now, still holding the gun and still aimed at Martin. At the other side of the platform away from the railings, Watson had been slowly moving, back to the point at the railings where Martin had first climbed. The pole discarded by Martin was lying on the floor and was picked up by Cummins. As he carried it to the rails he realised that Martin indeed was making an escape; he was beyond the reach of the pole already and was clambering successfully away from the platform. In a matter of minutes, he could be out of sight and then unable to be monitored. Watson could not understand what was happening. Ford was going to have to explain this. And where was this damned emergency route? Could it be that Martin was to avoid capture?

"This is it, Derek, your moment of freedom." Ford was shouting.

"What?" Derek Martin halted his progress.

George Ford stood right against the railings. He shouted at Derek Martin, "what's your memory like, Derek?" He then held the revolver in his tensed arm and cocked the firearm as if aiming at a target in a shooting competition.

"Don't George," shouted Maurice Watson.

Ford ignored him and pulled the trigger. Click. The gun made a soft clicking noise. It was empty. George opened the barrel, to reveal six empty chambers. He handed the weapon to Samuel Cummins.

"I apologise for the melodrama, inspector. I do hope you can indulge me a little further." He turned to Martin who had moved a further yard towards his freedom, but in the glare of the lighting could be seen sweating, on his forehead, and down the sides of his reddening face."Your memory, Derek, I asked you about your memory."

"You're a bloody fool, George. What are you talking about?"

"We worked on that route together, a long time ago, Derek. You can see what you're doing, you can see where you're going. But now it's all memory, Derek!"

With a sickening slur in his stomach and the sudden widening of his panicking eyes, Derek Martin, realised too late what was about to happen. And Derek Martin, and everyone else in the cavern was thrust into absolute darkness.

"You bastard, Ford!" Martin's fraught voice screamed in the blackness.

"No-one but you saw Elsa fall, because you pushed her. And no-one will see you fall, Derek. Of course I wouldn't kill you. You simply aren't worth it. You betray people. You cheat. You kill. I will not tarnish Elsa's memory by killing you, by killing anyone. I will not even kill you out of revenge, Derek. I will simply allow you to die."

The completeness of the darkness was matched by the silence now. George Ford had stopped speaking. Everything had been said. The rest would be silence.

Maurice Watson held his arm as it throbbed painfully. He almost imagined it made a sound in the dark silence. But it didn't. Samuel Cummins stood, deliberately silent, as if in respect to George Ford and in tribute to Ford's murdered wife. There was an intimacy with this darkness. There was a stillness too. There was a haven of thought inside this incredible silence. He listened. George Ford listened. And Maurice Watson listened. There was nothing now left to say.

As they continued to listen, the silence frayed slightly. A breathlessness could be heard, soft scrambling sounds. It seemed to last for several minutes. Then suddenly there was a stunted gasp from somewhere in the middle of the cavern's air. A stifled scream- like cry which was cut-off in its execution, a sliding sort of swishing and a slumping as a falling object dropped further away and a final softened smack and a return to silence. For a few seconds the silence and the darkness remained. Somewhere, further down, inside the darkness there would be a dead body.

A flick was heard and a sharp beam of torchlight sprang to life.

"Gentlemen," spoke George Ford, "I think it's time to go outside."

CONTENTS

22nd May 1956. Nottingham. 1

10th December 1989. South London. 3

8th August 1990. Scottish Highlands. 6

9th August 1990. Inverness. 10

12th August 1990. North Somerset Coast. 14

14th August 1990. Bristol. 16

15th August 1990. Inverness. 8 a.m. 18

15th August 1990. North Somerset Coast. 11a.m. 19

15th August 1990. Scottish Highlands. 11 a.m. 22

15th August 1990. North Somerset Coast. 2 p.m. 26

15th August. Inverness. 4 p.m. 28

16th August 1990. Scotland Yard 31

17th August 1990. South London. 8 a.m. 34

17th August 1990. Inverness. 36

18th August 1990. Scotland Yard 37

19th August 1990. Central London. 42

20th August 1990. Scotland Yard 45

20th August 1990. Scottish Highlands. 51

21st August 1990. Bristol. 56

21st August 1990. Central London. 59

21st August 1990. Inverness. 63

22nd August 1990. Bristol. 8 a.m. 65

22nd August 1990. Central London. 8 a.m. 70

22nd August 1990. Inverness. 10.a.m. 79

23rd August 1990. Scotland Yard. 9.30.a.m........................ 82

23rd August 1990. Inverness. 1.p.m. 88

24th August 1990. Scotland Yard. 93

25th August 1990. Heathrow Airport. 12.30 p.m.............. 97

25th August. Bakerloo Line. 2.30.p.m. 101

25th August 1990. South London. 5p.m. 103

26th August 1990. Inverness.. 109

26th August 1990. Central London. 9.30.a.m. 113

27th August 1990. Central London. 11.30.a.m. 117

27th August 1990. Central London. 12.15.p.m................ 120

28th August 1990. Scottish Highlands. 9.a.m.................... 124

28th August 1990. Scotland Yard. 10.a.m........................ 126

28th August 1990. Bristol. 4.p.m....................................... 130

29th August 1990. Central London. 10.a.m. 135

29th August 1990. Inverness. 10.a.m................................. 139

31st August 1990. Scotland Yard. 4.p.m........................... 145

31st August 1990. South London. 8.p.m........................... 155

1st September 1900. Scottish Highlands. 9.a.m................. 157

1st September 1990. South London. 5.p.m. 165

3rd September 1990. Central London. 10.a.m. 169

3rd September 1990. Scotland Yard. 4.p.m....................... 174

3rd September 1990. Inverness. 4.p.m............................... 179

4th September 1990. Richmond-upon-Thames. 9.a.m..... 183

4th September 1990. Scottish Highlands. 9.a.m. 194

5th September 1990. Somerset. 11.a.m. 198

5th September 1990. Inverness. 2.p.m............................... 203

6th September 1990. Manchester. 6.a.m............................ 209

7th September 1990. Scotland Yard. 9.a.m. 212

8th September 1990. Scotland Yard. 10.a.m. 221

9th September 1990. Yorkshire. 10.a.m. 230

9th September 1990. Central London. 10.a.m. ... 236

9th September 1900. Yorkshire. 5.p.m. 239

9th September 1990. Central London. 6.p.m. 252

9th September 1990. Yorkshire. 7.p.m. 256

12th September 1990. Scotland Yard. 10.a.m. ... 258

13th September 1900. Central London. 10.a.m. .. 263

13th September 1990. Richmond-upon-Thames. 11.a.m. ... 266